LAW & ORDER

DEAD LINE

J. MADISON DAVIS

UNIVERSAL

WOLF
FILMS

ibooks
new york
www.ibooks.net

DISTRIBUTED BY SIMON & SCHUSTER, INC.

An Original Publication of ibooks, inc.

ibooks, inc.
24 West 25th Street
New York, NY 10010

The ibooks, inc. World Wide Web Site Address is:
http://www.ibooks.net

Visit the Law & Order Web Site at:
http://www.uni-television.com/laworder

ISBN 0-7434-9798-8
First ibooks, inc. printing May 2004
10 9 8 7 6 5 4 3 2 1

Edited by Judy Gitenstein

Special thanks to Bill Fordes
for his invaluable assistance

Printed in the U.S.A.

A younger man! Goran Hagopian's wife, Hermine, had lost her mind. What did she think this greasy operator just off the plane from Yerevan wanted? A forty-eight-year-old woman? "The Quick Stop," said Goran to his assistant, Romero. "Why can't she see it?"

Romero tried to be sympathetic, but his English had failed him too many times before, stoking up Goran's anger when he'd tried to dampen it. What kind of pathetic *cabrón* would want Hagopian's hole-in-the-wall store? Romero shrugged as the service elevator opened, hoping a resigned "*¿Quién sabe?*" would shut Goran up.

"He thinks the Quick Stop will make him rich," said Goran, charging down the corridor. "The Quick Stop I bought by working two jobs! I should kill him. Hermine thinks she's in love. I should kill her. Isn't that what you'd do in Mexico?"

"I am from Santo Domingo," said Romero, gritting his teeth.

Goran drew his thumb across his throat and made a *skritching* noise. The door to room 547 opened as his index finger reached his ear.

1

"Are you the engineer?" asked the red-faced guest.

"You Mr. Coster? A problem with the air conditioner?"

"It's hot as a gol-darned oven in here." He pulled his white shirt away from his chest. "Look at that! It's ruined."

"So change it," Goran said sharply.

Coster gaped at his gray-haired wife, sitting by the open window and fanning herself with a tourist guide to Broadway. She raised an eyebrow, as if to say, "It's New York. What do you expect?"

Coster reddened like he was going to pop an artery.

"We fix quick as possible," said Romero, shoving Goran in. "No problem."

"There certainly is a problem!"

"Please, Emmett," said the wife. "The sooner they get started…"

Goran narrowed his eyes to slits, and Coster turned away. Romero noticed light between the frame that held the air-conditioning unit in the window frame. The narrow strip of foam that sealed it hung half out. The unit seemed to have been shoved. He wanted to ask if these people had bumped it. It would have taken a hell of a bump. But, strangely, the plastic front of the unit was undamaged, as if it had been tugged from the outside.

"Is it plugged in?" asked Goran.

"You think I didn't check that?" snorted Coster. He was auditioning hard to stand in for the guy who stole Goran's wife.

"Emmett…" sighed Mrs. Coster.

Romero leaned against the mullion and stuck his head out of the window to see the back of the unit. The corner of it was crushed, as if a cinder block had

2

been dropped on it. At first he thought there were feathers stuck in some kind of oil, but then it looked more like hair.

And dried blood.

He looked up. The bricks above him stretched like a Martian landscape to the sky. Something had been dropped off the roof? At the bottom of the air shaft, an aluminum can glinted. A potato chip bag rolled and danced near the ventilator from the coffee shop. Romero got a good grip and leaned farther out. He saw a bundle of discarded clothes between the rattling ventilator unit and the wall. Then, he saw the bundle had legs.

"*Jesus!*" he shouted. "Is a woman! Look!"

Mrs. Coster stopped fanning herself.

"Is woman!" Romero repeated. "Dead woman!"

Mrs. Coster gasped and Goran leaned out beside Romero. Their eyes met.

Goran shrugged. "It was too much to hope," he said. "Hermine weighs three times as much."

Detectives Lennie Briscoe and Ed Green stood in the stifling air shaft staring at the windows above them.

Briscoe tugged a uniform's sleeve. "Tell them to turn off the ventilator," he said, "or we'll all smell like French fries."

"A simple suicide and we're home for dinner," said Green.

"Dressed all in black, for her own funeral," said Briscoe. Suicides often dressed for the occasion, depending on the nature of the occasion. Some put on a tailored suit, others their college sweatshirt. A certain number left the world as naked as they came into it. No matter what they wore, dead never looked nice.

3

The ventilator stopped blowing its greasy plume, and the man from the medical examiner's office moved toward the body. This version of dead was particularly un-nice. In striking the air-conditioning unit, most of the woman's face had been ripped away. Muscle glistened. Bone gleamed.

"Been here a while," the examiner said, standing up. "There's not much blood, not even on what's left of the face, so she was lucky and went fast. I'd guess early morning. One to two. No later than three."

Green glanced up at the windows. "And nobody saw her for twelve hours?"

"The only reason anyone looks out here is if somebody else is taking a shower across the way," said Briscoe.

Green stepped closer to the body. "Straight up, it's hard to see down here." He pointed, "But over there…"

Briscoe drew a line of sight in the air. "The ventilator box would block the view."

"Dark bundle in the corner. Who notices?" said the M.E. "The birds hadn't found her yet."

"So that," Green indicated the mutilated face, "that happened in the fall?"

"Hit something on the way down is my guess. She dropped at least five floors."

Green made a noise of disgust. "If someone had seen that lying there, you think they would have called."

"Even if someone saw her here and didn't bother to report it, what's the difference?" said Briscoe. "Unless they saw her fall."

"You guys thinking up reasons not to question all the guests?"

4

"Us?" sneered Briscoe. "We just love to talk to dozens of *turistas*. It's why I never want to retire."

"Well, if you're done, we can haul her away."

"No I.D.?" asked Green. "Is she a guest? Just a jumper?"

"Nothing on her. No note. She's mid-forties. Five-six. About one-thirty-five. Slim enough to look good in stretch slacks. Didn't dye her hair." He lifted up the cover. "See the gray mixed in?"

Briscoe rolled his eyes. "I'll take your word for it."

Green avoided looking at the victim as well. "Is there enough there to get a sketch or something someone could recognize?"

"I wouldn't show the photo around," he said. "She's looked better."

"That's often the case with the dead."

"No, I mean from what's left, she wasn't wearing makeup."

Green thought about the clothing, or lack of it, on suicides. Did women usually make up before killing themselves? He made a mental note to find out.

The man from the M.E.'s office continued. "She was dressing down, you know what I mean? She had great cheekbones, a narrow nose. My guess is she would have been a knockout about twenty years ago. And judging from her hands, she hasn't washed many dishes or dug many ditches."

"Just maybe some gold, huh?" said Briscoe. "Any other deductions?"

"Just let me know if I'm right, which I usually am," he sneered, signaling a uniformed officer to bring the stretcher.

"With our luck, you will be," said Green.

5

"Nothing's more fun than the idle rich," said Briscoe. "Except the dead idle rich."

"Let's climb straight up," said Green to the day manager as Briscoe questioned the clerks.

The manager hunched over his keyboard, squinting as if he were going to rest his nose on the CRT's glass. The monitor looked like it was built for the ENIAC and the lettering blurred. "Six-two-seven's got a couple from Turin. Got in about noon."

"Who was in there before them?"

"Some jackass from Dubuque."

"Why 'jackass'?"

"Screamed how he didn't watch Pay-Per-View." The day manager tapped the monitor's glass. "He did. The equipment don't lie."

"Maybe what he watched isn't legal in Dubuque," said Green.

"That's why they love New York," said the manager.

Briscoe leaned into the doorway. "No one remembers a woman in black. Wrong shift."

"They get in at four," said the manager. "Seven-two-seven's a family of three."

"I'd think they'd report a missing mommy," said Briscoe.

"Here you go," said the manager. "Eight-two-seven. Checked in at five yesterday. Hasn't checked out. Paid a cash deposit for incidentals. Don't see that much, except from foreign tourists. 'Mrs. R.E. Chesko.'" He quickly picked up the telephone. "Reserved on Tuesday, by Internet. American Express Platinum."

"Don't kill yourself without it," said Briscoe.

"She planned ahead for her suicide?" said Green, thinking out loud.

"Not all that strange," said Briscoe. "But there are eight more floors above this one."

"I'm ringing eight-two-seven. There's no answer," said the manager. He dialed another number and spoke slowly, carefully, to the maid. "The privacy card is on the door. She thinks she hears the TV, but there's no answer."

"Tell her not to go in," said Briscoe.

As the door swung back, Briscoe and Green heard the loud *oooh* of a studio audience. On a 27-inch color screen, Maury Povich tore open an envelope with DNA results.

"Hello?" said Briscoe. "Police."

The bed was slightly rumpled, but the cover had not been pulled back. The window was closed, but the curtain rod was bent. Someone had pulled down hard on the sheer.

Briscoe rapped on the bathroom door. "Hello? Anybody in there? Mrs. Chesko?" The unlatched door swung back. Someone had used a single hand towel, then tossed it on the sink.

The manager reached for a black beret on the end table.

"Don't touch anything!" snapped Green.

Briscoe craned to look on the other side of the bed. "I remember those," he said. "I even remember using them regularly, back in the late Neolithic."

"What?" asked Green.

"Galoshes," said Briscoe. He pointed to a torn, bright blue foil square under the hanging edge of the bedspread.

"Mrs. Chesko and partner took precautions before she died."

7

"Proving that safe sex isn't always safe." Briscoe turned to the manager. "I don't want to read this in the paper," he warned.

"What are you saying? I don't want this in the paper."

"Then don't give them anything to write about," said Green.

"We should have an address," the manager volunteered.

"That would be a big help," said Briscoe, nudging him toward the door. "You print us all the records: phone calls, room service, if she watched any movies."

"Sure," said the manager. He had almost closed the door when Briscoe grabbed it.

"Wait. Have you got security cameras in the hall?"

"At the front desk and near the elevators. There's one on the delivery door."

"We're going to need those tapes."

Green was already dialing the crime scene investigators on his cell phone.

"No purse," said Briscoe. "She didn't even bring a toothbrush."

Green leaned toward the window frame as he spoke. "Right, eight-twenty-seven. A full workup. It's not for sure a suicide." He snapped the phone closed. "Maybe she was robbed."

"We should check the maid. Her stuff might have been lifted after she took the dive."

"And the trash cans in the area. Her purse could have been dumped."

Green pointed to a scratch in the paint on the windowsill.

"She reserves a room Tuesday to meet somebody on Wednesday. Gets here at five."

"About the time her boyfriend gets off work?"

"Or she does. Or they both do."

"So one of them works in midtown, wouldn't you think?"

Briscoe watched Green kneel to look under the bed. "I'd say if they had something to hide, that it would be close, but at least a couple of blocks."

"There's a subway stop on the corner."

"So maybe a lot of blocks," shrugged Briscoe. "They meet. They can't even wait to pull back the covers, but they do have the presence of mind to march with the Trojan. Slam-bam."

"She begs him to leave his wife," said Green, standing up. "He shoves her out the window."

"It works for me," said Briscoe.

"Say," said Green, "what is this?" He pointed to the corner of a rectangular item lying just under the edge of the television. Green pulled his pen and teased it out. It was a rectangular piece of plastic with a logo that said "SanDisk" and "128 MB" below that. On the long edge, it said "MEMORY STICK."

"It's a memory card, like for a digital camera," said Green.

"There's no camera, but did you notice the plug down there?"

Green bagged the memory stick and knelt to look at the electric socket beside the TV stand. A small charger about two by six inches had been hidden under the stand. A thin cord from the transformer curled among the cable wires in the corner.

"It's too big for a cell phone," said Briscoe. "A radio adapter? It says 'Sony.'"

"I'll bet a computer—a laptop or a notebook," said Green.

"If she had a computer, it's gone. It's looking like theft."

He answered a rap at the door.

A forensics technician carrying an investigation kit came in. "Hey, Lennie," he said. "What's the deal? Find a note?"

"No, but we got everything figured out," said Briscoe. "At least until you guys find the wrong kind of fibers."

"For a small fee, I'll plant what you like."

"Until I get a raise," said Briscoe, "I'll have to solve cases the old-fashioned way." He nudged Green. "Let's go find out who R.E. Chesko is."

T wenty minutes on the phone and Briscoe was wearing his "why me?" look. The "R.E. Chesko" on the credit card turned out to be Ralph Emerson Chesko, and according to the rules of American Express, his card wasn't supposed to be used by anyone other than Ralph Emerson Chesko, not even a wife, but since the reservation had been prepaid on the Internet, whoever it was had only needed the number. The identity of the body was now in question. The card hadn't been reported stolen, nor was there any unusual activity on it, but when the detectives tried to call the R.E. Chesko number, the phone had been cut off two weeks previously, for lack of payment. Since the address appeared to be in the toniest area of the Hamptons, this seemed peculiar. People with phone problems didn't normally live in that neighborhood.

While Briscoe went through the procedures to get the last couple of credit card statements, Green called the local police on Long Island, who said they knew nothing about the Chesko estate, other than that the house was on the historical register as the Boer Mansion and had been built in 1915 by a Dutchman in diamond mining. Green asked them to drive by and see if anyone still lived there. He drummed his fingers on his desk, then found the address and phone number of the nearest house.

"Can I help you?" answered a voice Green would have described as "very white," the voice you inherit when your family's first million came in doubloons.

"This is Detective Green of the New York City Police Department."

"Yes."

"You are Mr. James Riley Walston?"

"This is supposed to be an unpublished number."

"Well, Mr. Walston, I *am* a detective."

"Indeed. So you say."

"The reason I'm calling is that we were wondering if you knew your neighbor, a Mr. Ralph Emerson Chesko?"

"Too well, I'm afraid, but not well enough."

"Excuse me?"

"So, there are charges being preferred?"

"Against Mr. Chesko? What kind of charges?"

Briscoe, who had been on hold, peered across the desk.

"Why, the obvious!" said the man.

"I'm sorry. I was simply trying to contact Mr. Chesko about a stolen credit card. His phone seems out of service."

"Chesko bellied up six months ago. Moved within a month. People say things, but I still think he was on the up and up."

"I'm sorry?"

"He just got dragged down by the Williams thing. Falling dominoes. He lost more than his job, you know. Emily ran away as soon as the growth fund collapsed."

"Emily? Was that Mrs. Chesko? Have you seen her recently?"

"Not for, let me think, three months. Ah, well, Ralph shouldn't have been surprised. She was in it for the money. Anyone could see that. But, you know, Ralph didn't actually own the Boer Mansion. It was on a Preservation Society lease. Maintain it and you can live in it. Providing you don't alter it."

A housing subsidy for the rich, thought Green. Wouldn't want the non-moneyed moving into the nabe and ruining the ambience. "So you haven't seen Mrs. Chesko for several months?"

"Since she moved out. She was carrying the Moore."

"The what?"

"The Henry Moore. A mother and child sculpture. It seemed funny. The not-very-motherly Emily carrying an image of motherhood like it was her child. I imagine when the divorce is through, it'll turn up on the schedule at Sotheby's"

Green noted "valuable statue" on his notepad. "Mr. Walston, could you describe Mrs. Chesko for me?"

"If you'd seen her, you'd know her, and how!" said the neighbor. "A brick carriage house. Blonde, of course. Tried sultry Grace Kelly, but came out Judy Holliday."

Blonde? Green's pen hovered. "How tall would you say?"

"A long drink of water," said Walston. "Six, I'd imagine. I'm five ten. Yes, I'd say six."

The dead woman was definitely not six feet, thought Green. He tapped his pen on the desk. "The blonde was natural?"

"As natural as Iowa polyethylene."

"Could she have been blonde to cover a speckling of gray?"

Walston laughed. "Emily hadn't turned over her first batch of pubic hair!"

"Excuse me?"

"If the girl was a day over twenty-five I want her doctor!"

Green thanked Walston and hung up. "Damn!" he said. "She isn't Mrs. Chesko."

Briscoe rolled his eyes. "Don't tell me!"

"Mrs. Emily Chesko is about six feet, under thirty years old, and quite a looker."

"So the card is hot," said Briscoe.

Just then, Lieutenant Anita Van Buren approached. "What's with the jumper?" she asked.

"We don't know who she is," said Briscoe.

"Jumpers usually want you to know," said Van Buren. "It's their big moment."

"The credit card number must have been stolen," said Green. "Either by the Jane Doe or her boyfriend."

"They're faxing over the last couple of statements," said Briscoe, "but there's the other theft possibility, too. There is no purse, no wallet, and she might have had a small computer, you know, a laptop or something. Two accessories were left behind."

"Jewelry?"

"Not that we can tell," said Green.

"That doesn't mean she didn't have any," said Briscoe.

Van Buren shrugged. "A perp gains entry. She screams. He pushes. Or she backs up to the window."

"Fell?" said Briscoe.

"It happens," said Van Buren.

"Could be," said Green, "but the window wasn't easy to back out of, even completely open. She'd have to bend over. There's the condom wrapper, which could have been missed by the maid the day before. But it's more likely somebody was with her."

"Maybe the boyfriend took her stuff."

"I called robbery," said Briscoe. "They haven't had any thefts like this in midtown hotels. They've sent out their usual notices to the pawnshops for a Sony laptop."

Green shrugged. "It could have been a hotel employee, somebody with a passkey. But nobody knows anything, of course."

"The perp sneaks into her room, gets surprised when she comes back..." said Briscoe.

"Or they just filch it when she's already towered out."

"Took the whole purse?" mused Van Buren.

"If she had one," said Briscoe.

"Maybe it was an expensive one."

"That would fit," said Briscoe. "Otherwise it's just take the money and the fencibles and run. If the purse itself was fencible Gucci or something. Yeah, why not? We got a couple of unis checking the local trash bins."

"How'd you get out of the dumpster dive?" said Van Buren. "I'm not getting complaints about you using up manpower, am I?"

"Well, we've got to identify her, don't we?" said Briscoe. "Anyway, I collected on a favor."

Green suppressed a grin.

"Whatever. Just clear this up," said the lieutenant. "I need help on that Soho drive-by."

"Briscoe!" someone called. A uniform stood in the

doorway, holding several sheets of paper. "Detective Briscoe! Faxes."

Briscoe turned and raised his hand. The uniform handed him a set of American Express statements. "About time," he said.

"What are we looking for?" said Green.

"A clue," said Briscoe.

Green rolled his eyes and hunkered down over the papers. The top list began in mid-May. Lunch at the Plaza. Broadway tickets. Schmelling and Sons, Purveyors of Fine Food. The Wine Shop. The Wine Shop.

Must have been a good weekend, he thought. "Here's a ticket on Virgin Airlines. Maybe he's out of the country."

"And wouldn't know his card is being used," said Briscoe.

"There's a hotel charge for the Hotel La Place, St. Brelade, Isle of Jersey. Not a very large charge."

"Maybe it was just a one-night stand. Still, motels in New Jersey are cheaper."

"He bought something at a shop in Heathrow a day later."

"So he was either moving on from London or coming home." Briscoe rocked back. "The one night stand idea has me thinking. Maybe Chesko was having a fling with Jane Doe?"

"With a young trophy at home?" asked Green.

"Maybe he missed mama's home cooking."

They went back to scanning the charges. "Well," said Briscoe, "he's either back in the U.S.A., or somebody's buying on his card." He held up the list. "A week ago there was a big charge at a building supply store."

"Maybe there was a delivery," said Green. "What's the supply store?"

Briscoe's phone rang. "Brooklyn Lumber," he said, then snapped up the phone. "Yeah? Oh, Carl! So that was quick. Have fun? Yeah, yeah. So?" His expression changed. "No kidding?" He covered the mouthpiece. "The purse!"

"How does he know it's hers?"

Briscoe nodded, listening. "Nothing? You checked the whole thing out, right? Women's purses got all those hidden pockets and things. Right. And you? Okay. Bag it and bring it in. See if there are any cans you missed." He listened for a second and laughed. "Hell, Carl, you can take a bath anytime. When do you get the chance to break a case?"

"What's up?" asked Green.

"They found her leather purse in the hotel dumpster. Coach brand. There was the hotel receipt: American Express, R.E. Chesko."

"So who is she?"

"That's the catch. There's a grocery receipt, cash, from a store in the Village. A couple of eyebrow pencils and a cheap pen with the NYU logo. Everything else is gone."

"So the thief took the wallet, and if we're lucky, the card."

"And they might use it yet," said Briscoe. "Maybe they're just spending her cash right now."

"We could see if anyone remembers her in the grocery," Green suggested. "But, first, let's see where all of these building supplies went."

"What you want to bet to a vacant lot? Charge the stuff, have it delivered, move it in an hour. It will be emptier than the last scene of *On the Beach*."

Green hesitated for a moment, then decided not to ask. He began dialing.

SHAMIR'S PAWN AND USED
EIGHTH AVENUE AND TWENTIETH
THURSDAY, AUGUST 22

"So I called. I don't need no grief." The pawnshop owner's breath smelled of cardamom seed. His fingernails were manicured and his mustache was neatly combed. Shamir was a big man in a big Hawaiian shirt. In the neighborhood, he was often called "Shamu."

Briscoe looked around at the usual pawnshop assortment of dusty musical instruments, electronics, and a case full of rings.

"I saw it on the bulletin. The notices come on the fax. You got here quick."

"We were in the neighborhood," said Green.

"On our way to a vacant lot," muttered Briscoe.

"The last time I call in something, a detective don't show up for two weeks."

"Robbery's pretty busy," said Green.

"So the customer comes back to redeem it. The guitar. The creep steal it, pawn it, then see in the paper it once belong to Sid Vicious and he wants it back."

"Sid Vicious, eh?" said Briscoe.

"So what happened?" said Green.

"I say it's all his. Hey, I don't need to be shot by

18

no gangsta. Not my fault the cops, I mean 'officers,' don't come."

"Right," said Briscoe sarcastically. Shamir gave him a look.

"We appreciate your trying," said Green. "You got a Sony laptop?"

"I look down the list, I think maybe it's it. The woman wasn't right. You are lucky I called after last time. I almost sent her away."

"It was a woman?"

"Yes." Shamir held up the pawn slip. "Ermilia Santonio. She showed me a green card for I.D."

Briscoe's eyes met Green's. "A maid?" he asked.

Green flipped through his notepad. There were nine maids on duty at the Waterloo on the two days. An Ermilia Santonio was number five on his list, but they hadn't talked to her. Green held up his notepad. "Bingo," he said.

"You said you knew the woman wasn't right?" asked Briscoe.

"On a laptop, I want to see if it works. You can get NYU students here who crash their machines and try to pawn them. This woman, she could be a student. Students come in all shapes now. But she had a hard time opening the latch. When I asked her what the thing would do, she just said 'many things.' So I asked her where she got it. She said her brother gave it to her. I turn the thing on, it has a password and she can't tell me what it is. She says she forgot and her brother's out of the country."

"So you suspected it was stolen?"

The man twitched his nose. "How would I know? I figured I'd see if it turned up on the lists."

"You could have called in immediately."

"Hey, maybe I shouldn't. I feel like you're accusing me."

"*Tut, tut,* Shamir. You shouldn't be pawning stuff you think is stolen," said Green.

"And if I didn't, she'd have walked out of here," said Shamir. "I'm out thirty-five bucks, and this is the thanks?"

"Come on, buddy," said Briscoe. "If it hadn't shown up on the list, you'd have gotten yourself a computer on the cheap. But we're not interested in that, okay? Show us the machine."

Shamir gave them another half-lidded glare and unlocked the mesh door of his cash register cage. He brought out a black briefcase and set it on the counter. As he unlatched it, Green stepped forward.

"Let us handle it," he said. "There might be fingerprints."

"Fingerprints?" said Shamir. "This is something important, eh?"

"We don't know," said Briscoe.

Using a handkerchief, Green slid the computer out of its case. It was a thin silver Sony Vaio, model number PCG-R505GCP4. Green pointed at a slit in the side. "A memory stick goes there."

"Is there anything to identify it?" asked Briscoe.

"If it's registered, the serial number will be on record," said Shamir.

Briscoe nodded. Green opened the top. "You tried it?"

"You need a password."

"And you put your hands all over it, I suppose."

Shamir turned up his palms. "What do you expect?"

Green pushed the button and waited until the screen lit. "PASSWORD:" appeared.

He typed in "CHESKO."
Nothing.
He entered "RECHESKO."
Nothing.
"RALPHCHESKO."
Nothing.
"RALPHECHESKO."
Nothing.
"A kid could bust it in twenty seconds," said Shamir.
"And I don't suppose you know one," said Briscoe.
Shamir smiled.
"You didn't...?"
"I call you right away!"
"You pawned a machine like this for only thirty-five bucks?" asked Green.
"Hey, it was charity," he said. "You never know what's bad with a computer, do you? I felt sorry for her. I figured maybe it was worth that in parts. Now I don't even get that."
"You win some, you lose some," said Briscoe. "We're grateful, okay? We're just trying to figure out if this is the one we're looking for."
"These disks were in the case pocket," said Shamir. "This isn't like one of those spy things? I read in the paper about laptops being stolen from the Alamo."
"Alamagordo?" asked Briscoe.
"Chinese guy."
"We don't go after spies too often," said Briscoe.
Green took the diskettes and looked at the labels one by one. "CHECKBOOK," the first read, then "LETTERS." The third was a photo-editing program. "SHAFTED," he read on the fourth one. "What does that mean?"

"Anything else in the case?" asked Briscoe. "Like a charging cord?"

Shamir shook his head.

"You get an address for this Ermilia Santonio?" asked Green.

"On the slip. If you find her, I want my thirty-five bucks," said Shamir. He reached into his shirt pocket and shoved a curled piece of paper at them. "If she ain't got it, what you say you do something about this parking ticket?"

"And they call Trump the master of the deal," muttered Briscoe.

"Santonio's way uptown," said Green, checking the address.

"We'll go by way of the invisible building supplies," said Briscoe. "The odds on two addresses to nowhere are getting too short to bet."

Green clicked off his cell phone as they turned onto Twenty-Second Street. "The hotel says Ermilia Santonio is off for two days, but they have the same home address."

"Amazing," said Briscoe. "Given the traffic, she'll die of old age before we get up there." He craned his neck looking for house numbers. "Well, whaddya know, Ed? It's not a vacant lot."

"It's not exactly the Dakota."

"It doesn't look occupied," said Briscoe, pulling up to the curb, "but it's not an empty lot."

The roughhouse had received delivery of 1200 square feet of prefinished light oak flooring and 1500 square feet of subflooring, all paid for on R.E. Chesko's platinum American Express. Plywood, however, covered the front windows and a folding steel gate, the kind a shopkeeper would use to close his store at night, protected the entryway. Green leaned his head out the car window and spotted the building permit on the other side of the steel gate. They could at least get the address of whoever was doing the renovation.

As he crossed the sidewalk, however, he heard music coming from under the stairway to the front door. He peered down the steps into the basement and saw another steel gate, with an open door behind it.

Briscoe caught up. "What've we got? A crack outlet mall?"

"Listening to Mozart?"

"What? The poor can't have taste?"

They climbed down the stairs.

"Hello?" shouted Green. "Anybody there? Police!"

A salt-and-pepper-haired man cautiously looked out. "Can I help you?" he asked. He was the kind of man who aged well, thin and outdoorsy. His white overalls were smudged on the bib and thigh with something caramel-colored, but he wore them more like a model in a Ralph Lauren ad than a working carpenter. In his right hand he held a goblet of red wine.

Green raised his badge. "Did you just get a delivery of flooring?"

"A week ago," he said. "Is there some problem?"

"We're Detectives Green and Briscoe. Can we talk to you?"

His brows narrowed. Sweat rushed down his nose. "If I'm being served, you can stick it through the bars."

"Detectives don't serve papers," said Green.

"You expecting a lawsuit?" asked Briscoe.

He shrugged. "They arrive as regularly as the tide. Fortunately, they also fall away with great regularity. But if you want to take the flooring you'll have to use a crowbar on half of it." He looked at the wine in his hand as if surprised it was there and set it on a ledge on the wall to fish for his keys. "I'm not quite down to boxed wines, yet, but they'd have me at Mad Dog 20/20 if they could."

Briscoe leaned to look past the man, but saw nothing unusual. "You must be Ralph Emerson Chesko."

"In the flesh."

"Your neighbor told me you used to manage a growth fund," said Green.

"At the Monticello Investment Group. 'Brother can you spare a dime?'" said Chesko.

"So you're working construction?" asked Briscoe.

"It's not exactly the Hamptons, is it? I've always liked working with my hands, but I never expected to do it twelve hours a day." He raised his palms to show calluses and an assortment of Band-Aids.

They stepped across the threshold. A large electric fan whined on the floor as if it were about to give up, directing air at a sofa with a sleeping bag on it. On the arm, a carton of Chinese food with red-lacquered chopsticks teetered in the artificial breeze. Chesko reached to turn off his portable CD player, while Briscoe peered up at the opening where a section of old flooring had been removed. Upstairs, hanging from a nail in the cracked plaster, a bare lightbulb dangled above a saw table.

"I'm doing subflooring today. I don't believe in just slapping good wood over the old. This house is the bottom of my new ladder. It had squatters, but I acquired it from the city for back taxes. I'll remodel, sell it, and use it to finance another. One rung, then another. I'm redeeming my soul with honest labor," he said cheerfully.

"So what happened with your growth fund?" asked Green.

"Tanked," said Chesko. "I made three big mistakes. First, that damned fiber optics thing. I knew it was risky, that's the only way to get real returns. Who could have guessed that—" He stopped abruptly, smiled. "Something tells me that you're not really interested in that."

"We're interested in your American Express card. It was used to book a room at the Waterloo Hotel."

Chesko looked genuinely confused. "Hotel?"

"A woman checked in with it."

"That's crazy!"

"Maybe the number was stolen?" asked Briscoe. He was thinking of the building supply store. If the number had been stolen there, Green and he were on a wild-goose chase. Anybody could be using it. "The woman prepaid for the room online."

"Oh," said Chesko. "You see, I've got the card in my duffel bag over there. But I know who has the number. Both my ex-wives. But Emily's catting around Palm Springs, as far as I know. And Barbara has no reason to book a hotel room."

"Barbara?"

"My first ex-wife. Emily's in the process of making it double-down."

"Is Barbara about five-six?" said Green. "Around a hundred and thirty-five pounds? Dark hair? Touch of gray?"

"I'm not sure about the weight. She put on a few after the divorce. Not that she got fat."

"Did Barbara wear a black beret?"

Chesko winced. "Christ, yeah, that's her. The Jacqueline Kerouac of the twenty-first century. Ever since the divorce, she's decided she's some kind of artiste, always wearing black and that stupid beret, babbling about a 'room of her own.' Of course she left out the rest of that Virginia Woolf quote, the part about having the 'independent means.' Call me Mr. Means. *I* was supposed to provide that. Everything first class: her fancy computer, her business-class software, all her supplies. Even the damned paper. I think she really believed her manuscripts would be archived. We're talking ten thou a month, fellows. How's that for Bohemian? But I paid until the roof fell in."

"So she went Beatnik on you?" said Briscoe.

Chesko shook his head. "She had no more business playing writer than Mike Tyson. It's embarrassing. A woman like her. Or like she was."

Green's eyes met Briscoe's. "What do you mean 'was'?"

"When I met her, she was a runner-up for Miss Connecticut. Even after a decade of marriage, I could walk into a room with her and guys would swivel their necks so hard they'd need a chiropractor. Then, it was the garden parties and the salad recipes and the linens and the apricot glaze on the quail. Yawn! I don't know how she could get wrapped up in that so much. Maybe it was the painkillers. She might as well have put pills in the candy dish. God, after twenty years she was boring!"

"So you traded her in for a sporty V-8," said Briscoe.

Chesko shrugged. "Why go on suffering? Maybe I was getting older and thinking about not having any kids. Maybe I just wanted someone who wasn't thinking about the linen sale at Bergdorf's when we made the beast. I know there was an age difference with Emily, but so what? Call it a mid-life crisis. Is that terrible?"

Briscoe toed a pile of sawdust and tried to shift closer to the fan.

"But it's classic, guys. I've been punished, and how!

I ended up with a young and beautiful woman who secretly took the pill to save her figure and was thinking about money when we made the beast. After the fund collapsed, Emily hit the road."

"You get what you pay for," said Briscoe.

"No one believes I haven't socked a bundle away somewhere, but I really haven't. They think I couldn't be that stupid. I believed in what I was doing. Why else would I have put all my own money in? I wasn't one of these bastards drifting down to the penthouse in their golden parachutes. I'm sleeping here!"

Briscoe and Green looked at each other.

"That's what integrity gets you. I don't care what Barbara is saying, I'm tapped. I know I'm in violation of the settlement, but I warned her I couldn't keep it up." He stuck his arms out. "So arrest me. She can't get a nickel if I'm in the poke."

"We're not here about your support payments, Mr. Chesko."

"I'm tired of paying for her crazy notions. The well is dry. She should get a job."

"She has crazy notions?"

"She's going to write the great American feminist novel, rake me over the coals for being a shit, and have me pay for her groceries while she does it. It's nuts and I'm sick of hearing about it."

"So you said," said Green.

"Well, you won't be hearing about it anymore," said Briscoe. He rocked back on his heels to watch Chesko's reaction to what Green was about to tell him.

"I'm afraid it appears that Barbara Chesko may be dead."

Chesko squinted, looked from Green to Briscoe and back again. "I don't understand."

"A woman fitting your description of Barbara fell down the air shaft of the Waterloo Hotel. From the eighth floor."

"She was the one who checked in? What was she doing in the Waterloo Hotel?"

"We don't know," said Green.

"For certain," said Briscoe. "It appears there was a man with her."

Chesko staggered unsteadily backward to the sofa, groping for it with his spread fingers. "She's dead?"

He lowered his head into his hands.

"Are you all right, Mr. Chesko?" asked Green.

"Yes. I think so." He shook his head. "No, I'm not 'all right.' We were married for twenty-three years."

"So, you met her at the Waterloo?"

Chesko looked up and squinted again. "Why would I do that? To rekindle our romance? Do you think there would be anything interesting after twenty-three years?" He winced. "I didn't mean that like that. We were a good couple once."

"I wouldn't know much about twenty-three years, but it's always interesting if she isn't your wife," said Briscoe. "Even if she's an ex-wife."

"She has an apartment in the Village. Why a hotel? If she had a boyfriend, why wouldn't she just take him home? What's the point? And using my card number!"

"Maybe that was the point," said Green.

Chesko shook his head again, this time as if he knew that this was exactly the kind of thing she would do. Then, suddenly, his jaws clenched and his nostrils flared. "Maybe she was looking for another 'patron of the arts.'" He shook his head. "It's just like her. Pathetic. How could she fall out the window?"

"That's what we'd like to find out. We were hoping the man who was with her could tell us," said Briscoe.

"You wouldn't have been that man by any chance?" asked Green. "Maybe she was all right when you left?"

Chesko's hands were shaking. He crossed his arms and sighed. "I've told you. You've got the wrong turkey, fellows. Not me. And I have no idea who'd have wanted to bang her."

Briscoe raised an eyebrow.

"They're going to love this," muttered Chesko. "Everybody's going to blame me! The *Post* will be after me again. I took my investors' money, then pitched my wife off the roof to get her life insurance." He waved both hands down. "Christ!"

"We're just trying to find out how she died," said Briscoe. "Did she have insurance?"

Chesko looked at him coldly. "I don't believe this."

"Did she?" asked Green.

"She used to. When the fund tanked, I stopped paying for it. Look, I'm very upset. Do you have to badger me right now? Is there something suspicious about her death? You said she fell."

"I'm sorry, Mr. Chesko," said Briscoe. "We don't mean anything by it. It's our job, you understand."

Chesko stared at them for a few seconds, then lowered his head. "What I wouldn't give for that big bottle of Napoleon cognac I used to keep in my office."

"There's always Mad Dog 20/20," said Briscoe.

T he super, a gaunt man named Voskov, flipped along the key ring. "No, haven't seen her since I picked up the rent Tuesday. She's pretty quiet. A good tenant."

He tried a key. It didn't work.

"She ever have guests?" asked Briscoe. "A boyfriend?"

"I saw her with a guy once. It's none of my business."

The lock clacked and the super bumped the door with his shoulder. "It's tight," he said. "I tried to loosen the frame with a hammer, but it's an old building..."

"Maybe you relocked it," said Briscoe.

Voskov turned it back the other way until it clacked. This time when he bumped it, it opened with a squeak. He shrugged and went inside. "Mrs. Chesko? Mrs. Chesko? The police are here!"

"If she answers, I'm running," said Briscoe, checking the side room.

"Amen," said Green. "Anybody been in here since Tuesday?"

Voskov shook his head. "Not me. No."

31

Green put his hand on the super's shoulder. "You're not in trouble. Barbara Chesko's dead." Voskov looked around as if he expected to see the body. Briscoe emerged from the bedroom.

"I don't come in unless they ask me. Somebody might get in when I go to lunch, but I haven't seen anybody."

Briscoe held up an eight-by-twelve photograph. "I found this on the desk. There's five of them. Is this her?"

Voskov nodded.

"Bingo, Ed. Barbara Chesko with a face."

Green studied the photograph. From her torso up, Chesko stared defiantly into the camera, arms crossed, chin raised, hair pulled back. She was wearing a black turtleneck. Green remembered the body with half its face torn away and winced. "That's her."

"You smell that?" asked Briscoe.

"Gas?" sniffed Voskov with wide eyes.

"More like oil," said Green.

Voskov nodded in relief. "The exterminator came on Wednesday. Every six months."

"So someone *was* in the apartment after Tuesday," said Green.

"Sure, sure. But he's nobody, just the exterminator."

"Thank you, Mr. Voskov. We're going to look around a while." Briscoe gently pushed him toward the door.

"When can I run an ad for the apartment?"

"We'll let you know," said Briscoe, closing the door. "In addition to the insecticide," he added, "I smell a rent hike."

"Life goes on," said Green. "You know, this isn't exactly one of those studio portraits."

"Looks a little frightening," said Briscoe.

"Women can get that way when they're dumped."

They examined the tiny apartment. There was a kitchen area to the left, with a small cappuccino machine. The refrigerator contained yogurt, a tub of tabbouleh, soy milk, and some leftover pasta with mussels. A pint of expensive ice cream sat in the freezer. The dishes and the sink were clean, except for a cup waiting to be washed. A dry herbal tea bag was stuck to the bottom. Nothing in the trash can under the sink was unusual. Junk mail and orange peelings. Two cockroaches dead on their backs.

"See any sign of a boyfriend?" asked Briscoe, checking the medicine cabinet. "If she provided the protection at the hotel, she didn't leave the box."

Green gave the bedroom a quick look, then paused at the desk. The room was so small the desk chair bumped against the queen-sized bed. Green could actually sit on the bed and reach the desk. The "computer" Briscoe had mentioned earlier consisted of a Sony docking unit with a wireless keyboard, speakers, a cable modem, and a wireless mouse. None of this equipment looked like it had been manufactured more than six months ago, meaning, as with most computer stuff, it had only been obsolete from about the time Barbara Chesko had first plugged it in.

"The pawned laptop would fit in this dock," said Green.

"It would be a strange coincidence if it didn't," said Briscoe.

"This looks pretty high end for your usual PC user," said Green, "like it would run to a few thousand."

"Exactly what the ex complained about," said Briscoe.

Just to be certain, they searched the room and into two pieces of luggage in the closet, but found no laptop. Santonio must have lifted it out of her hotel room, along with her purse.

Green sat on the bed, opened the desk drawer and found a stack of letters, but was distracted by a date book. As he moved toward July he saw a hair appointment, a phone number, an appointment at "K&S!" in late July. On August 21, it said "Waterloo," but nothing about whoever she was meeting. Every two weeks on Thursday nights going on into October it said "Writing Group, 8 sharp!" with different addresses. The last one had been on October 17. She wouldn't make the one scheduled for tonight. He bagged the address book because of the various unidentified phone numbers scribbled here and there on different pages.

In the middle drawer there was a stack of bright white paper and underneath an unopened box of Hammermill 100% cotton bond.

In the front of the file drawer at the bottom of the desk were a number of thin folders labeled "Apartment," "Divorce," "Visa," "Bills," and "Receipts." Behind them, folders nearly the thickness of a telephone directory were unevenly stuffed with different shades of paper. Green pulled out one of the folders and flipped it over to the title page:

SHAFTED

The Story of a Marriage

**a novel by
Barbara Chesko**

Sixth Draft

Green shook his head with a slight smile. "Lennie, get this!"

Briscoe swung his head into the door. "Find something?"

"It's the 'great American feminist novel,' as Ralph Chesko described it."

Briscoe read the title page. "A moving commentary on the ennui of modern marriage, I'm sure. Very original."

Green opened to page one and read out loud. "'This is the story of a marriage, my marriage, my marriage to William Shaft, also known as Bill. Bill was everything a woman could wish for. He was—'" Green broke off, shaking his head.

"'He was just my Bill!'" said Briscoe, rolling his eyes. "Is this supposed to be a comedy? *Sex and the City* revisited?"

"'He was tall, handsome, and destined for financial success. He was just out of the Air Force and was known as Major William Shaft. Little did I know how it would all end up twenty-one years later, with Major Shaft's cheating (both the financial and the marital), anger, and heart-rending betrayal.'"

"Please," said Briscoe, "*I'm* rending." He took a breath. "Aw, hell," he added, "we shouldn't be making fun of her. Maybe this was a first draft or something."

"It says 'Sixth.'"

"Is this woman published?"

He lifted several of the letters out and skimmed them. "'It doesn't meet our needs at this time,' 'Thank you for thinking of us,' 'Unfortunately, we feel the market is glutted with novels of this type at this time,' and so on, and so on." He flipped a few more. "This one's not bad." He handed it to Briscoe.

"'While I have utter faith in your talent and the story you have to tell, I'm afraid the editorial board has decided to pass on this at this time. I know it may be a lot to ask, but my personal feeling is that your work is very close to fruition'—I like that 'fruition'—'and that perhaps another revision, a really close line edit, might provide exactly the polish that could lead to a contract.'"

"It sounds like she was getting there."

"Go figure." Briscoe handed the letter back. "They hadn't actually signed her."

"Most people can't write a book."

"You know what I mean. Horseshoes and hand grenades."

"That might be it," said Green. "This letter was sent on May 17. What if she got shot down?"

"Suicide?"

"She rewrites the whole thing, gets her hopes up, and they say no. She gets distraught and so on."

"It works for me. Santonio lifted her purse and laptop and maybe some jewelry after she jumped. She put the room on Ralphie's card just to zing him one more time. Shafting Mister Shaft," said Briscoe.

"It looks like the lieutenant gets her wish," said Green. "We'll be on the drive-by tomorrow. Think of the fine class of people we'll get to canvass."

"The deaf *and* the blind. Hear no evil, see no evil. We need something to confirm her state of mind. Is there a turndown?"

Green flipped more letters. "Not that I can find. If they hadn't decided yet, or she wasn't finished editing, she's not likely to have killed herself over it."

"Unless she got so depressed she couldn't bring herself to finish," said Briscoe. It would be too convenient that she got turned down Tuesday and killed herself Thursday, wouldn't it? I never pull a case like that."

"So it hinges on this: if she's still got hopes for her book, she isn't likely to have done it and we're looking at murder. If she's been rejected…"

"I hate trying to read a dead vic's mind."

Green skimmed more letters. "There are several from an editing company. They go back over a year. The most recent…it says they've completed the 'line edit.' It's dated July first."

Briscoe counted on his fingers. "The publisher says get a line edit, whatever that is. It's finished by July. The book gets turned down. She kills herself. That makes too much sense."

"*If* it got turned down." Green plucked out the May letter from the publisher and began dialing on his cell phone. "Let's find out." He waited and listened. "Answering machine. Leave a message?"

"Tomorrow," said Briscoe. "Maybe Chesko knows. We can stop by there before we chase the goose. What are the odds we can't find this Ermilia Santonio?"

"What are the odds that if we do, Santonio says she didn't push anybody?"

"Then it's robbery's problem."

"Wait," said Green. "Instead of going back to Chesko…" He picked up the date book. "The writers' group. 'Glenda's' it says. They're meeting tomorrow at ah—eight. They'd know about her book prospects, right?"

"They'd maybe know if she was depressed," said Briscoe. "I doubt Ralph would have noticed, even when they were married."

"Let's make sure Voskov gets this place locked," said Green.

"Huh?"

Green twisted his hand holding an imaginary key. "He turned it one way and couldn't get in. He turned it the other and could."

"The door was unlocked when we got here. Sure." He thought for a minute. "What are you thinking about?"

"I don't know. Maybe it was just the exterminator. Maybe not. There's a small chance the laptop Shamir gave us wasn't Barbara Chesko's. Hers could have been stolen out of here."

"Don't complicate things." Briscoe moved his hand creating a marquee in the air. "Ed Green for the Defense."

"There's more than one Sony laptop out there."

"Take that manuscript and the letters. Maybe the book shows she was unraveling. And let's remind Mr. Voskov not to touch anything."

"Let's find Ermilia Santonio."

"But unless she confesses," said Briscoe, "we'll still have to look for Chesko's recreational partner. There was somebody in that room using a condom."

"Now, *you're* complicating things," said Green.

"**E**rmilia Santonio?" said Green, holding up his badge.

A man stared out past the door chain. His left eye was white as if whatever had slashed the scar running from his forehead to his acne-scarred cheek had also taken its sight. He said, "She went back to Guatemala." He moved to close the door, but Green held it firm.

"Can we come in?" said Briscoe. "We just want to ask a few questions."

"What do you want?"

Green spoke in Spanish. "We're police detectives. We're not from immigration. It's about her job."

The man answered in English, but stepped back from the door as he did. "Her job? Which one? I told you, she's gone." Green could see that the man was wearing a full length jumpsuit. The embroidered logo on the chest said "Waterloo Hotel."

"We want to ask Ermilia about some missing property. It belongs to her or her sister or somebody in her family."

This seemed to confuse the man somewhat.

"Do we have to talk through the door?" Briscoe asked.

The man disconnected the chain. Briscoe nudged Green and tapped his own chest to draw attention to the man's jumpsuit.

They stepped into the tiny living room. The one lamp was very nice, as if new, but the end tables and the sofa had been around for a long time.

"So," said Briscoe, "you work at the Waterloo, too?"

The man stopped. He was either confused or nervous. "Waterloo?" was all he managed.

"Is that where she got the laptop?"

The man shook his head. "Ermilia works in a bodega on a hundred and fifteenth."

"But she's a maid at the Waterloo hotel, isn't she?"

He hesitated. "We both work there," he said slowly. "I have three jobs. She has two."

"Three, huh?"

"A man has to live. This is New York."

"So was it you who got the laptop? Or was it Ermilia?"

"What are you talking about? We can't afford no computer."

Green shoved him against the wall and pinned him there with a spread hand. "We don't like it when you play dumb. It tries our patience and makes us think you don't trust us."

"What's your name?" asked Briscoe.

"Guillermo," he said. He wasn't a guy easily scared. Like a lot of immigrants he expected to be roughed around. He accepted it as his destiny.

"Guillermo who?" said Green.

"Guillermo Santonio. Ermilia is my wife."

"Now was that a nice thing to do?" said Green. "Send her all the way downtown to pawn that laptop?"

"I didn't send her nowhere," said the man.

"So why'd she pawn it all the way down there?"

"On Fridays, she cleans apartments in the Village."

"When you stole the laptop," said Briscoe, "was Barbara Chesko in the room?"

The man's eyes grew wide. "I stole nothing! God is my witness! Barbara Che—?"

"Chesko. You didn't catch her name? She's the woman you pushed out the window."

"No! I don't know what you are talking about. I found it." Santonio went pale as he suddenly realized why they were here. "*Madre de Dios*," he mumbled.

"What is it?" said Briscoe.

"The woman who fell."

"Yes, her."

"What about her? Do you have something you want to tell us?" asked Green.

"The computer was hers?" He looked quickly from Briscoe to Green and back. "I heard about her from Romero, the handyman. I didn't think anything. He said she killed herself. She was robbed? I had nothing to do with that. I was never there!"

"In her hotel room?"

"No!"

"You used your passkey," said Green.

"No! I don't get a passkey! I clean the lobby and the trash bins. I work in the basement. They took the passkeys."

"Who?'

"The managers. A month ago. More. Six weeks."

"Why'd they take your keys, Guillermo?"

"They take everybody's keys. They say there was pilfering."

"You a pilferer, Guillermo?" demanded Green. "Is that it?"

"I didn't steal nothing!"

Green's forearm banged Santonio against the wall again. "Maybe you just wanted the woman? Had her, killed her, took the laptop as payment for services rendered."

"No!"

"How'd you get the laptop, then? She woke up and saw you and you pushed her out the window."

"No! It was in a trashcan. The first thing I do every morning. The corner tore through."

"The corner of the laptop?" asked Green.

"It tore through the plastic bag. I thought maybe the computer was broke. I thought I could get it fixed, maybe sell it."

"Maybe you had a little struggle with the woman who owned it. You didn't really intend to kill her, did you?"

"I don't go to the rooms."

"Look, *amigo*," said Briscoe, trying once more, "tell us the truth. The laptop and the purse were on the bed. She comes out of the bathroom—"

"*I don't go into rooms*," Santonio said through gritted teeth.

Green's eyes met Briscoe's. They had tossed out the accident suggestion as a phony lifeline, but he hadn't gone for it. Usually, a guilty suspect, feeling the waters rise, will grasp at any kind of rope floating near. Either Guillermo was a particularly savvy criminal or he hadn't murdered her.

Briscoe shrugged. Green lifted the pressure he had been applying to Santonio's chest.

"First Ermilia accuses me of stealing it," said

Guillermo, "now you. I tried it and it light up, but it needs a password. I go to work. What does she do? Get thirty-five dollars from a pawnshop to buy baby clothes! It has to be worth two hundred."

"You have a baby?"

"Soon," said Guillermo. "Two months."

"I hope you'll be able to see it born," said Green. "We're going to go down to the station. If you're lying to us…"

"No, please. I have to go to work. I swear. It was in the big corner trash can. I thought I was lucky."

"When did this happen?" asked Briscoe.

"I don't know. I get to work at seven-thirty. Must have been about eight-thirty, eight forty-five."

"Why didn't you turn the laptop in to lost and found?" said Briscoe. "Isn't that what you're supposed to do?"

"It was in the trash! Someone threw it out. If it's in the trash, nobody wants it, right?"

"You wanted it. Where can we find Ermilia?"

"She had nothing to do with it."

"With what?"

"Finding the computer." In exasperation, he muttered something in Spanish.

"What was that?" asked Briscoe.

"He says we have wax in our ears," said Green.

"I'm getting old, Guillermo," said Briscoe, leaning toward him, "and Ed is easily confused. We need things repeated until we get them right. So where is Ermilia?"

Guillermo licked his lips again. "At work. The bodega. Please, don't upset her. It could harm the baby."

"We'll have to check this out, Mr. Santonio. You'll

have to come with us. What time did you say you got to work?"

"Seven-thirty."

All they'd need was proof Santonio was in the hotel around the time Barbara Chesko died, Briscoe knew, and they might be able to close the case. Without physical evidence they wouldn't be able to pin murder on him, but there was still a possibility in the DNA on the bedspread. "Let's get Ermilia and straighten this out," said Briscoe.

"I work in forty-five minutes."

"At the hotel?"

"No, my other job. I clean fish."

"We'll call your boss for you," said Green, taking out his cell phone.

"Please," Santonio pleaded, "the police, you know. I'll get fired and I didn't do nothing. Let me call in sick. It's not easy to get a job. The baby."

"I thought you had three jobs," said Briscoe.

"We are needing every penny. Please."

Still holding the cell phone, Green looked at Briscoe, who said, "When we get to the station."

Santonio's hand flashed out, shoved Briscoe into Green, and snatched the cell. As they lurched back, the detectives automatically reacted as if he had gone for their weapons. "Damn!" said Briscoe. Green reached at Santonio and just scratched the collar of his T-shirt as he ducked and rolled into the bathroom, slamming the door.

Reassured by the warm feel of their pistols still in their holsters, they pulled their pieces and crashed flat against either side of the door.

"Is there a window?" asked Green.

Briscoe shrugged.

"Guillermo," shouted Green. "Don't do this."

Briscoe tried the old metal door. The paint was

chipped where it had been dinked. "Locked." They heard him talking.

"Who's he calling? His wife?" said Briscoe.

"Come on out, Guillermo," said Green. "Your baby's going to need a father. Don't let this get out of hand!" Briscoe backed to the window and watched the fire escape.

"Come out, Guillermo, or we'll have to break in!"

"Call for backup?" asked Briscoe. "We'll need a battering ram." He tried to unlock the window to step out on the fire escape, but it had long been sealed by layers of paint.

Green thought of what Santonio might have in the bathroom. A gun? A razor? Keeping his gun leveled at the door he backed up.

The detectives tensed at the sound of the latch turning. "Doan shoot!" they heard. "I give up. Doan shoot!"

"Open the door!" shouted Green. "Slowly!"

"Keep your hands high!" said Briscoe.

The door creaked back. Santonio was on his knees on the floor, his hands over his head. Green then saw a dark shape in Santonio's hand. Every muscle in his body went rigid.

The cell phone.

A flush of cold sweat instantly covered the detective. He had nearly fired. Green trembled with relief, then anger.

"Get flat on that floor!" shouted Briscoe.

"I could have killed you!" snapped Green, reaching for his handcuffs. "Just give me an excuse to hurt you!"

Green, Briscoe, and Van Buren stood in the twilight of the one-way mirror. On the other side, Guillermo Santonio sat still, his arms crossed. He sniffed every minute or so. He had wept in the car.

"I pushed the redial," Green was saying to Van Buren, "and it was the bodega. He was warning her."

"And she's gone, I assume," said Van Buren.

"The way Ed drove, we're lucky to be alive," said Briscoe, "but she didn't even take her sweater. The owner acted like he didn't know her, but we didn't let him get away with that."

"We circled the block in each direction," said Green, "but she had about fifteen, twenty minutes to scoot."

"That was pretty dumb, fellows," said Van Buren.

"Hey, it was a phone," snapped Green.

"Watch it, Ed," she warned.

He spun away. "Okay," he sighed. "It was dumb."

She studied the suspect. "He looks pretty tough."

"All he needs is a knife in his teeth," said Briscoe. "He says he was adopted by missionaries after his parents were killed. That blind eye was courtesy of the Guatemalan military."

"He's legal?"

"A U.S. citizen like you, me, and John Walker Lindh. Ermilia isn't. The green card in her apartment is a phony."

"They're not married?"

"Afraid to get anywhere near the legal system. She must have sneaked in, then met him."

"But if she just married him, she'd be okay, right?"

"Maybe not if she sneaked in first. They'd make her go back and apply to be admitted."

Van Buren nodded. "Which they'd never do."

"On the other hand, if she gives birth…" said Briscoe.

"She's the mother of an American citizen."

"I checked with the hotel," said Briscoe. "It's true that they collected all the passkeys six weeks ago and issued new ones only to employees who need them regularly. Guillermo isn't supposed to go up to the rooms."

"But he could have gotten his wife's," said Green.

"Is the hotel admitting it has a theft problem?"

Briscoe shook his head. "'Had,' they say. Six or seven rooms were boosted in June."

"Why didn't they tell you this?" said Van Buren.

"They don't want it to get out. Lawsuits. Publicity. They say they don't have a problem anymore."

Van Buren rolled her eyes. "Maybe we should check if anyone else 'fell' out a midtown window. See what thefts *were* reported."

"I've got a list on the way."

Green reached for the doorknob. "So, are we going to question this turkey or not?"

"You read him his rights?" They nodded. "Maybe Lennie better," said Van Buren. "You're a little anxious, don't you think?"

47

"Maybe I don't like being jerked around."

"That's what I mean, Ed."

Briscoe jumped between his partner and his lieutenant. "I've got such a history of being jerked around, it bores me." He walked past Van Buren and opened the door to the interrogation room. Santonio acknowledged his presence with only a quick glance.

"Thirsty?" asked Briscoe. "I can get you a soda. A coffee."

Santonio shook his head.

"I don't blame you on the coffee. It's terrible here."

"Could use a smoke."

"Can't do that," said Briscoe.

Santonio seemed to be searching the corners for cobwebs.

"Look," said Briscoe. "It didn't really help Mrs. Santonio to make her run."

"She didn't do nothing, but you would punish her all the same. Cops are all the same. Judges are all the same."

"She pawned that laptop, Guillermo. That makes it look like she stole it. She's a maid. She has a passkey."

"Ermilia is no thief."

"But you need money for the baby."

"We work hard! Do you think thieves would work like we do?" His voice ground like gravel. "All I want is for my son to be born in a country where the government cannot do this"—he pointed to his bad eye—"to a ten-year old boy." He broke down and began to mumble *Madre de Dios*, *Madre de Dios*, over and over.

Briscoe glanced at the one-way mirror, shrugged, and handed Santonio his handkerchief. Eventually,

48

Santonio said *gracias*. Briscoe put a hand on Santonio's shoulder and spoke quietly.

"Look, Guillermo, Ermilia could be in a lot of trouble. She ran from the police. If we have a lot of trouble finding her…"

"All I care is that you do not find her until my son is born. Then you cannot send her back."

Briscoe tugged at Santonio's arm to look him in the eye. "I can understand your troubles, Guillermo, but the district attorneys? You'll just be another notch on their guns."

Santonio seemed to be resigned to his fate, not really rising to Briscoe's threats. Briscoe continued, but Santonio held to his story. Filling out some paperwork on a clipboard, Van Buren remained in the room with Green. After nearly forty-five minutes, he said, "Good cop's not working."

"And you want to play bad cop, I suppose?" said Van Buren.

"Different strokes," said Green.

She tapped on the glass. Briscoe came out. "Yeah?"

"What do you think, Lennie?"

"I think he's scared," said Briscoe. "He loves his wife."

"Did he kill Barbara Chesko?"

Briscoe shrugged. "I doubt it. Not deliberately, anyway."

"My turn," said Green, but just as he moved toward the door, Santonio stood, went to the barred window and gripped it. They watched as he pulled at the bars as if to try to rip them out of the frame.

He turned, then, looked straight at the one-way mirror and shouted, "I want a lawyer! A lawyer! Get me a lawyer. I am not saying nothing else!"

"Well," said Van Buren, "it took a while for the ghost of Ernesto Miranda to dial, but the call seems to have come in."

So, where we're at," said Briscoe to Assistant Medical Examiner Rodgers, "is that Guillermo Santonio is willing to plead guilty to robbing Barbara Chesko's hotel room. His court-appointed attorney is trying to get a light sentence because he's fessed up."

"Court-appointed attorneys are good at throwing their clients on the merciless mercy of the court," said Rodgers.

"Some of them give the D.A.s a real bad time," said Green.

"My theory is if you don't have enough money to hire an attorney, you should break out of jail and rob somebody else to pay for one. Otherwise you don't stand a chance."

"I'll stay tuned for the *Nightline* discussion of criminal justice in America," said Briscoe. "What I'm suspicious about is why the guy suddenly confesses."

"You?" Rodgers asked Green.

"Could be. He says he got a passkey from his wife, and makes a big deal about how she didn't know, but the hotel collects them when the maids clock out."

"He denies ever seeing Barbara Chesko," said Briscoe.

"But if he wants to cop to the laptop," said Green, "he's welcome to the jail time."

"He's just covering for his wife," said Briscoe. "Which is why the D.A.'s office sent us back on the bricks. It could be that Santonio's confessing to burglary to avoid a murder charge."

"Hence, your friendly M.E., a.k.a. 'me.'"

"Can you place the guy in the room? Is there anything here that indicates Mrs. Chesko was forced out of the window?"

"Can't say about him," Rodgers said. "But there are signs that she didn't go gently."

"So you *are* saying she was pushed?" asked Green.

"Maybe. Maybe not."

Briscoe spread his hands. "Come on, doc. Help us out here. We just want to know where to file the case. S for 'suicide,' M for 'murder,' or A for the ever popular and always easy on the taxpayers 'accident.'"

"Door number one, number two, or number three: all have something going for them. No note, eh?"

"No," said Briscoe sharply.

"Well, she has paint under her fingernails. It was scratched off the windowsill." Rodgers stepped to the counter and opened a file. She spread the photographs on the counter. Green winced then forced himself to look.

"I didn't find any pre-death contusions that indicated anyone had struck her or gripped her arms or anything like that." Rodgers lifted one of the photographs. "There is a scratch on her left forearm. It could have been raked by someone trying to grab at her as she fell."

Green held out his arm and slowly pulled it back. "Or she jerked away from someone, then fell."

"Or it scraped the wall on the way out or down." The M.E. pointed. "They're not showing real clear, but you can see them."

"It looks like four parallel scratches," said Briscoe.

"And it could have been done by four fingernails. Looks like it," said Rodgers. "I'd testify it looks like it. But it could have been something else."

"Thanks a lot," said Briscoe.

"My, didn't we wake up sarcastic today? I just gather the physical evidence, Lennie. They were fresh scratches. They didn't bleed long. About as long as it takes to fall eight floors."

"But, look," said Green, "she grabbed at the window frame, so we can rule out suicide, right?"

"Who's to say she didn't change her mind at the last second?" said Rodgers. "In the split second between the trigger's release and the powder's ignition, the suicide decides to live. Bang anyway."

Briscoe raised an eyebrow. "You spend too much time down here communing with your clients."

"I could get out more, it's true. But this one isn't speaking clearly to me." She lowered the arm back on the slab. "I can tell you she had sex before she died. Both lower orifices. Nonoxynol-9, so the penetrator used a condom."

"Both orifices," said Briscoe, "so it took at least five minutes."

"If she was lucky," said Rodgers. "There's no sign of resistance. No sign of vaginal bruising. No evidence of rape. But then, sometimes there isn't."

"And the nonoxynol, it matched the wrapper we found?"

"The wrapper wasn't totally dry, so I'd say yes. But it means nothing. It's the most common spermicide and one of the most common condoms. Most stores sell them."

"Anything else?"

"There's a bit of a fingerprint on the corner, but you couldn't identify anybody from it. Not enough detail. Too few points of comparison. We could try to see if there's anything odd about your suspect's prints, like a scar or something, but that would be a long shot. Send down his prints, anyway."

"Santonio says Chesko wasn't in the room when he stole the laptop. We're asking for a DNA sample and he seems willing."

"Bring it on, then," said Rodgers. "But I'll have to see if there's anything we can compare it to."

"Look hard," said Green. "We were hoping you could help."

"Maybe she was just looking for a quick one and picked up somebody," suggested Rodgers. "Then maybe it depressed her."

"She reserved the room a day ahead," said Green. "It doesn't seem like a pickup."

The M.E. shrugged. "Maybe it was depressing anyway."

"What about pubic hairs?" asked Green. "White guy? Black?"

"I didn't find any. I could look again, but a hair won't tell you much if you don't get a follicle for the DNA."

"Come on, Doc," said Briscoe. "I'd like to wrap this up before Christmas."

"Look," said Rodgers, "we can almost certainly get

DNA off the bedspread, and hope it isn't just her fluid, or maybe off the condom wrapper."

"We'd already planned on the neighborhood pub crawl," said Briscoe. "And checking on boyfriends. I've got a hunch the stain came from her ex."

Green gave him a quizzical look. "Where the hell did you get that?"

"Can you think of any better revenge on your ex than throwing yourself out of the window after having a reunion?" said Briscoe.

Green shook his head. "That's like a soap opera."

"I've known two cases of it not necessarily by window." He paused. "I'm not kidding. One splattered her brains with her husband's forty-five at Sunday dinner."

"I'll raise you by four," said Rodgers. "My favorite was the guy who drank battery acid at a strip joint. His ex was performing with a snake." Green winced. "Yes, a reptilian snake of the genus Python. Not one of the usual two-legged snakes."

"I fold," said Briscoe. "Wait a minute. You said you could get DNA from a condom wrapper?"

The M.E. smirked. "A guy's in the heat of passion. He's got one hand busy unzipping or groping or something. He's in a hurry. He tears the condom open with his teeth, leaving some saliva on it."

"That's good," said Green.

"And they teach you that in pathology school?" said Briscoe.

"You learn a lot communing with the dead," said the M.E., "and in bed, my first husband usually qualified."

Glenda Atterby was in no hurry to open her door, even though she had been notified by the doorman. Briscoe leaned on the bell several times, then pounded the door with the heel of his fist. "Police!" he said. Green held up his badge in front of the peephole.

"All right, already!" they heard her say, as she unlocked her door.

"Are you Glenda Atterby?" asked Briscoe.

"Yes, and you've interrupted Melva Patterson's reading."

Six women sat in a circle in the living room behind her. The one in a wing chair had a grim expression. She put down her manuscript, sipped red wine from a balloon glass, and avoided looking in the detectives' direction. "I hate being interrupted," she said.

"I'm sorry to disturb your soirée, but we understand that Barbara Chesko had an appointment to be here tonight."

"She's not here. Oh, God! There's nothing wrong, is there?"

"Can we come in?"

Atterby backed away, then rushed to her group.

"Barbara!" She spun back to Briscoe. "She never misses! Don't tell me—"

"I'm afraid it's bad news. Mrs. Chesko, she's dead."

One guest shrieked and bit down on her fist. One threw herself against a heavyset woman and sobbed on her shoulder. The woman looked surprised, then annoyed, then rolled her eyes. Patterson gulped her wine. The other two froze in astonishment.

"Oh my God!" said Atterby.

"Was she murdered?" asked Patterson.

"Why would you think she was murdered?" asked Green.

"Because you're policemen!" said Atterby.

"We're just trying to find out about her," said Briscoe.

"How did she die?" Patterson insisted.

"She fell."

"Fell?"

"From a window."

The women sat stunned. "Oh my God!" repeated Atterby, groping for a chair. "All that talent!"

Briscoe and Green waited to let the shock subside. The heavyset woman seemed unable to decide what to do about the woman sobbing on her shoulder. Finally, Atterby recovered enough to shake her head and say, "Just as her novel was about to be published!"

"Really?" asked Green. "She sold her book?"

"She was planning to bring her contract tonight," said Atterby. Several of the women looked surprised, then horrified.

"Tonight?" asked Briscoe.

"Bummer," said Patterson, knocking back more wine.

"It was a surprise," said Atterby, more to explain to the other women than to the detectives. "She told me she was going to bring some special news, signed and delivered."

"When did she say this?"

"She telephoned me Friday. Maybe it was Saturday. Yes, Saturday."

"Did she say it was a book contract?"

"She didn't have to. It was all she wanted in the world. It was all she lived for."

"We knew she would be the one to break in," said a woman squatting on a throw pillow.

"There's so much luck involved," said Atterby. "But she was really on track."

"How do you mean?" asked Briscoe.

"She had an editor really interested in her work. He was helping her put the manuscript in shape. He even recommended an editing professional to work with her."

"So," said Green, "she was a pretty good writer."

"'Pretty' is condescending," said the heavyset woman. Her voice was as hoarse as a cheese grater. "She was a good writer."

"Better than good," said another. "We must never forget her."

"She was a *great* writer," said another and dissolved in tears. Her friend soothed her.

"Better than the rest of you?" asked Green.

"And what is that supposed to mean?" snapped the hoarse woman.

"I mean, if she was 'really on track,' as you say, about to get published, you all must be pretty, I mean, good."

Atterby smiled. "We are. No one is allowed to bring

58

negativity into our group. We are here to be positive."
Several of the women nodded seriously, several wiping
tears.

"So, some of you must be on your way as well,"
said Green.

"Our luck will come," said Patterson. "We each just
need to find the right editor on the right day. Am I
right?"

Several women nodded. One rubbed at the back
of her hand.

"So, did you know this editor who was interested
in Mrs. Chesko's novel?" asked Briscoe.

"Barbara kept it a secret," said Atterby. "She didn't
want to jinx it."

"And we didn't want to know," insisted the heavyset
woman.

"Why not?" asked Briscoe.

"There would be a temptation to exploit that, an
imposition on our friendships, so it's against group
rules. Each of us wants to make it on her own. She
would share when it was right for her. We didn't ask,
did we?"

"None of you?"

There was a momentary silence. Patterson hesitantly
spoke. "Ah, Kirstner and Strawn." She glanced at her
friends. "We went to Barnes and Noble after the ses-
sion at Hannah's." She turned toward the hoarse
woman. She was presumably Hannah. "Barbara
mentioned that the new book by Suzanne Lewiston
had been edited by the man who was interested in
her novel."

"She didn't say who?"

"No, just the publisher: Kirstner and Strawn."

The editor who had been encouraging Barbara

59

Chesko wrote on Kirstner and Strawn stationery, Green remembered. Chesko's date book had also listed an appointment at "K & S."

"Her husband—her ex, I mean. What did he think of her writing, do you know?" said Briscoe.

"Him!" said Atterby. "He was just another man who wants one woman chained in the kitchen and another one chained to his bed."

"He kept telling her she needed to give up writing and get a job," said Patterson. "And then, a month ago, he claimed he had no more money. It was an outrage."

"He had some business reverses, they say," said Briscoe.

"Like that means he didn't have a golden parachute!" said Atterby.

"His bimbo left him," said Patterson. "Poor boy!"

"The hurt he put Barbara through!" said the sniffler.

"But it brought out her creativity," said Hannah. "It made her stronger!" Several of them nodded.

"Listen," said Briscoe, "we're trying to talk to all the people who knew her. Did she date? Did she have a steady boyfriend? Anything like that?"

"I think she was pretty fed up with men," said Patterson.

"She wasn't you know like *that*," said another. "Just not wanting to get involved."

"Well, was there anyone she might be seeing casually?"

"She never mentioned anyone," said Patterson.

"Maybe she had a reason to keep it secret? Like he was married?"

Briscoe had clearly said the wrong thing. Atterby

bit each word. "After what happened to her, I hardly think she'd do that!"

"We were just trying to find out why she was in a hotel in midtown," Green explained. "Any ideas?"

"Maybe her apartment was being painted?" said Hannah. "People get sick from the fumes."

Briscoe interrupted. "How did she seem lately? Was she moody? Did she seem depressed?"

"She was on cloud nine the last time I talked to her," said Atterby. Most of the others hadn't seen her for several weeks. One saw her in a coffee shop, but didn't get a chance to talk.

"You think if her book got turned down, she might have...?"

"Killed herself?" said Atterby.

"Gotten depressed, let's say," said Briscoe.

"She was a strong woman!" said Atterby. "Isn't that right?" The women nodded. "She'd have been disappointed. I don't know what I would do, but I know she would pick herself up and go back at it twice as hard!"

This set the crying woman to bawling. Briscoe raised an eyebrow at Green, his "Oh God, that's enough" signal.

"We'll get in touch if there's anything more," said Green.

"Will you let us know what happened?" asked Atterby.

"That bastard hired someone to throw her off the roof," said Patterson. "You can bet on it. She didn't kill herself."

"We never said she did," said Briscoe. "All we know so far is that she fell."

Patterson rolled her eyes.

"Is there anything you know about this you haven't said?" Green asked Patterson. "Rumors about Mr. Chesko? Anything Barbara might have told you?"

"All I know," said Patterson, "is that money can buy more than bimbos. There are people in this city who'd murder anybody for a buck ninety-five."

"And don't we know it," said Briscoe. "But was Barbara afraid for her life or anything like that?"

"If you want to know if I can tell you anything specific, well, no. I can't. But that doesn't mean it didn't happen. I know a thing or two."

"I'll bet you do," said Green.

"If you think of anything," Briscoe said, passing out cards, "give us a call, ladies."

The door closed behind them.

"'Ladies'?" asked Green, pushing the elevator button. "One of them will probably file a complaint."

"Hey, I didn't say 'girls,' did I?"

"They're just a group of people with a common interest."

"And knives in their fanny packs. You think they didn't resent her for lining up Kirstner and Strawn?"

"No, I don't think so."

"You need a couple of ex-wives," Briscoe laughed.

"You're a bitter man, Lennie Briscoe. Bitterer than they are."

"Thank you for sharing that, Ed. I'll try to have pleasant dreams."

Van Buren appeared out of nowhere, looming over Briscoe and Green's desks with a Diet Sprite and a granola bar. "Tell me you've wrapped up the jumper. I need help on that drive-by."

Briscoe raised his head from the smoked turkey sandwich he had split with Green and swallowed. "Curiouser and curiouser. There's something hinkey about it."

"You think Santonio pushed her?"

"We're not sure," said Green. "We checked into the details on the pilfering. There was a batch of small robberies—seven to be exact—at the Waterloo starting in April. A couple of wallets, purses, video cameras, a Nikon, that kind of thing. The guests were out of the room. The pilfering ended about a month later."

"The Santonios?"

"They were there during that period, but they were also there before the pilfering and after. The management suspected a bellhop named Michael Donelly. The thieving started a week after he was hired and stopped when he was busted for possession."

"Could he have come back?"

63

"He was voluntarily deported back to Ireland. He was in jail in Derry on the day Mrs. Chesko died."

"So it doesn't rule out Santonio. Are we going to charge him with murder? You're homicide detectives. If there's no crime, don't waste the time."

"We can't even prove he was in the room," said Green. "The DNA is back already."

"Already? They've improved!"

"It was a no-brainer," said Briscoe. "They haven't finished the full workup, but the blood type doesn't match. Whoever had sex with Barbara Chesko was an O. Santonio is AB."

"So we can't place Santonio in the room," said Green.

"He might have told his wife," said Van Buren.

"If we could find her." Briscoe exploded his fingers. "Poof! Thin air."

"She'll try to contact him, don't you think? Their phone?"

"They can't afford one. There are fingerprints all over the hotel room, but neither Santonios' are there. Bunches of others." Briscoe shook his head. "I'm telling you, the guy is confessing to cover up for the mother of his child."

"So, you really believe he found the laptop in a trash can?"

Green reached to his desk and opened the lower file drawer. The security tapes from the Waterloo were stacked behind the file divider. "They don't cover the hallways, just the entrances. The lobby, basically, and the café."

"We haven't gone through all seventy-two hours yet," said Briscoe, "but somebody who resembles

Guillermo goes to empty the trash about the time he said."

"Which is actually the time he does it," added Green.

"What do you mean 'resembles'?" said Van Buren.

"The tapes are really lousy," said Briscoe. "They haven't bought new ones since the Betamax went South. And I think there's dust on the lens. It goes in and out. It's like watching reruns of *Birth of a Nation* in a blizzard."

"Not only that," said Green, "the camera's not in position for a good look at the trash can where Guillermo says he found the laptop. The camera's aimed at the front desk, of course. The trash can is behind the corner of the desk area."

"They weren't expecting anyone to rob the trash," said Briscoe.

"We can see Guillermo cross the lobby with his cart at eight-twenty something, but we can't see whether he finds the laptop."

"He says he hid it in the bottom of his cart," said Briscoe. "You can see him bend over, but not what he's doing."

Van Buren shook her head. "Look, fellows, we don't even have a good circumstantial case for murder. Maybe we should just charge him with the theft."

"You know," said Briscoe, "that's even a stretch. It was Ermilia who pawned the laptop. Nobody else has ever even seen Guillermo with it."

"All he's got to do is say he confessed to protect his wife," said Green.

"He doesn't have to say anything if we can't corroborate any detail of the confession." Van Buren thought a moment. "But maybe he'll just plead, go on probation, and later we'll get something more. Meantime, you keep trying to find Mrs. Santonio."

Green caught Van Buren looking at his half of the sandwich, which he hadn't touched. "You want this? I'm not hungry."

"No," she said sharply.

"I think the missus took it," said Briscoe, "but that doesn't mean she pushed Chesko."

"There's no reason she might not have gotten desperate and pushed Chesko. Maybe she told this to Guillermo and that's why he's covering up. We'd better get something. The D.A.'s office doesn't think he'll be held very long. Maybe the end of the day."

"And he can walk out the door and disappear with Ermilia," said Briscoe.

"Exactly," said Van Buren.

"A suspect to a murder?" said Green.

"What murder?" said Briscoe. "You don't have to be a judge to think like one."

"I don't know what else we can do," said Green. "We have no leads on her. We could see if Guillermo calls her from jail, but, you know, if this is a suicide, what's the point?"

She crumpled the wrapper of her granola bar and glanced at Green's half sandwich again. "Do we have any idea who's the donor of the fluid on the bedspread?"

"Not a clue," said Green. "Her friends don't know of anyone she dated. Nor her neighbors. A lonely, middle-aged woman. Dumped by her husband. No love interest. It smells like a suicide."

"Now I know it doesn't always go to form," said Briscoe, "but she had sex and then committed suicide?

And, then, she was really working hard to be an author."

"Twenty-five rejections' worth," said Green.

"I can't picture her suffering through that many turndowns only to kill herself before she gets to Barnes and Noble."

Van Buren's lips pursed to her most skeptical expression. "I thought that's what authors and artists did. It makes them immortal." She paced one step in each direction. "Well, then, wrap it up. Likely suicide, whatever."

"You sure you don't want this sandwich?" asked Green.

"No!" said Van Buren. She glanced at Briscoe. "What?"

"Nothing."

"I don't want the sandwich. Is that a big deal?"

Briscoe shook his head. "That isn't what I was thinking."

"Here we go," said Green.

"I'm just thinking we're going at this wrong," said Briscoe.

"Make my day," said Van Buren, crossing her arms.

"Maybe one of the Santonios stole the laptop, maybe one of them found it. But so what? There's the ex. He was tired of supporting her," said Briscoe. "I can't shake the feeling there's something with the ex."

"You 'can't shake the feeling'? Do you have any concrete reason why he should want her dead? Husbands off their wives. Abandoned wives are usually not the problem. The guy has moved."

"Ten thou a month," said Briscoe, "is a lot of typing paper."

"One hundred percent cotton paper," said Green.

"So he goes to court and gets the payment modified," said the lieutenant. "Rich guys use lawyers to do their dirty work."

"Maybe he was trying to reconcile with her," said Briscoe. "That's a good way to stop paying."

"Are you speaking from experience?"

"Very funny," said Briscoe.

"All I'm hearing is 'maybe' this and 'maybe' that. Does he look dirty? Big insurance? Anything like that?"

Briscoe shrugged. "We'll check it out. He could use the dough, he says."

"If I don't hear something better, we're closing this file."

"The ex has another motive," said Green. "Barbara was writing a nasty book about her married life with Ralph, a.k.a. Bill Shaft."

"What do you mean?"

Green held up the manuscript. "Mr. Chesko may not have been the kind of man who inspires women to forget his weaknesses."

Briscoe mopped a blob of mayonnaise from the corner of his mouth. "We gather from talking to the woman's writing group that it hits below the belt. Embarrassing personal stuff. Maybe lily wilting and such."

"And this would make him kill her? What does it say?"

"Well," said Green, "we haven't read it straight through."

"Not enough pictures for me," said Briscoe.

"But it rakes him over the coals. And there was a good chance of it being published."

Van Buren looked at the title page. "*Shafted*?"

"See? She loves it," said Briscoe.

"Oh, right!" said Van Buren.

"It'll go to the top of the *Times* chick-book charts."

"Don't give me a motive to murder *you*," she said.

Green rocked back in his chair. "Never mind the humiliation factor," he said, rubbing his chin. "What about the growth fund? What if she threatened to say something about his business?"

"Like she casually drops the passwords for his Swiss bank account? Something like that?"

"Maybe not that, but maybe how he snatched the loot, something that reveals fraud or embezzlement or insider trading."

"Did he read the book?" asked Van Buren.

"I don't know. He acts like the thing isn't very important, but that might mean he's trying to keep us from reading it."

"Hell," said Briscoe, "the writers' group has heard at least some of the thing, and she was sending copies all around town. Wouldn't somebody notice it was incriminating?"

"We're not talking about murder. It's not like she's accusing him of killing her brother or stealing the *Mona Lisa*. Anybody would notice that. But if there's something in the manuscript that lays out his business practices, something the editors and the writing group wouldn't recognize…. Some accounting thing or something. Anyone else might think it's just business talk in a novel about a businessman."

"But if he read it, he'd recognize it immediately," said Van Buren. "These finance guys have to take a number to get into court these days."

Green tapped his desk with his index finger. "A lot

of people think Chesko pulled something with the growth fund. As long as he was paying to finance her fantasy life, maybe she didn't feel any particular calling to squeal on him."

Van Buren raised her hands. "I'm still hearing 'maybe.'"

"What if she tried to blackmail him?"

"It's still maybe, but it's an interesting one."

"She wasn't timid about turning Ralph Chesko into Bill Shaft," Briscoe reminded her, "and freely discussing his, ah, shortcomings." He waggled his head.

"True," said Van Buren, "but I like the money angle better. If it was just about humiliating him, why'd it take him six months to react?"

"The book wasn't about to be published," said Green.

"Maybe you should find out exactly what the story is on the growth fund," said Van Buren.

"You sure you don't want the sandwich?" asked Green.

Van Buren snatched up the pickle that lay beside the sandwich. "Get something or get off it," she said, holding the pickle like a blackjack. She spun and marched back toward her office.

"Dieting," whispered Green.

"I heard that!" said Van Buren as her door slammed.

SECURITY AND EXCHANGE COMMISSION
DIVISION OF ENFORCEMENT OFFICE
233 BROADWAY
MONDAY, AUGUST 26, 2:00 P.M.

S.E.C. Supervisor Milt McKinney hung up the phone and laced his fingers. "I told you it would be routine getting clearance," he said. "But I have to follow the rules, and nothing goes out of this room."

"We understand," said Briscoe.

"The file is on the way in," McKinney said. "At this point, I can't let you read it or give you copies or anything, but Washington will clear it if it's a part of a homicide investigation and I'm clear to discuss the details."

"We appreciate it," said Green.

"I don't think you'll find it very interesting, though. I could understand if Chesko himself had been murdered," he smiled. "If I'd lost as much of your money as Chesko had lost for his clients, you might be gunning for me."

"How much are we talking about?" asked Briscoe.

"Well," said McKinney, "Chesko managed the High-Yield Monticello Growth Fund for the Monticello Investment Group. He was another one of those 'financial geniuses' for a while."

"What do you mean by that?"

"I mean he was lucky. Over a three-year period, he was a point and a half ahead of any other growth fund. There were articles in *Forbes* and *The Street.com* about him. He made the cover of *Money* and was interviewed by everybody. The fund's assets shot up to nearly five hundred million at one point."

"He took care of five hundred million?"

McKinney nodded. "Managed it. We're not talking about a detective's retirement fund."

"So, naturally," said Briscoe, "his clients were disappointed when it tanked."

"That's putting it mildly," said McKinney. "When it dropped, the investors immediately began calling. The American Federation of Wire and Spring Workers lost a major chunk of their pension fund. You probably saw that in the papers. In today's climate, they assumed it couldn't happen without Chesko's doing something illegal. Really, they just wanted their pound of flesh. They accused him of churning, misrepresenting proceeds, skimming, breach of fiduciary responsibility—you name it. We even looked into the possibility that the Monticello Group had committed a failure to supervise. When we found nothing substantial, they screamed that Monticello or Chesko or both had bought us, the vice president of the United States, and on and on."

"Besides the Wire Workers, who else invested?" asked Green.

"I can get you a list, but keep in mind it's embarrassing for an investor to lose this much. And, after all, there were no illegalities."

"I notice you keep saying there was nothing illegal," said Briscoe. "Anything slightly shady, but not strictly illegal?"

"Well," said McKinney, "'financial geniuses' like Chesko normally dance along the edge. If a guy's going fifty-seven in a fifty-five zone, do you ticket him or not? Usually not. Chesko pushed the envelope, but he never tore it. There wasn't—"

The door opened and a woman brought in a file. "Here it is," said McKinney. He thanked her and she left. A scent of cinnamon dawdled behind her.

"Did you suspect anything you couldn't prove, or was it that he really was clean?"

McKinney opened the file. "That's like asking whether someone is innocent, isn't it? No adult human being is innocent. But many of them are not guilty of specific crimes."

"So Ralph Chesko was not guilty."

McKinney scanned the top page. "He was cleared. He used poor judgment. He went out on a limb, sawed a bit too much, tried to recoup those losses by climbing out farther, and sawed it off. His risks worked for several years. Luck: a lot of people have it for a while. Then they start to believe they've got the market figured out."

"Sounds like playing the ponies to me," said Briscoe.

"Not quite, but the psychology's similar. Remember when day trading was such a rage?" McKinney took off his reading glasses. "With Chesko's fund, several things came together at once, precipitated by that Chapter Eleven in one of the fiber optic networks. Chesko tried to make up the lost ground by shorting and then had to cover."

"*Hablo inglese?*" said Briscoe.

McKinney smiled at Briscoe's attempt at Spanish. "He goofed big-time at least three times in double or nothing scenarios. Shorting can be dangerous."

"But not crooked?" asked Green.

"As I said, we left the file active in case something else turns up, but we have essentially cleared him. The investors went on to file complaints with the National Association of Security Dealers, an industry watchdog, then with the Investor Protection and Securities Bureau."

"That's the state agency?" asked Green.

"Right. It's under the New York Attorney General. It enforces the, ah, Martin Act, the New York State Securities Act."

"Could all these investigations have missed something?" asked Briscoe. "Money can be hidden; books can be doctored. Maybe you guys looked in the wrong place."

"Jack Lionel is one of the best investigators of this kind of thing. He's with the IPSB, and I wish he was with us. He went over Chesko's books with a louse comb and found no more than we did: minor irregularities. Accounting errors that were maybe not entirely inadvertent, but nothing significant. Believe me, detective, there was serious screaming from serious people about the fund. That's why the state attorney general assigned Jack to it."

"Is it possible," asked Green, "that the investigators might have looked in the wrong direction, so to speak?"

McKinney seemed annoyed with the question. "The SEC, the NASD, and the IPSB all investigate very large amounts of money. Between you and me, Jack can be a real s.o.b. at times. The attorney general wants him that way. Jack the Hammer, he's called. If there had been violations, Jack would have found them. He lives to mount heads."

Briscoe glanced at Green and then eased into his question. "Look, we have a kind of weird situation. Barbara Chesko wrote a novel before she died. There's some mention of financial stuff in it. It might as well be Iranian for all we know, but we were thinking someone familiar with this sort of thing might recognize these people or the deals."

"A novel? Ralph Chesko's wife?"

"Ex-wife. We think it's based on her life," said Green, "only she's changed the names and so forth."

"She might have inadvertently, or even deliberately, revealed something about some crooked dealing," added Briscoe.

"And you think he might have done it?"

"That's what we're trying to figure out."

McKinney nodded thoughtfully. "Ah," he said. He drummed his fingers for a second. "I'd put one of our guys on it, but I really think Jack Lionel knows the whole case better."

Briscoe grinned wryly. "In my experience, you federal guys don't like to pass up a prime T-bone."

"I don't smell any blood, frankly," said McKinney, "but I'll call Jack for you. Maybe something can be done on the state level, but I wouldn't count on it."

A heavyset, bald man with a ring under his eye for every number fiddler he'd bagged, Jack Lionel chewed an unlit cigar as he searched on his garbage barge of a desk.

"So, what was it you were looking for?" he asked.

"Anything," said Green. "Anything at all."

"Is there anybody in the book who is recognizable?" asked Briscoe. "Is there anything illegal going on?"

Lionel sat back, opened his mouth like a hippopotamus who expected them to throw peanuts, and said, "Yes and no."

"Well?"

"Yes, there are some recognizable people. No, it doesn't inculpate anybody."

"Who is recognizable?"

Lionel flipped a few pages of the manuscript. "This guy sounds like Martin Schoenbauer. He was chairman of Lyons Macintosh and I know that he was involved with Ralph Chesko."

Green twisted his head to look at the book. "Which one is he?"

"Hasenpfeffer, Gustav Hasenpfeffer."

"I must have missed him," said Briscoe.

"He grabs a waitress's derriere on page fifty-two."

"Well there's a crime!" muttered Briscoe.

"I said I recognized him. He's a grabber all right, and he's paid for it: off the record, out of court, and on the QT."

"Is he the kind of guy who'd meet a woman in a hotel?"

"Is the Pope Polish?"

"Okay, he's not gay. Would he meet a woman in a hotel and kill her?"

"Don't ask me. As far as I know he just grabs ass, then pays the settlement. He never learns."

Green looked up from his notepad. "Was there anything strange about his deals with Chesko?"

"No," said Lionel, "they made a lot of scratch together. The book doesn't say anything about it anyway."

"Okay, anything else?" asked Briscoe.

"This guy Loren Lunch is probably Warren Buffett hardy har but just the name is used. And then there's Bubblehead."

"My favorite," said Briscoe.

"He bears a lot of resemblance to Ethan Merivale at Hutton, but the trick is, he isn't."

"How do you mean?"

"Physically, mannerisms and stuff, he's Merivale, but his business dealings in here mean Bubblehead is Leonard Cooper, not the brightest bulb in the rack. He and Chesko worked together at Merrill Lynch when they were just starting out. Nothing there, either."

"Rumors? Off the record stuff? Anything at all?"

"Nada. Zilch. Zero."

"What about his trip to the Isle of Jersey? Isn't that like the Caymans? You can hide your money there?"

"We investigated that. All legal activities are confidential there, with the key being 'legal.' Jersey's pretty reliable. Chesko has an account, but it is relatively modest. I think it's his jack in the hole."

"'Jack in the hole'?" asked Green.

"It's not good enough to be an ace," said Lionel. "I think he was just making sure he couldn't go entirely under. It's enough to get you a nice retirement home. No. I'm sorry to tell you the book doesn't say much about finance and what it does say is stupid." Lionel laced his fingers. "Gentlemen, I'll never forgive you for making me read this."

Green flipped his notebook closed. "So much for that theory."

"Chesko's clean, then," said Briscoe. "Thanks for your trouble."

"Clean?" said Lionel. "I operate on the assumption nobody's clean. I just haven't caught him yet."

"Everybody's guilty, eh?"

"Money corrupts," said Lionel. "A lotta money corrupts a lot."

Lionel offered the manuscript to them. "McKinney told me he didn't see anything either, but I don't think he read it all."

"A weak stomach?"

Lionel snorted. "McKinney told me this thing was going to be published. By what book company, for God's sake? If it's a public company, I'd short it."

Green was thinking and spoke hesitantly. "So this *is* terrible, right?"

"That?" asked Lionel. "It doesn't even rise to being so bad it's funny. It's just boring. Let's just say that if I had time to read anything other than balance sheets, it wouldn't be this."

"So why do people say it's good?"

"Hell, Ed, it's all a matter of taste," said Briscoe.

"But it isn't," said Green.

"A matter of taste? Of course it is. You ever sit through a critically acclaimed movie? Ever tried to read a book called *Gravity's Rainbow*? My daughter told me it was a work of genius. *Sheesh*."

"Look," said Green, "Mickey Spillane is one thing, Alice Walker is another. But this isn't about taste. This book is terrible. Who could think it wasn't?"

"Well, the writers' group for what that's worth," said Briscoe.

"That's a support group," said Green. "They'd praise each other's laundry lists. 'No negativity.' Remember?"

"What's your point?" asked Lionel. "So it's bad. A lot of books are bad."

"There was that editor who liked it," shrugged Briscoe. "They said she was about to sign a contract."

Green shook hands with Jack Lionel, who was gaping at them, still waiting for the peanuts to fly. "We've taken up too much of your time. Thank you for your help."

Briscoe looked confused but followed Green to the elevator. When the door closed and they were alone, he eyed the excited Green and asked him, "So what gives?"

"Look, Lennie, I counted a dozen letters from an editor named Rosserman to Barbara Chesko. Every one of them tells her that her book could be the next big thing." He measured the air with two fingers. "But there are an inch thick of turndowns. A few of them say things like the plot is weak. One says 'We've seen too much of this before.' Most of them just say it doesn't fit their needs."

"There's no accounting for taste, Ed," said Briscoe. "They didn't like it, Rosserman did."

Green pinched the bridge of his nose. "What am I trying to say? Look, does it make sense that he sees talent when no one else does? I'd sure like to hear why. Wouldn't you?"

Briscoe raised his hands. "Wait a minute. What's that got to do with her dying?"

"Why would he do that?"

"Huh?"

"Why would he tell her her book is good when he knows it isn't?"

"She could have killed herself because she was strung along," said Briscoe. "Maybe he finally told her the truth about *Shafted* and dumped her at the same time."

"Bingo, Old Spice man," said Green.

"So, he's Mr. Condom. And I was afraid we were going to have to make a case against Mr. Bubble-head!"

Briscoe and Green took an elevator to the eleventh floor and emerged to face a trio of closed beige doors with buzzers at the side. An annoyed and nasal voice asked simply "Yes?" and they identified themselves, asking to see Robert Rosserman. Several seconds passed and no one opened the door. Briscoe was about to lay on the buzzer again when a woman with thick glasses and a pencil on her ear came out. They squeezed past her and walked in.

On each side of the corridor a row of doors stretched to a ceiling-high bookcase at the end. They passed three doors before they saw an open one. In a windowless office a woman squinted at her CRT, then at one of the many manuscripts piled on her desk.

"Rosserman?" asked Briscoe. She silently pointed through the wall to farther down the corridor.

"Thank you," said Green, but she didn't look up.

They passed an office in which a man was arguing on the phone, but the paper sign taped to his door identified him as "Albert Ilsing." The last office on the left had the distinction of a dirty window and a brass plaque identifying Rosserman. A bushy headed man leaned back in his chair, his feet on his desk, flipping the pages of a thick manuscript. He didn't look up until he turned a page, delicately laying it face down on his blotter.

"Yes?" he asked.

"You Rosserman?" Briscoe asked.

"And you are?"

"Detectives Briscoe and Green. We'd like to ask you about Barbara Chesko."

Rosserman dropped his feet to the floor and set aside his manuscript. "Barbara?"

"Chesko."

"You sent her this letter," said Green. He held it out. "In fact, several letters."

Rosserman glanced at it. "Oh, Chesko. Sure. How is she?"

"Not too well, I'm afraid."

Rosserman hesitated. "Well, rejection is part of the game."

"And what kind of rejection is that?"

Rosserman blinked. "Her novel. We turned it down." He smiled. "Is that suddenly police business?"

"And when did this happen?" said Green.

"Last week. What's all this about?"

"We heard you worked closely with her."

"Closely. Well, I wouldn't say closely. I encouraged her. I saw a raw talent that needed to be shaped and matured."

"Some of her writing group was under the impression that she was about to sign a contract," Briscoe said.

Rosserman sat back, lacing his fingers across his stomach. "Really? Well, good for her."

"With you."

"Me? Lord, no. Not with me. It must have been someone else. There are lots of publishers. Maybe print on demand."

"She never mentioned it to you?"

He thought for a moment. "Not that I recall. I'm sure I'd remember if I heard she'd gotten an offer."

"It would be difficult to remember?"

Rosserman smiled. "Well, no. But things get a bit hazy when you're responsible for twelve books a quarter. I can barely deal with my published authors. Those we reject, well, those numbers would surprise you."

On the shelf on Rosserman's wall Green noticed a book with an African mask on the spine. He tugged it out and opened it as Rosserman spoke. "What can you tell us about her?"

Rosserman shrugged. "She sent in a manuscript about a year ago. I recognized a certain raw talent, but it didn't measure up to professional standards. I recommended some editing, which was done, and then she resubmitted it. It was much closer, but needed restructuring I thought, then a really thorough line edit. It came back for this last time, but, unfortunately, there was no place in the publishing schedule, so I couldn't even submit it to the board. I recommended she get a good agent to shop it around."

"It seems like you went to a lot of trouble for her."

"Not for her," said Rosserman. "For her book. I believe it demonstrated a significant raw talent."

"You know," said Green, "that interests me. How do you recognize 'raw talent'?"

"They either have it or they don't," said Rosserman. "It's like picking out horseflesh. An editor develops an eye for it."

"But," Green continued, "What exactly do you see? If you've got somebody whose talent is undeveloped, how can you see it?"

Rosserman's eyes flashed. "You just know," he said. A moment passed as Rosserman picked at imaginary lint on his canvas trousers. "You guys get a sense of when somebody's guilty, right? I mean aren't you officers supposed to have a sixth sense for when somebody's lying?"

"That sixth sense is only in potboilers written by undeveloped talent," said Green.

"It's experience," said Rosserman crisply. "You can recognize when a writer's got it."

"Raw talent," Briscoe nodded. "So you said. And when did this happen, the turndown?"

"I called her Monday. No, this Tuesday." He hesitated.

"And?"

Rosserman contemplated his laced fingers. "She was quite distraught. She threw quite a scene."

"On the phone?"

"No. I decided against a letter and called her about eleven. She showed up here about two, but I was on the phone doing some negotiating on sub-rights."

"Sub-rights?"

"The right to publish a book overseas, paperback rights, movies. These were translation rights, I think. Italy. Mondadori? Well, she had to wait, so I couldn't get to her until nearly four-thirty and I guess I'd be pretty steamed up by then myself."

"That's two and a half hours," said Green, raising his eyes from the book he was still flipping through. "If I were her, I'd take that as a large hint. Maybe you hoped to wait her out."

Rosserman leaned forward. "She read, I guess. I don't know for sure. Jenna, our secretary, told me Barbara had stomped out just a few minutes before."

There was a moment of silence.

"I feel awful about it," he continued. "To tell the truth, I forgot she was out there. I thought she had left. Maybe I hoped she would. I had a lot of sympathy for her."

Briscoe glanced back at the narrow hallway.

"She was around the corner past the bookshelf. There are some chairs around there. A coffeemaker. Would you gentlemen like a coffee? There are sodas, too."

"No, thanks," said Briscoe.

Green closed the book he had taken from the shelf. "This one of yours?"

"I edited it, yes."

He pointed to the blurbs on the back. "Toni Morrison, Norman Mailer, John Updike, *The New York Times*—it got a lot of praise."

"Yes it did," said Rosserman. "I'm very proud of it." He picked at lint on his canvas trousers. "I only wish the bean counters felt the same way."

"Meaning?" asked Briscoe.

"It didn't even sell into the mid-list. That book," said Rosserman, "is literature. Any book Antoine Day Kwulu writes is literature. But literature isn't always what people buy."

"That happen often?"

Rosserman sighed. "Too often, I'm afraid. It's a tough business. You can spend months of twelve-hour days looking for a manuscript that has it, and then you can spend hours upon hours working with a writer. When it's just right, when you know that the manuscript is really on, it may nonetheless get tossed into the remainder bins like a day-old doughnut."

"It really takes that kind of time, editing?" asked Briscoe. "Sounds like being a cop."

"If editing isn't your life, you shouldn't be an editor."

"Must be tough on your marriage."

"I'm not married. Not anymore. We got out of college and she wanted to be an actress." He smiled. "The Apple was too big for her, but I stayed. Never remarried. It's hard to meet the right kind of woman in this city."

"Maybe you're too picky," said Briscoe. "Breathing was usually good enough for me."

Rosserman looked a bit distant. "She's now back in Topeka, married to the former quarterback who used to shove my head in the middle school toilet. He sells cars and he's no better at that than he was at quarterbacking. My daughter's at Washington University, in St. Louis. It's pretty expensive."

"Well, if the quarterback ever wants to write his memoirs, you can shove his manuscript in the toilet."

Rosserman scrutinized Briscoe as if to judge the intent of the remark. "It's a shame a woman like Barbara had to be subjected to the realities of the market," he said seriously. "But there you are." He lowered his eyes.

Green put the Kwulu novel on the desk.

"To tell you the truth," said Rosserman, "from what I knew of her I liked Barbara. She was very intent on becoming a successful writer. She pursued her dream with all the intensity a person can muster. It's sad, but it happens. It's just that most aspiring writers don't work so hard at it."

Green leaned forward on the desk.

Rosserman looked up at him. "You're welcome to take *The Walk to Djibouti* with you, detective."

"No thanks," said Green. "We're really just curious why you're not being straight with us."

Rosserman looked at Briscoe, then back at Green. "I've told you all I know."

"You've been referring to Barbara Chesko in the past tense."

His eyes went back to Briscoe. "That doesn't mean anything."

Briscoe smirked. "A woman goes apeshit in your office and you have to be reminded of her name a week later?"

Rosserman tilted his head to the side. "I felt sorry for her. She really embarrassed herself."

"And you, I imagine," said Green. "The thing is, two detectives show up at my office, I'd want to know why they're there. You're not very curious, Mr. Rosserman."

Briscoe leaned in on him. "We generally don't spend a lot of time trying to figure out why somebody got her book rejected. The taxpayers would take a dim view of that. And you know it."

"I thought you would tell me," said Rosserman.

"But it wouldn't be news to you, would it?" said Green.

Rosserman patted his fingers on the edge of his blotter.

"Would it?" said Briscoe.

Rosserman licked his lips. "All right. I knew she was dead."

"You pushed her?" asked Green.

"Pushed?" Rosserman turned pale. "No! That's ridiculous!"

"Why were you in the Waterloo Hotel with her?"

"I wasn't in the hotel with her!"

"Weren't you?"

"No!"

"So how did you know she was dead?"

Rosserman blinked. "The news?"

"Try again," said Green. "And don't make me angry."

"I wouldn't make Ed angry," said Briscoe. "Ed's got a temper."

"All right," Rosserman said. "Yes, I knew she was dead. Someone called me Monday morning. She told me that Barbara had committed suicide and that I was responsible. It was very upsetting. I didn't want the company involved."

"What time was this call?"

"Ten. Ten-thirty. I'd just gotten in."

"Who was the woman?"

"I don't know," said Rosserman. "She yelled it and hung up."

"What exactly did she say?"

"She said, 'I want you to know that you're responsible.' And I said, 'For what?' And she said, 'For breaking Barbara's heart, you bastard. She jumped off the Waterloo Hotel.'"

"Is that exactly what she said?"

"Not word for word. I can't remember."

"And what did you say back?"

"I was stunned. I said 'what?' I don't know what I said. I think I asked who this was, but she didn't say. She just repeated it and said I was as guilty as if I'd pushed her."

"Why didn't you think it was a crank call?" asked Briscoe.

"I...It just sounded right. Barbara was very upset Tuesday. I knew she wasn't altogether. I was worried about her."

Green straightened up. "And you didn't make any effort to find out if it was true?"

"I went through the papers." He pointed at the trash can. There was a *Times* and *Daily News* in it. "I didn't know how else to find out without getting Kirstner and Strawn into the picture. I thought I might try to telephone her apartment later, but if she was alive I didn't really want to talk to her again." He lowered his head. "She was very needy."

"This caller, you don't have any idea who it was?"

"No."

"You don't have caller ID?"

Rosserman pointed at a simple pushbutton telephone.

"And what did she want?"

Rosserman looked up. "Nothing. She just said she wanted me to know I was responsible."

"There wasn't any hint of blackmail, she'd be calling again, anything like that?" asked Green.

"She didn't threaten to place you in that hotel room?"

"No!"

"Because she knew you were there?"

Rosserman slapped his desk and shot to his feet. "I wasn't there! If you've got something you want to accuse me of, you accuse me. But until then, I've got nothing to say. What kind of crap is this?"

Green held up his handcuffs. "Maybe you'd like to continue this conversation at the precinct house?"

Rosserman paled and seemed to sag. "Please," he said, "this is ridiculous. The woman killed herself. There's no reason to drag me and Kirstner and Strawn into it. I feel bad enough as it is."

"How do you know she killed herself?" asked Briscoe.

"I told you," said Rosserman. "She was needy. She was distraught. It seems obvious. If you had known her..."

"So why'd you tell her she had talent?" asked Green.

"Look," said Rosserman, "I never promised to publish her. Never. Talent isn't everything. She had a long way to go."

"Your letters don't say anything about having a long way to go."

"I encouraged her, that's all."

"And when you met her at the hotel," asked Briscoe, "what did she say?"

"As God is my witness," said Rosserman, "I didn't meet her on Wednesday. I was here until nearly eleven, then went home to a bottle of El Presidente."

Briscoe eyed him and nodded slowly. He exchanged a glance with Green. "You'd better be telling the truth this time," he said. "If we find out otherwise...."

"I swear," said Rosserman raising his right hand. "I had nothing to do with it. I'm sorry for her, but it wasn't my fault."

"If we need anything, we'll get in touch," said Briscoe.

They had just stepped out of the tiny office when Rosserman called out. "Detective!" He came out into the corridor with a copy of *The Walk to Djibouti* and handed it to Green. "Here, take a copy." He turned toward Briscoe at the end of the corridor. "Take anything you want, as well."

Briscoe stared past the books at the area in which Barbara Chesko had waited. Folding chairs, a coffee urn and a copier. Behind the desk, a woman glared up from her keyboard. She had so much makeup on, it looked like her face would crack if she smiled. He figured she'd managed to avoid smiling for a decade.

He gave her a nod. "It must have been fun to sit with her for two and a half hours," he muttered. "It looks like the room outside the principal's office."

"That's Jenna Marshak," said Rosserman quietly. "She's been here since both Kirstner and Strawn were alive."

"I think I married her ugly stepsister," said Briscoe, moving toward her. "Say, Jenna," he said, "do you remember when Barbara Chesko was here Tuesday?"

She glanced through the top of her bifocals at Rosserman.

"These are policemen," he said.

"I couldn't help but hear," she said. She pointed to a chair. "She sat there from around two something to after four and then packed up and left."

"She say anything?"

"Just went over her manuscript with a pencil. Wrote notes on her laptop. Asked for Mr. Rosserman several times. He was on the phone. I went to take minutes at the marketing meeting at three, she was still here when I got back."

"Wednesday," said Green. "When did Mr. Rosserman leave the office?"

"I told you..." began Rosserman. He was silenced by Green's hand on his chest.

"For lunch?" said Jenna. "He was back about one forty-five. After that he was here all afternoon."

"Until when?"

"Four-thirty or so, a little after. He came back, well, it was almost seven. I left about eight. He was still here." She glanced at Rosserman.

"You work that late normally?"

"The new catalog was out of format," she said. "Computer problems. The odd pages were off center and the fonts—"

Briscoe interrupted. "When Barbara Chesko was here, can you tell me how she seemed? Was she upset? Angry?"

"She was doing a slow burn. She was no worse than most."

"Most of them?"

"Writers are volatile," said Jenna. "They're not always stable. They're not realistic about the publishing business."

"And she wasn't realistic?"

"I only read the published ones," said Jenna. "Mr. Kirstner used to say the great, unpublished author is a myth."

"That makes it tough for the raw talent," said Briscoe.

She shrugged. "Good is good and bad is bad," she said. "This is not a charity. It's a business."

"We'll find our way out," said Briscoe.

The outer door clacked behind them. "How splendid are the offices of the publishing world," said Briscoe, pushing the elevator button.

"I smell a lot of fish on that guy," said Green. "If there wasn't something wrong, why spend so much effort to avoid answering us?"

"We could drag him down to the precinct and watch him flop, but we've wasted enough time. She towered out of this world."

The elevator creaked open. "My head says yes, but…"

"Look," said Briscoe. "He shtupped her. Maybe not Wednesday, but sometime. She was 'needy,' and 'it's hard to meet the right kind of women in this city.' That made her more needy and it still proves nothing. Why would he toss her out the window? Breaking up's not that hard to do. He spends all day turning people down. And if he pushed her, how are we going to prove it?"

"I hate to let a murderer walk," said Green. "If he is one."

"I can't get the scratch marks on the window frame out of my head," said Briscoe. He gave a little shiver. "But, it wouldn't be the first time the bad guy walks free."

"Maybe it isn't the first time. For him, I mean."

"It's worth a look," said Briscoe, "but that's about it, don't you think?"

The only legal action against Rosserman was a ticket for parking a rental car in front of a hydrant near the Port Authority Terminal in 1999. But that wasn't the only mention of him in the records. Roughly two years ago, he had been attacked on the subway by an elderly man with a cane. According to the brief assault report, Harold Rauch, 72, had followed Rosserman into the 51st Street subway station, shouting that Rosserman owed him money. As Rosserman tried to flee through the turnstile, Rauch grabbed him. Rosserman shoved back and Rauch whacked him. He received six stitches on the forehead, but after Rauch's arrest, he declined to press charges.

"Just another day in the city," said Briscoe.

"Who was Rauch?" asked Green. "He filed suit against Rosserman, but dropped it." The editor had been a codefendant in two civil suits: Rauch's in 2002 and another a year later. In both cases, the judge ruled he was not a party to the action. His co-defendants made a sealed settlement in the second suit.

Briscoe scanned to the bottom of the assault report and dialed the home number. A woman answered. "Yes?"

"Is this the Rauch residence?"

"I'm Berman now. I used to be Rauch."

"This is Detective Briscoe from the police department. Is Mr. Harold Rauch in?"

"Papa died sixteen months ago. What is this about?"

"I'm sorry to hear it, Mrs. Berman. We were following up on some old records, and there was a report of Mr. Rauch's altercation in the subway two years ago."

The woman's mood changed. She seemed to be speaking between grinding teeth. "He should have killed him."

"Killed who?"

"Roseman!"

"Rosserman?"

"The bastard breaks Papa's heart, cheats him, and it's Papa who gets arrested. What are you bringing that thing up for? Papa never did a wrong thing in his life!"

"According to this, your father struck him with a cane."

"Not hard enough! All that bad karma, the mental agony, you don't think that can't unleash cancer? I saw it! My father was totally vital until then. He survived Korea and Vietnam. Six months after this, the cancer."

"I see," said Briscoe, clearing his throat. "We're just checking on some things. The officer didn't write down the nature of your father's disagreement with Mr. Rosserman."

"He robbed him!" she shouted. "He told Papa that his book could be a best-seller, then he told him it wasn't good enough."

Briscoe raised his eyebrows. "Your dad wrote a book?"

Green looked up from Barbara Chesko's papers.

"He was career Army. He was at Inchon and was one of the first advisors to South Vietnam. He trained some of the Bay of Pigs soldiers. He had a fabulous life. He wanted to let people see the things he'd seen, to know what it was like."

"And he wrote a book and sent it to Rosserman?"

"Not just Rosserman, he sent it to about a dozen publishers. But Rosserman was the one who built up his hopes."

"How's that?"

The woman spoke as if trying to communicate with an idiot. "He told him his book just needed a little editing. He gets Papa all hepped up and then won't even answer his phone calls."

"So Mr. Rauch attacked him?"

"He didn't go there to do that."

"I understand. But he did hit him."

"He caught Rosserman sneaking out of the building and tried to reason with him down the block to the subway. The man wouldn't talk. Papa reached out for the bastard's coat and Rosserman shoved Papa. If he'd have fallen he could've broke his hip! He swung the cane to protect himself."

"I see."

"My Papa was a man of action. He didn't take guff."

Briscoe made eye contact with Green. "So your dad was angry about how Rosserman handled his book? But you're saying he was robbed. What do you mean by that?"

"Besides his *life*?" snapped Mrs. Berman. "The editing money! Forty-five hundred dollars!"

"Rosserman got paid to edit your dad's book?"

"No, but he sent Papa to those people in New Jersey. The McDonalds. They marked all over the book, but when Papa had the whole thing retyped according to their directions, Rosserman just said it needed more work. Well, Papa wanted to know what work. Rosserman just said 'It lacks coherence,' or something like that. As if Papa was senile. As if he was born yesterday. He wanted him to get more editing. They were just trying to get more money. So Papa went to see him and that's what happened."

Briscoe scratched his ear. "I'm not clear on the money."

"That was what the McDonalds charged."

"But Mr. Rauch didn't give any money to Rosserman?"

"You think he didn't get his share? Baloney. I wasn't born yesterday, either, you know. That crook never had the slightest intention of publishing Papa's book."

"Maybe he just didn't like it," said Briscoe. "I don't mean to run down your dad's book or anything…"

"Look, fella, if Rosserman had just said it wasn't good enough, Papa wouldn't have cared. He talked about paying for publishing it with one of those companies that do that, but after those crooks took his money, he didn't think he could spare what was left. He was afraid he'd end up ninety-five years old and warehoused in a V.A. hospital. That's how healthy he was."

"So your dad's book was never published?"

"I made copies for the family." Her anger subsided into unsteady words. "I buried the original with him in an archive box. Somebody will appreciate it in the future."

"Maybe he meant the book mostly for the family to remember him by," said Briscoe. "That's a good thing." Mrs. Berman said something inaudible. Briscoe thought she was crying. "I'm sorry to have disturbed you, Mrs. Berman," he said, hanging up.

"I'm beginning to suspect Rosserman's a prick," he said, then summarized his conversation with Mrs. Berman. "He got this guy Rauch as worked up as Barbara Chesko."

"And," said Green, "recommended him to the same people who edited Chesko." He held up a letter from Chesko's apartment.

Briscoe held it at arm's length under the desk lamp. "Redux Incorporated. Avery and Monica McDonald. Of Princeton, no less." He skimmed the letter. "'If you avail yourself of our services, we cannot guarantee publication. However, we do sincerely believe *Shafted: A Memoir of a Failed Marriage* has the potential to be a best-seller.' Wasn't it just *Shafted: The Story of a Marriage*?"

"She must have changed the title."

"Maybe it was the McDonalds' idea. That commercial touch that makes it a best-seller."

"There are about fifteen letters from either Avery or Monica McDonald. In the first couple, it seems like they are trying to persuade her to hire them." He handed one to Briscoe.

"'Dear Ms. Chesko,'" he read, "'I was chatting the other day with my good friend Bob Rosserman at Kirstner and Strawn and he mentioned your novel. He was quite impressed with the manuscript, but, as I am sure he explained, in these tough days in publishing, even the finest raw talent can be rejected simply because it lacks the sheen of professional editing. Here at Redux Incorporated, we provide those professional services.' Et cetera, et cetera." Briscoe pointed to the logos at the bottom of the letter. "And they take MasterCard and Visa."

"So of course they like the book, Lennie. They'd like any book whose writer has a credit line."

"*Shafted* has raw talent, you notice."

"It's groceries and a new carpet to the McDonalds," said Green. "But that doesn't explain why Rosserman liked it."

"Wouldn't the publisher hire the editor? I mean, someone sends in a manuscript, *My Life as Madonna's Boy Toy*. The boy toy wouldn't have it edited or ghost written or whatever, would he?"

"Maybe they take it out of your fees. The record companies charge their own bands for the studio time, hotels and all. They deduct it from sales. That's why one-hit wonders end up cutting the ribbons at car dealerships."

"But this is 'we take MasterCard.' There's nothing in here about Rosserman fronting the money, or anything like that."

Briscoe looked for Ralph Chesko's American Express statements, the ones that had the Waterloo Hotel charge and a couple of others. "There was no charge for Redux on these."

"The letter's older than those statements right? And, anyway, they don't take Amex," Green said. "Chesko kept everything in her files. "We can see—" He fumbled for a folder.

"If she paid them," said Briscoe, "what does that prove?"

Green put down the folder marked "Visa" without opening it.

"It proved Rosserman thought the book needed it and Barbara was willing to pay for it."

"So what's worth killing Barbara Chesko for?"

"You're right. No." Green thought. "But I still don't like the Rosserman guy lying to us. Why?"

"Everybody lies," shrugged Briscoe. "He didn't want to be involved. He hasn't got a motive."

"Well, I say we go scare him, get him to admit he screwed her in more ways than one, then either he confesses to pushing her—those odds are ninety-nine point nine to one."

"Or he faces up to making her suicidal."

"I *would* like to rattle the guy."

"If we did that to all the guys who jerk us around, we'd never get anything done," said Briscoe.

"We get things done?" said Green.

"But this must happen a lot, don't you think? Artistic temperament and all that? How many books does he turn down?"

"But how many does he recommend get edited? Mrs. Berman thinks he did that deliberately."

"I don't follow," said Briscoe.

"So that these people, the McDonalds, can get a fee."

They thought for a moment. Briscoe spoke first. "Hell, maybe they're just friends. Professional courtesy or something."

Green turned to his computer monitor. "Let's Google them." He typed "Redux" into the search engine. There was some material on a weight-loss medicine called Redux, a review of the re-release of *Apocalypse Now Redux*. Redux Incorporated appeared at the bottom of the search page. He went to the web site.

"The publishing world is tough," Green said, "and so on, and so on. You can't get anywhere without that professional touch."

"Yadda, yadda," said Briscoe. "When do we get to the convenient payments?"

"You click to the next page." Green scanned it. "They don't get specific. They say they follow publishing norms."

"Are you getting the feeling we don't know enough about 'publishing norms'?"

"I thought people wrote books and sent them to a publisher and the publisher printed them. Who knows? Who thought about it?" Green clicked another link. "'Avery McDonald has published books with several major publishers,' it says. He's the coauthor of a diet book, a Mack Bolan mystery under the name of Don Pendleton, a Star Invaders novel, and *The Man's Guide to Studliness*."

"'Studliness'! A book about me. It tears away the veil over my style," said Briscoe.

"Some thrillers—*Death March*, *Death Watch* and *Death Mask*, and a *Happy Hours* novelization called *Be-Bop Bennie*."

"*Happy Hours*?"

"That's that old situation comedy. A retired nun raising a Chinese kid, a Mexican kid, and a short African-American kid. He was Bennie."

Briscoe blinked. "No wonder the nun retired."

"They weren't her kids. They were orphans. They form a rock band. You never saw this? It's on cable."

"Ah, the wonders of the electronic civilization." Briscoe shook his head.

"*Be-Bop Bennie* isn't the only book the guy wrote."

"Maybe it ended his career."

"Monica McDonald worked as a literary agent, a magazine editor, and published a dozen romances before writing *Insider Secrets for Publishing YOUR Book*." Green flipped open the Visa folder still lying on top of Barbara Chesko's papers. "Bergdorf's, cash advance. Several cash advances. Five thousand."

"Maybe she was paying the rent by credit card," said Briscoe. "The ex had cut her off."

"Nothing like that the month before. The month before. Look there: seven thousand six hundred and forty-five. Redux!"

Briscoe whistled. "This would have been the last time. April, right?"

Green flipped several more statements. "Four months before that, forty-five hundred."

"That's what Rauch paid."

"And here's another a year ago. Sixty-seven hundred!"

Briscoe whistled again. "Added up, it's real money."

"Ralph Chesko's money." Green toted it up with a pencil. "Eighteen thousand eight hundred and forty-five."

They thought for several seconds. How did this connect to what happened to Barbara Chesko in the Waterloo Hotel? Did it?

"All right," said Briscoe. "Let's go a little further with this on Monday. I'll call Dennis Gross in Fraud. You see if you can get hold of this guy McDonald."

STARBUCKS COFFEE
575 FIFTH AVENUE
TUESDAY, SEPTEMBER 3, 10:30 A.M.

"**A**re you sure I can't get you gentlemen something?" said Avery McDonald, setting his large latte on the tiny table.

"Too rich for my blood," said Briscoe, sizing McDonald up. He wore a tweed jacket, even though it was at least eighty that day, and carried a black cane with a brass knob at the top. His wild eyebrows and narrow goatee were flecked with silver.

McDonald grinned. "When they test my cholesterol, they have to strain out the arabica. I'm a total junkie for this. Total."

The Princeton, New Jersey address for Redux had turned out to be a mail drop only. The phone number was in Peekskill. They had left a message on his answering machine and McDonald had called back early that morning from his cell phone. It was he who suggested the coffee shop. Briscoe was thinking the same thing that had blipped his radar on Rosserman: McDonald was a bit too cheerful, a bit too uncurious about why detectives would want to talk to him, and maybe too sure he could handle them.

"So," said Green, "you come down to the city often?"

"Thank God for the trains when they're running. The business is here, but day-to-day life is better up there. Peekskill is my retreat from the hurly-burly. It's a happy coincidence I am here today. Monica and I are pitching a new concept in horror fiction. It's very *on*, very—" he made quotation marks with his fingers "—*happening*, as we used to say. It could be the next big thing."

"Barbara Chesko," said Green.

McDonald sighed. "Oh, yes, I heard about that."

Briscoe and Green waited.

"Bob Rosserman mentioned it. Have you found a reason yet?"

"Reason for what?" asked Briscoe.

"The poor dear's suicide."

"That's why we're talking to you," said Green. "She made some rather large payments to you over the past couple of years."

"And? They were for editorial services." He said it as if protesting. "I did a lot of work with her novel. It was really in shape when we were through. It's a shame she didn't hang in," he sighed. "Unfortunately, creative persons are not always stable."

"Are you saying Barbara Chesko was unstable?"

"*De mortuis…*" he said dryly. "Not much more than most writers. On the other hand, she *did* kill herself, didn't she?"

"Her book wasn't good enough to be published?" asked Briscoe.

"Even after all the work?" added Green.

"Who says?" said McDonald. "It's not a dichotomy. That it isn't published yet doesn't mean it isn't publishable. Do you know how many times John Kennedy Toole tried to sell *A Confederacy of Dunces*?

He gave up and killed himself, and the novel won the Pulitzer Prize! A publishable book, even a brilliant book, may take considerable time to find a publisher. Did you know there are only half a dozen major publishers these days? It's a tough market. But all anyone needs is a good manuscript on the desk of the right editor on the right day. Shazam! It's a bestseller."

"Shazam," said Briscoe flatly.

McDonald shot him a sharp glance. "Who is complaining?" he said. "She never complained, so what is it? Her ex-husband?"

"Is it normal to get complaints?" asked Green, earning the same sharp glance. McDonald calmed himself and leaned forward.

"Look, gentlemen, people come to us with their manuscripts. Monica and I read them over and if we feel there is a realistic possibility it could be published, we offer to give it the polishing that might make it stand out on an editor's desk. That's all we promise. We can't promise it will be published. We can't promise it will be a bestseller. If we had the ability to do that, we would knock out bestsellers ourselves and retire. Some of our clients refuse to understand that. Even the best manuscript can go overlooked. Like John Kennedy Toole's!"

"And you edited this book?" asked Briscoe.

This time McDonald's glance narrowed to a glare. "No. It's just an example. The point is, we never promise anything other than the best editing money can buy."

Briscoe eased into his question. "You know, Mr. McDonald, I checked with a friend of mine in the Fraud Division."

"Oh?"

"Detective Gross? There have been several complaints."

"Then I'm sure the detective explained there wasn't anything fraudulent going on. Monica and I deliver exactly what we promise. We give our clients every opportunity, but we cannot guarantee a book contract." He tapped the table with his index finger. "Our contract is very specific about that. Very."

"Eighteen thousand ought to buy quite a job," said Green.

"We don't charge eighteen thousand!" said McDonald.

"When you add up Barbara Chesko's payments, they come to over eighteen thousand," said Green.

"That wasn't one job. It was several. We did everything we could for her. Once I spent three eight-hour days with Barbara going over that manuscript. Normally we don't do that. Normally we don't meet our clients face-to-face."

"And that's why she paid you that much?" asked Green.

"I'm a professional. I've got twenty-five years of experience. It's peanuts compared to what consultants get in other fields!" He shot his hand up, nearly upsetting his latte.

"Don't get excited, Mr. McDonald," said Briscoe. "We're trying to understand the ins and outs, if you know what I mean. On a policeman's salary, it seems like a lot of money."

"It just burns me! Books are so important. But the guy who designs a logo for a hamburger chain gets millions!"

"Uh-huh," said Briscoe.

"Do many people pay you as much as she did?" asked Green.

"Some." He crossed his arms. "You're aware we gave her a discount? We had great faith in her manuscript. Normally, a line edit ought to come up to twenty dollars a page, and wouldn't have included the face-to-face time I spent with her."

"Mr. McDonald," said Briscoe, "do you remember a man named Herman Rauch?"

"Rauch? Is he the editor at HarperCollins?"

"He was one of your dissatisfied customers," said Green.

McDonald shrugged. "I don't have many dissatisfied customers, but I do not recall him. People want to blame me for their luck. I give them all they pay for. That's all I can do."

"You charged Rauch forty-five hundred."

McDonald shrugged. "I must have liked his book."

"But you don't remember him? He sued you."

"I know he sued me. All right, yes, I remember him. I just don't remember his book. He was the one who tried to kill Bob Rosserman."

"He whacked him on the head," said Briscoe.

"Aren't you unhappy when somebody turns down a book you've worked on?" asked Green.

"This is a profession. Editors have their own factors."

"But didn't Rauch's book meet the highest professional standard? Didn't Barbara Chesko's?"

"Look," said McDonald, "we gave the man half of his money back just to calm him down. We didn't have to do that. The contract says we don't have to do that. But you know what attorneys charge."

"Did Barbara Chesko ask for her money back?" said Briscoe.

"No! She was happy with the job! Very! Maybe that's why she was so disappointed when Bob turned her down."

"He told us a committee turned the book down."

"The editorial board, then." He raised his watch. "I have an appointment at twelve."

"We just thought you'd want to clear this up," said Green.

"Well?" demanded McDonald. "She killed herself. What's that got to do with me?"

"Maybe nothing, but I'd think you'd want to clear it up."

"That's just being a good citizen," said Briscoe.

McDonald opened his mouth to say something, but Green spoke before he had a chance. "You and Rosserman are good friends?"

"We're business acquaintances. We're on good terms."

"So he sends you clients?"

"If he thinks it will help the manuscript. If he sees something in the manuscript that might be improved."

"And what does he get out of this?"

McDonald glanced at them both. "We usually give him a finder's fee. It's a gesture, an appreciation."

"And how much would that be?"

"Oh, just a consideration."

"How much is a consideration? A bottle of scotch?"

"Why don't you ask him? I don't like to…"

"So, just for an example, what did he get each of the three times you went to work on Barbara Chesko's manuscript?"

"I don't remember the amounts. Something like a

couple of hundred dollars. We give the same fee an agent would get, about fifteen percent. There's absolutely nothing illegal about this, nothing at all. People don't have to hire us if they don't want to, and *if* they do, we do exactly what we promise to do."

"But don't your clients think this editing of yours is going to get their books into print?" said Briscoe.

"I am totally up front with them. I can't be responsible for how they misinterpret it."

"'It'?"

"If they think we are guaranteeing publication, they are misinterpreting. The contract is very clear."

"And Mrs. Chesko, did she misinterpret?" asked Green.

McDonald stood. "I have no idea what she thought. I feel sorry for her. But them's the breaks, gentlemen." He shot his cuffs, slipped the strap of his leather bag on his shoulder, and picked up his cane. "I have an appointment."

Briscoe and Green neither said nor did anything to stop him. They watched him glance back at them as he charged out the door and bumped into a passerby before heading north.

"Coffee jitters," said Green.

"'Them's the breaks,'" said Briscoe.

Len Kupferman was friendly enough, but looked a bit wary, as if he expected Briscoe and Green to pitch an idea for an awful book. His office was piled with manuscripts. Post-it notes hung from his ancient desk lamp like leaves on a dying oak.

"Well, it is true," he said, sitting on the edge of his desk, "that publishing operates in its own peculiar ways. Everybody has notions about how it works, but only the people who are in it really grasp it. What can I help you gentlemen with?"

"We're a little confused about some things," said Briscoe, settling onto a plain wooden chair, "and we appreciate your talking to us on short notice. I remembered you from Captain Dowd's party."

Kupferman squinted. "Oh, yes! That was what? Three years ago? Mike's book did pretty well. Our L.A. people are still trying to sell it as a movie. Mike could be the next Wambaugh."

"Mike was a good cop," said Briscoe. "I miss him."

"He lived a lot of stories before his retirement."

Green scratched at the skin between his lower lip and chin. He had something on his mind. "Is he a good writer?" he asked.

110

The question seemed to befuddle Kupferberg momentarily, as if Green had asked how many ears Dowd had. "Why, yes. The book went through three printings. Did you read it?"

"I get enough cop stories at work," said Green.

Kupferberg smiled. "I imagine you do."

"The reason we're asking," said Briscoe, "is like this. Suppose a book comes that's got good stories, but the person who wrote it isn't exactly Ernest Hemingway. What happens?"

"Well, there aren't many Hemingways, especially not in the Hemingway family. You mean someone whose writing isn't up to snuff?"

"Right."

"It depends on the content. It depends if it's salable. Say a celebrity comes in. Eminem wants to tell all about growing up. This will sell, but we discover Eminem is no writer. It's worth the publisher's while, then, to hire a ghostwriter."

"*Baseball Been Very, Very Good to Me* by Chico Escuela, as told to Joe Blow."

"Exactly," said Kupferman. "Usually, they pay Joe Blow a little extra to keep his name off it. If the person isn't a celebrity, then he'd better have a hell of a story. Mike Dowd had a hell of a story. Several, in fact. The Murphy Commission stuff. The Henderson murder."

"So there was a ghostwriter on Dowd's book?" Kupferman hesitated, so Briscoe reassured him. "Look, it goes nowhere. This is background. The case doesn't have anything to do with him."

"Well, as a matter of fact, there was no ghost."

Briscoe couldn't tell if Kupferman was covering for Captain Dowd, even though it really didn't matter.

"But it needed editing, right? Mike didn't just retire and turn into a writer."

"I worked with him to shape it. Not many agents like to do that, but I started out to be a playwright, so I like to get my hand in once and a while."

"So you edited it. Would an agent normally do this?"

"No, I didn't really edit it. Mostly I made suggestions about how the material should be organized. What should be left out, put in, like that. An in-house editor at Ballantine worked on it for the page-by-page, line-by-line stuff. Mike was very cooperative. As I said, most agents don't have the time and I don't know of any who do the actual editing, except in unusual circumstances. When a book is accepted, a house editor works with the author and then a copyeditor goes over it for typos, contradictions, grammar, and so forth. That's normal with any book. I remember we had some trouble with Mike's copyeditor. She was touchy about politically incorrect dialogue. She was another one of those kids not long out of Vassar." Kupferman laughed. "Officers never use sexist or ethnic obscenities, do they?"

"Never in my career have I heard one," said Briscoe.

"I didn't think so," said Kupferman.

"Who pays for the editing?" asked Briscoe.

"The publishing house."

"The writer doesn't hire them?"

"Not ordinarily. Some of the more successful authors do, so they can get top dollar for their manuscripts. But most writers don't make very much. They can't afford it." Kupferman shrugged. "Usually there isn't much editing at all, except that done by the writer. If the book isn't written well enough, publishers don't buy it. There are a lot of other choices. Why do you ask?"

"Suppose we've got a writer who's got some good stories. Would a publisher ever advise the writer to hire an editor?"

Kupferman chuckled. "As an insult."

"I don't get it," said Green.

"What I mean is that it would mean the thing is unpublishable. If it weren't, the house would hire an editor."

"But couldn't an editor make it publishable?"

"Oh, rarely," said Kupferman. "Like I said, if the story was compelling enough, for whatever reason, maybe a book doctor could turn it into something. There are some book doctors who do miracles. There's a great guy up in Croton who can give a moribund book the equivalent of a heart, lung and liver transplant, but there has to be some sign of life to work with in the first place. Most honest book doctors contract with publishers. They don't do most of their work with individuals."

"Would the story of the breakdown of a marriage be the kind of thing that a publisher might recommend to a book doctor?"

"*Sheesh*," said Kupferman. "Bill Clinton's marriage maybe. How many marriages break down? Is there a murder? International intrigue? I've had two wives and I don't even want to remember the name of my attorney."

"It wouldn't even fly as a woman's book?" asked Briscoe.

Kupferman shrugged. "If it was extremely well written, literary in quality, I'd be willing to look at it, but…"

Green rested his elbows on his knees and clasped his hands. "The thing is, we are having a problem understanding why a publisher recommended a book be edited, when there was nothing to the book in the first place. No real celebrity. A businessman. Nothing but the husband fooling around. Why?"

"Who was the publisher?" asked Kupferman.

"Kirstner and Strawn."

"That's a good house," said Kupferman. "They must have seen something in it. Maybe they thought it had literary potential."

"The author hired an editor named Avery McDonald."

Kupferman gaped. "McDonald? Kirstner and Strawn recommended McDonald? Don't tell me they're in bed with McDonald? That's not possible."

"Am I missing something here?" said Briscoe.

"Kirstner and Strawn is an old and distinguished publisher! They have a better rep than that!" Kupferman shook his head. "Where you've got a lot of dreams, detectives, you attract a lot of bad actors. Can I go off the record here?"

"We're just trying to understand," said Green.

Kupferman leaned toward them and spoke in a half-whisper, neatly enunciating his words. "Avery and Monica McDonald are slime. They buy mailing lists and advertise in writing magazines. You send them a manuscript, they think it shows potential. If you just send them the money, they'll fix it up for you."

"So they fix it up?"

"No, they pretend to fix it up. They mark it up, make worthless suggestions, then send it back with good luck on it."

"But they do edit it?"

"Only in the most perfunctory fashion. They're taking advantage of people. I've got a client who worked for them for a couple of months. He was broke and trying to finish his degree at Columbia. He answered an ad for editors and found himself working for them. He did two books a day at two hundred fifty a pop."

"I couldn't *read* a book a day," said Briscoe. "Not even Marvel comics."

"Precisely," said Kupferman. "I'll give you his number."

"So, then," said Green, "the only reason an editor at Kirstner and Strawn would recommend the McDonalds would be?"

"There isn't any reason. No decent one, anyway."

"So what are the indecent reasons?"

"Bribes. Kickbacks. I've heard of editors and agents getting fees for referring victims to so-called editors like this," said Kupferman. "Any editor who threw a writer to those sharks would know what he was doing. And I guarantee that unless something is different in the main office of K and S, any editor who did it there would be out on the pavement."

Briscoe and Green looked at each other. Motive?

"You know what it's called among agents?" confided Kupferman. "'Reflux.' After a few drinks, it graduates to 'Refux.' The latter is more accurate."

LIEUTENANT VAN BUREN'S OFFICE
27TH PRECINCT
TUESDAY, SEPTEMBER 3, 3:03 P.M.

Robert Rosserman's sweaty hands quivered as he took Van Buren's. "How do you do?" he said, then sat stiffly in a chair.

"I'm John Ellis with Hartman and Price," said the slim young attorney.

"Do you know detectives Briscoe and Green?" Van Buren asked. Ellis took their hands in succession.

"A pleasure," he said. Everyone sat. Ellis placed his briefcase in his lap and stretched his forearms across it. "I'm sure you're wondering why we're here."

"To discuss Mrs. Chesko's death?" asked Van Buren.

"Exactly," said Ellis, "and to ask for a little mercy."

Briscoe looked past Ellis. "You need a lawyer? Why would you need a lawyer, Mr. Rosserman?"

"Lennie," said Van Buren. Rosserman brushed at his trousers.

"He doesn't," said Ellis, "but he thought it might help in case there was a misunderstanding. Mr. Rosserman and I asked for this meeting to correct an error of judgment on his part."

"I'm sorry," said Rosserman. "I didn't think it mattered."

116

Briscoe opened his mouth to speak but Ellis raised his hand to cut him off. "It was an error of judgment, out of the best of motives. It was more an error of omission than commission."

"And exactly what was this error?" said Van Buren, tilting her head.

"She killed herself," said Rosserman.

Ellis gave him another "let me handle this" look.

"Are you speaking of Barbara Chesko?" said Van Buren. "Do we need to record this conversation?"

"Hear us out. Bob meant well, but it was a mistake."

Van Buren smiled at Ellis and raised her eyebrows.

"Well," said Ellis, "you already know that Bob turned down Mrs. Chesko's manuscript around noon on Tuesday. About two, she showed up at his office, distraught. Bob had an important telephone call to deal with."

"Sub-rights," said Briscoe.

"Besides which," said Ellis, "he was hoping she would sit, reflect, calm down. Unfortunately, the call became complicated. He forgot she was out there. Am I being accurate, Bob?"

Rosserman nodded.

"About four-thirty Bob came out to go home and Mrs. Chesko confronted him: the editor in the office down the hall, Albert Ilsing, heard it, the secretary, Jenna Marshak, heard it, but Bob told Mrs. Chesko the editorial board had turned down the book, and after a while, she left."

"But there was no editorial board, was there?" asked Green.

Rosserman rolled his head. "I couldn't take that thing to the board. I'd have been a laughingstock!"

"But you told us it had raw talent!" said Briscoe.

He clenched his hands. "It wasn't ready to publish."

"Okay, so you admit you lied to Mrs. Chesko," said Green. "And you admit you lied to us. What else?"

Ellis snapped open his briefcase. "He should have given you this." He lifted out an envelope and handed it to the Lieutenant. "The suicide note," he said.

Briscoe stood and read it out loud over her shoulder:

YOU HAVE USED ME. RALPH USED ME. AVERY USED ME. I AM ALL USED UP AND WON'T TAKE ANOTHER DAY OF IT. MY LIFE HAS BEEN OVER FOR YEARS. LET THAT BE ON YOUR HEAD. NOT THAT YOU'LL CARE. YOU'VE SHOWN ME HOW MUCH YOU CARE.

"But I do care," mumbled Rosserman. "I thought she'd get over it."

"And when did you get this note?" asked Van Buren sharply.

"It was in his mailbox the day after she died," said Ellis.

"The mailboxes are by Jenna's desk," said Rosserman, "just a few feet from where Barbara waited. The envelope was between a couple of manila envelopes. If I'd have gone through the box on Wednesday, I might have known. I might have stopped her."

"So," said Green, "you knew she was in the Waterloo Hotel?"

"No!" said Rosserman. "I meant if I had known about the note and known where she was—"

Ellis placed his hand on Rosserman's forearm. "Bob is really broken up about this. He could have simply

118

shredded the note and you would never have known about it."

"That's true," said Van Buren. "Unless he thinks the note will clear him."

"Clear him?"

"Of suspicion of murder," she said.

Ellis momentarily looked like he had wandered into the women's rest room. "Murder? Who said she was murdered?" He looked at Rosserman. "She jumped out of the window."

"Or was pushed," said Briscoe.

Ellis glanced at his client as if to ask him if this was the real reason Rosserman had asked him to come. "Well, certainly, that letter proves she wasn't pushed," he finally said.

"Maybe he should be charged with withholding evidence," said Van Buren, "and we can see where that leads."

"You see?" said Rosserman to Ellis, before facing Van Buren. "For God's sake! I brought this to you on my own. There's a shredder not twenty feet from my desk. I simply was trying to keep K and S out of the papers. We're a respected publisher. We don't need this kind of tabloid publicity."

"He came here to inform you," said Ellis, "but also to ask you not to punish his employer. A little discretion. These accusations are ridiculous."

"I didn't hear any accusation," said Van Buren.

"Are you sure this is just to protect the beloved and eminent reputation of Kirstner and Strawn?" said Briscoe. "What about you, Mr. Rosserman? Do your bosses know that you referred Mrs. Chesko to Avery McDonald?"

Rosserman blinked. "I suggested they might help. I was trying to help her."

"So, then, it's just a coincidence you get a fee?"

"Who said anything about a fee?"

"That's how it works, isn't it?"

"I didn't force her to use Redux. That was entirely her choice. I certainly didn't do it for the finder's fee."

"Money never motivates me, either," said Briscoe, "but I'm sure your bosses wouldn't approve of this little favor."

"I did nothing wrong!"

Ellis's eyes had been banging from side to side watching the exchanges and trying to figure out where they were going. "That's enough," he said. "I now see why Bob asked me to come along. Mr. Rosserman has turned over a significant piece of evidence. That's what he was here for, and he acted in good faith. If you have accusations or innuendos, you'd best be careful with them. Now, am I to assume that this meeting has ended?"

Van Buren glanced at Briscoe and Green. They had nothing to add. "But keep yourself available," she said to Rosserman.

"I think," said Ellis, "that any further contact should be through me." He reached into his briefcase and held out a business card. "In fact, I am advising Mr. Rosserman that he shouldn't speak about this matter, unless I am present."

"Catch you later," said Green. Rosserman glared back at him.

When Ellis closed the door, Briscoe said, "I think he was disappointed in the outcome."

"I think he wasn't sure we'd buy it," said Green, picking up the note. "Why else the lawyer?"

Van Buren looked down at the note. "Nevertheless," she said, "I suppose that about ends the case."

"Not that there was one to begin with," said Briscoe.

"We could see if the note has her fingerprints," she said.

"Oops," said Green, dropping it to the desk. "But it won't."

"It won't? How do you know? She didn't write it?"

"It smells," admitted Briscoe. "As soon as we question him, it turns up. Do I detect a little consciousness of guilt?"

"Oh, it's easier than that," said Green. "We need to go back to her apartment to make sure, but she didn't do this. At least not at home. The paper is wrong."

Rosserman was reaching for his phone when Briscoe and Green stepped into his doorway. His hand hung suspended. "How did you get in?" said Rosserman. "What now? My lawyer told you—"

"We walked in," said Briscoe. "This isn't the Pentagon."

Rosserman took a deep breath and weakly smiled. "I'm sorry. You startled me." He rubbed his forehead with his fingertips. "This whole thing with Barbara is upsetting. I've got a call in to Los Angeles. Rough day."

"About to get rougher," said Green. "You got a blank piece of paper?"

"A blank? What for?"

"Got one?"

Rosserman blinked, raised both hands as if bewildered, and opened his desk. He lifted out a sheet of letterhead.

"Not that," said Briscoe. "Just plain white paper. Like you'd print out a memo or something."

He shuffled a few things around in the drawer. "I'm out. Jenna keeps all that down by the printer."

"I'll go say hello," said Briscoe.

Rosserman watched Briscoe until the detective was out of sight. "Has this got something to do with Barbara's note?"

"I'd say so," said Green. Rosserman continued to look confused. Green stared at him until Briscoe returned.

"Bingo," said Briscoe. He held up a sheet of plain white paper. "They got tons of this."

"It's ordinary laser printer paper," said Rosserman.

"The same kind of paper that so-called suicide note was printed on," said Green.

Rosserman raised his eyebrows. "'So-called'? It's not like there's anything special about that paper. It's fifteen dollars a crate. There are tons of that in every office supply store."

"But not in Barbara Chesko's apartment," said Green.

"Huh? So?"

"Funny thing about Mrs. Chesko," said Briscoe, "she was soaking her ex."

"Or maybe she was just high-styling it," said Green. "Whichever it was, with this writing thing of hers, she had to do it all first class. Brand-new Sony computer. Expensive printer."

Rosserman's eyes went back and forth between Green and Briscoe. "She took it very seriously."

"And all her manuscripts and letters were on one hundred percent, watermarked, acid-free paper."

"Like her manuscripts required preserving," muttered Rosserman.

"The point is," said Green, "she didn't have any of this cheap paper in her apartment."

Rosserman closed his eyes trying to grasp what

they were saying. "That kind of paper's everywhere. What are you saying?"

"We're saying Barbara Chesko didn't own any," said Green.

"We're saying you lied to us again, Mr. Rosserman," said Briscoe. "That suicide note didn't come from her."

Rosserman spread his hands. "What are you saying? Of course it came from her. Who else?" The recognition dawned ugly. "That paper didn't come from *here*. Why would I write her suicide note?"

"Hmm, let me think," said Briscoe. "Could it be that her death wasn't a suicide? Could it be you pushed her?"

"Are you crazy? This is a nightmare!"

"You lied to us, man. We don't like that," said Green.

"It implies guilt, wouldn't you say?" added Briscoe.

"She could have gotten that paper *anywhere*," said Rosserman. "This is nuts!"

"Well, maybe we should talk about how nuts it is down at the precinct," said Briscoe.

"You're arresting me?"

"Not yet," said Green. "But it'll go easier if you help us straighten this out."

"Maybe we could arrange an arrest," said Briscoe. "How does 'suspicion of murder' sound?"

"That's crazy! She was unstable. She killed herself! You can't prove her note was written by me. I didn't do it. It could have been printed anywhere. How do you know she didn't have any of that paper? How do you know she didn't get it printed at Kinko's or somewhere? This is nuts."

Briscoe leaned close. "If we have to prove this,

you're going to make it a lot harder on yourself. I'm already in a pretty bad mood."

"I found the note in my mailbox!" He pointed back toward Jenna's office.

Briscoe grinned. "You know, when I first started out we could identify which typewriter had been used for which document. There were little distinguishing nicks on this or that letter. You can see detectives using this fact in old movies."

Rosserman glanced at Green then locked back into Briscoe's stare. Briscoe continued. "Now people feel safe because they have laser printers, but guess what? Each laser printer is slightly different as well. It's like little dots and they come out a little different. Like a fingerprint."

"I didn't write the note!"

"I'm not a technical sort of guy," said Briscoe. "But I know some, and I'll bet they can prove the printer in the work area was where the note was printed. Or do you have one of your own?"

"We all use the joint printer. I didn't do it! For God's sake!"

"You didn't push her?" asked Green.

"No! And I didn't fake a note either!" He twisted his head from side to side, trying to find something to say. "I want my lawyer. This is nuts! I'm not saying another word."

He reached for his phone. Green slapped his hand over the receiver before Rosserman could lift it. "I hope he tells you to come clean with us," he snarled.

"When we come back," said Briscoe, "you're going to have a very bad day."

"I didn't do it," said Rosserman, nearly choking on the words.

"We'll leave a receipt for the office printer," said Green.

"What do you think, Mr. Rosserman?" said Briscoe. "You think her note was printed on it?"

Assistant District Attorney Serena Southerlyn was
ten minutes from an arraignment, and only the one
elevator was running. She charged up the stairs
clutching a thick case file against her chest, shaking
her head against what Briscoe and Green were asking.
"Come on, guys," she said. "You know it's weak. Why
are you even asking me?"

Briscoe and Green chased after her. Green spoke
first. "Look, we know we haven't got enough, but
there's probably DNA on the blanket and maybe the
condom wrapper."

"Probably? Maybe?"

"The M.E. thinks there is."

Southerlyn looked at her watch. "So ask him for a
blood sample."

"His attorney seems like he'd go along, but
Rosserman refuses."

"We gave him the old 'you can prove yourself innocent right away' routine," huffed Briscoe, "but he
wouldn't go for it."

"Which means he was in the room," said Southerlyn.

"The guy faked a suicide note in his office," said

Green. "Maybe fifteen people had access to the printer, but he is the only one we know of that had any connection to Barbara Chesko."

"And he's got a motive," panted Briscoe. "When we explained why we were taking the printer, his bosses found out he was directing suckers to the McDonalds. They canned him on the spot."

"Are there fingerprints on the suicide note?"

"Not Barbara Chesko's," said Green. "Rosserman's attorney. Rosserman's. Mine."

Southerlyn stopped. "*Yours?*"

Green shrugged. "Van Buren's."

"Good work."

"We handled it before we knew what it was," he protested.

"His attorney claims that Barbara Chesko or somebody else printed the note and put it in his mailbox," said Briscoe. "But there's nobody else's fingerprints on it."

"Other than half of the twenty-seventh precinct?"

"The tech tells us that Chesko's laptop doesn't have the suicide note on it. Not the computer in Rosserman's office, either. And it's not on the secretary's machine."

"Does he have a home one? A laptop? Even if he erased it, it doesn't really go away, you know," said Southerlyn.

"We'll check if he has another machine," said Green.

"Is it possible," asked Southerlyn, "that somebody else wrote the note and stuck it in Rosserman's mailbox?"

"That's a stretch," said Green.

"Juries like a nice stretch," said Southerlyn. "They

vote 'not guilty' if the stretch reminds them of Perry Mason." Southerlyn stopped at the landing. Her cheeks were flushed. Briscoe looked grateful.

"And she wasn't having a relationship with anyone else?" Southerlyn asked.

"No one else knows of anyone else," said Green. "No one saw her pick up anyone. We didn't see her with anyone in the hotel lobby tapes. She checks in alone and goes upstairs."

"Does Rosserman have an alibi?"

"He says he worked late and went home to a TV dinner."

Southerlyn thought for a moment. "The circumstantial evidence is good, I think. Tell him to get ready to roll up his sleeve. I'll get an order by tomorrow, before the judges begin leaving for Labor Day."

Briscoe hung on the stair rail, catching his breath and watching Southerlyn's hips swinging up the staircase.

"If I give my body to medical research," gasped Briscoe, "will they come carry me down these stairs?"

Executive A.D.A. Jack McCoy was the last to arrive at D.A. Arthur Branch's office, and, to his surprise, the secretary directed him to the conference room. Had he forgotten a meeting?

The morning had gone too easy, he was thinking. A knee-breaker had made a surprise change to a guilty plea and word had come that the Court of Appeals had refused to listen to arguments on behalf of Martin Brunley, a child molester who both he and Branch thought might get a hearing. The percentage of sons of bitches on the streets of Manhattan had therefore decreased very slightly, maybe infinitesimally, but it was an improvement—two wads of dirty gum that could no longer stick to innocent people's shoes.

"Jack," said Branch as he stepped through the half-open door. "You all know each other, I assume?"

McCoy nodded to Lieutenant Van Buren, Detectives Briscoe and Green, and A.D.A. Southerlyn. The fifth person was a jowly man whose suit said "cop." He offered a hand. "Jack McCoy."

"Dennis Gross," said the man. "Fraud."

"Well," said McCoy, adjusting his shoulders as he sat, "What's all this about?"

"Thanks for coming in. I chatted with Lieutenant Van Buren earlier," said Branch, "and thought it would be easier if we all got our heads together on this. There is some rumbling at City Hall, and I need to make sure I'm on the right page."

McCoy clasped his hands and rested his forearms on the table. He tried to think what case they all had in common, but drew a blank. "What do you mean by rumbling?"

"Let's just say there's interest in influential places."

"The *Daily News* is hinting conspiracy in the death of Barbara Chesko," said Southerlyn, offering him a folded tabloid.

"Barbara Chesko?" McCoy skimmed the article. "Oh. She was married to that growth fund guy. Wasn't this a suicide? That isn't our business. Ralph Chesko looks dirty on her death?"

"He's clear as near as we can tell," said Briscoe.

"The paper is just raising suspicion," said Branch. "The 'merely a coincidence? slash could it be a conspiracy?' teaser."

"They're not accusing him," said Southerlyn, "but there's that paragraph in the financial column there..." She pointed.

"'Yet, Wall Street gossips frequently speculate on what Barbara Chesko, an apparent suicide, might have known about her husband's business dealings over the past decade.'"

"Ralph Chesko takes that as tantamount to an accusation of murder," said Branch. "He's not amused and thinks the investigation is being dragged out. It's been what? Almost two weeks since the body was discovered."

"So?" said McCoy. "The *Daily News* has its conspiracy theories, he can have his. Let him write a letter to the editor. What's that got to do with us? Two weeks isn't long."

Branch tugged his ear. "See the blisters? I didn't discuss the case with him. I just listened."

"Arthur," said McCoy, "why didn't you just hang up?"

"There's nothing wrong with hearing him out," said Branch.

McCoy knew that there was more to it than that, or Branch wouldn't have listened. He looked at the cops. "Has someone been leaking hints Chesko might be involved in his wife's death?"

"No," said Van Buren. "In fact, we don't think he had anything to do with it."

"The papers know something we don't?"

"As near as we can tell," said Green, "Mrs. Chesko didn't know much about his business dealings and the AG and the SEC is sure he didn't do anything chargeable when his fund went down."

"In the article, a spokesman for the Wire and Spring Workers Union mentions a trip to the Isle of Jersey," said Branch.

"He took a trip there," said Briscoe, "But it was months ago, and the SEC says that it's all legitimate."

"I don't get it," said McCoy.

"Jack," said Branch, "there are alternative explanations and, if I understand what the detectives are saying, little evidence either way. The woman had a reason to commit suicide however weak it may seem."

"I disagree," said Southerlyn. "Barbara Chesko

didn't have a 'weak' reason for suicide. She spends all that time writing the novel, then editing it, then getting her hopes up about her novel. *Then*, these creeps Robert Rosserman and Redux shatter her dreams. She's been scammed. She feels humiliated and foolish."

"Aging, ditched by her husband, ripped off, and wondering how she could have been so stupid," said Branch.

"Exactly," said Southerlyn. "And if it's a suicide, who drove her to it? I think we've got to do something about Redux. If this isn't a scam, what is?"

McCoy raised his eyebrows helplessly and turned to Gross. "So there's fraud, then?"

Branch asked the detectives to summarize what they knew about Redux. He needed to hear it all spelled out himself, anyway, he said, "to fend off the jackals."

As Briscoe finished, McCoy turned to Gross. "I'm not sure I heard anything specifically illegal."

"Well, it's borderline, isn't it? There are scams and then there are scams. Legal-wise," said Gross. "That's what the A.D.A.s tell us."

"But if that editor is even close about the amount they take in," said Southerlyn, "they take advantage of a lot of people."

"Income taxes on half a million last year," said Gross.

"You can't protect people from being stupid," said McCoy.

Branch set down his notes. "It stinks, though. Take some time to look into the fraud aspect, Serena, if you think you can build a winnable case."

"I'd like to," she said.

"You think maybe this editor Rosserman shoved her out the window?" asked McCoy.

Green answered. "If Kirstner and Strawn knew he was picking up fifteen percent for referring clients to Redux…"

"He would have been fired," said Briscoe.

"So to protect his job he killed her," added Green.

McCoy smiled. "I never knew book editors had jobs worth killing for. I heard it was a low-paying job with long hours."

"It's not funny a man should be killed," said Branch, "but it's often funny he should be killed for so little."

McCoy smiled. "Chandler."

"Right," said Branch.

McCoy dropped his smile. "Can you place him in the hotel?"

"Everything is circumstantial," said Briscoe, "unless the DNA helps. That's not back yet. But he doesn't have a good alibi. He lied to us and cooked up the suicide note."

"Sounds like consciousness of guilt," said McCoy.

"So maybe her feelings turned to anger," said McCoy, "and she threatened Rosserman with fraud charges." He turned to Gross. "I assume that's why you're here."

"I'm here because of Redux," said Gross. "We've had complaints against this Redux—twenty in the last three years."

"Isn't that a lot?"

"Not necessarily. A lot of service occupations draw complaints. Remodelers. Decorators. Most of the complaints were dropped. Some of the officers recognize the McDonalds when the complaints come in and merely file the report."

"They don't investigate?"

"It's a judgment call," said Gross. "A few days' wait may save a lot of work that goes nowhere. One investigator called and got some of the complainant's money back, but mostly we don't waste our time. We suggest they talk to a civil attorney. What Redux does, well, it's hard to call illegal." He explained the Redux contract and how it specified there was no guarantee, after the editing, that the manuscript would become a book.

"So, blinded by their hopes, people overlook this?"

"Exactly," said Gross. "There's a similar scam for songwriters. You send in lyrics. They write back what great potential you have. The wannabe likes to believe he has potential, of course, or he wouldn't be writing songs. The company offers to make a demo record to send to all the famous singers. This costs you plenty. They mail it to a hundred people, all recognizable celebrities from Trisha Yearwood to Ice-T. Guess what? The singers throw the demos in the trash with the rest of the junk mail. It's all the same: there is no way that any of this gets you into the business."

"But it's deceptive," said Southerlyn.

"Of course it is," said Branch, "so are most herbal diet plans, but it doesn't necessarily make them criminal."

"Guaranteed way to kill roaches," said Van Buren. Everyone looked at her. "You never heard of this? There was a guy in the nineteen forties or sometime who sold a guaranteed way to kill roaches. You sent in a dollar and he mailed you two blocks of wood with directions to smash the roaches in between them. His defense was his ad was literally true. Like the McDonalds' contract."

"But the post office department shut him down, didn't they?" asked Serena. "Mail fraud?"

McCoy interrupted. "This isn't really the point, is it?"

"You're right," said Branch. "The death is."

"The question is," McCoy continued, "was Barbara Chesko murdered? And if she was, who did it? It sounds to me the most likely person is Rosserman. Ralph Chesko has nothing to gain, unless she knew about something illegal in his business. Nobody seems to think she did. The McDonalds have no motive," McCoy continued. "Chesko's no threat. The McDonalds evidently survived a number of fraud complaints and will survive many more."

"Survived and prospered!" said Gross.

"Really?" asked McCoy. "That many people are writing books?" McCoy was amused. Southerlyn looked at him coldly.

"That many people are paying for their editorial services. God knows how many are writing who don't hire them," said Gross. "We talked to one of their editors once. She was a smart kid. She argued with Avery McDonald and tried to get unemployment. She claimed they were making up to ten thou a week."

"That much?" said McCoy.

"But the kid couldn't tell us anything we could take to court," said Gross. "She was the classic disgruntled employee. IRS audited them and they found nothing but a couple of unreceipted deductions. The McDonalds were sloppy at sending out 1099s, but that just made the IRS go after the people who got paid."

"But, unless you can find a way Barbara Chesko could have hurt them, they have no reason to kill her," said McCoy.

"So what is our action, people?" said Branch.

"We need more evidence against Rosserman," said McCoy.

"The DNA should do it," said Briscoe.

"And that would prove what?" said Branch. "That he had sex with her. Where is the evidence she was pushed?"

"If we can prove he made up the suicide note?" said Green.

"Rosserman turned in the suicide note himself," said Briscoe, "which could have been a way to get himself off the hook, but it would have been just as easy to do nothing, as his attorney pointed out. There's a shredder in his office."

"A lot of guilty people go over the line trying to prove their innocence. They think they can fool us," said McCoy. "Maybe the M.E. could find us something?"

Briscoe shrugged. "We'll ask, but..."

"Look, people," said Branch, "in the final analysis we're hardly any farther along than when the detectives showed up at the scene. Get the DNA results for Rosserman and maybe he will tearfully confess and save us a lot more trouble. We know he's a liar. But it seems to me you can't go anywhere with homicide unless he breaks down. It's far too circumstantial."

"We should at least make him suffer for playing three-card monte with us," said Briscoe, stretching and rising.

Southerlyn reached out for Gross's arm. "I'll want to see the files on Redux."

"Say when," said Gross. "I've got a file five years thick."

McCoy lingered in Branch's office while the others

drifted out. "Cleveland Sharpe copped a plea," he told Branch, "and the Supreme Court refused to hear Martin Brunley's appeal."

"That *is* good," said Branch. "maybe the liberal press of New York City will lay off me for an hour."

"What was this meeting really about?" asked McCoy, glancing back at the doorway. "That bit of nonsense in the *Daily News*?"

Branch seemed, as was usual with him, to be carefully composing his response. "On one side, they say he absconded with the union's pension fund. On the other side, he's an innocent victim of the markets." He paused. "Ralph Chesko has been a big donor in the past, to a number of campaigns."

"To you?"

"To a lot of people," he answered.

"I thought he was broke now."

"Just about, as far as anyone knows, but the party doesn't just toss supporters over."

"Who will return his calls when they're sure he's really broke?" said McCoy.

"Don't be totally cynical, Jack. Certain important persons are sincere about helping him. Just because Chesko donated doesn't mean he, ah, wasn't friends with important people."

"So Chesko is upset about the news article?"

"Less that, I think, than the fact that the McDonalds relieved his ex-wife of eighteen thousand dollars of the support money he sent. I really don't think that would bother him if he had a million or two stashed in an Isle of Jersey bank."

"Her murder doesn't bother him? Just the support money?"

"At the least, I'm sure he doesn't want to be accused

of it. Maybe he feels guilty about divorcing her. Talk to him yourself," said Branch. "Horse's mouth and all that. Assure him we're doing everything we can."

"Political hand-holding isn't my business," McCoy said.

"Who are you kidding, Jack?" said Branch. "This is America. Hell, this is the universe! Politics is everybody's business. For good and ill." He paused again. "All right, Jack, I'll call him myself. But keep a close watch on this case."

"We'll build the case against Rosserman," said McCoy. "If we can."

When the detectives delivered the DNA order to John Ellis, he had shrugged and said he had talked to his client thirty minutes before. "He would have changed his mind by this afternoon," said Ellis. "He was offended, that's all."

"Well, now, he doesn't have to change his mind," said Briscoe, dropping the order on Ellis' desk.

Afterward, they canvassed the Waterloo Hotel and surrounding neighborhood again, just in case somebody had seen Barbara Chesko with a man.

It was a long, frustrating afternoon. They tried every employee they could find at the Waterloo. Bellhops, clerks, maintenance people, maids, the wait staff in the coffee shop. There was also a high-class Greek restaurant in the hotel, but no one there remembered Rosserman. They then moved on to nearby businesses. Some people remembered talking to the detectives when the body was discovered. None of them could identify the picture of Bob Rosserman. Many would try to avoid looking at it, out of fear of becoming involved. If you urged them to take another look, they were usually relieved to be able to say they didn't recognize him. Others of them would say they thought he might be familiar, though they didn't know why. People who wished they could be helpful often said that. They always wanted to know why you were asking, hoping they were participants in something they would later see on the news.

Briscoe and Green slid onto bar stools. The bartender, a narrow-hipped man with massive shoulders, stood at the far end of the bar, wiping out the cylinder of a blender and talking to a bulldog of a woman delivering cases of bottled beer.

"You know how in old movies they say, 'My dogs are barking'?" said Briscoe loosening his shoes. "Mine have died and are howling in doggy hell."

Green couldn't help smiling. "Doggy hell?" He shook his head. "The way you turn a phrase, you ought to write a book."

Briscoe gave him a "drop dead" look.

"Hey," said the bartender, "New York's finest!"

"Is it that obvious?" said Green.

He gestured toward Briscoe. "You were a regular."

Briscoe squinted and looked around. "You're right," he said. "The memories are coming back and they aren't pleasant. I guess the evil side of my subconscious drew me back."

"And if I remember correctly, you did have an evil side."

"Sorry. Get me a club soda," said Briscoe. "Lots of ice. Do I remember this place being busier?"

"It's always quiet after Labor Day weekend," said the bartender.

Briscoe laid pictures of Barbara Chesko and Bob Rosserman on the bar. "You ever seen either of these two?"

The barman picked up Chesko's picture and stared

closely at it. "No. Don't think so. They come in together?"

"We're not sure."

"I recognize the guy," he said. "He's been in here."

"When?"

"I don't know. A week, two weeks ago."

Briscoe straightened up as if his feet no longer hurt.

"He had an argument with a guy in the booth over there. They were hunched down together, eyebrow to eyebrow. This guy here"—he tapped the picture—"was really worked up, just barely holding himself together, but he kept his voice down."

"Can you remember when this was?"

"Wednesday. My wife's birthday. I bought her some cannoli and had to exchange them."

"What?" said Briscoe. "They weren't the right size?"

"Cockroach in the filling." He rolled his eyes. "It was sticking out like a hood ornament. My wife woulda freaked."

"Yummy," said Briscoe. "Do you remember what time these two guys argued?"

"Sometime after six and before eleven. I do noon to three, then pick up my daughter from school. Her mom gets home at five-thirty and I come back."

"Can you pin it down better?"

"Let me think." He filled a tumbler with club soda. "Later. I think. I don't know. Was it Wednesday?" he asked himself.

"Are you sure it's him?"

"I think so. I think it was just after I came in. Like six-thirty or seven. I was steamed about the bug and I saw them over there and hoped they wouldn't get into a knockdown, because I was in a pretty bad mood. I wasn't about to dig the nasty thing out. I mean, where there's one there's usually two."

"Where there's two there's a million." Briscoe thirstily gulped a mouthful of the club soda and wiped his chin.

"I was afraid the littler guy'd whack him with his cane."

Briscoe set down the glass and gave Green a look. "A cane?"

"Nothing spectacular. It had like a doorknob on the end."

"Could you identify these men if you saw them again?" asked Green.

The bartender thought. He closed his eyes and tried to remember. "The one guy had curly hair, the other...ahhh. It was the guy with the curly hair who got animated. He came to the bar. I didn't get a close look at the other one. The small guy."

"Small?"

"He looked small in the booth."

Briscoe rolled his eyes.

"Hey, I'm trying to help," said the bartender. He snapped his fingers. "A goat!"

"Goat?" asked Briscoe.

The bartender touched his chin. "A goat!"

"And a cane," said Green.

Briscoe and Green nodded. Briscoe jumped to his feet and pulled out his wallet. "Police money is no good with me," said the bartender.

"But it really hit the spot," said Briscoe, throwing two dollars on the bar. "Buy your wife a roach-free cannoli."

The woman who opened the door of the huge Victorian house had John Lennon glasses and the stocky figure of a woman who was more muscle than fat. Her hair was parted down the middle, as straight as if she ironed it. She was wearing a worn Army shirt, stone-washed jeans, and sandals.

"Is this the McDonald residence?" asked Briscoe.

"Who wants to know?"

He raised his badge. "Are you Mrs. McDonald?"

"I'm Monica McDonald, if that's what you mean. What's up?"

"Is Mr. McDonald in?"

"And what is this in reference to?"

"It's in reference to seeing Mr. McDonald," snapped Green.

"Will this take long? We're going to drive to our place in Maine and he's taking a shower. If you've got papers to serve…"

"Mr. McDonald knows us," said Briscoe. "We called him on his cell. He said he'd be here."

"He didn't say anything about it, just that he wasn't in a hurry to drive to Maine. He likes driving in the dark."

144

"Can we come in?"

"Is that necessary?"

"Is all this dancing necessary?" said Green. She said nothing, but backed away from the door. At first Briscoe thought he smelled pot, but then recognized it as a sweet incense.

There was little furniture in the room, but a dozen overstuffed Madras pillows composed a sitting circle around a low circular table. It was the kind of arrangement in which you'd expect to see a hookah in the center. Instead was a carton of manuscripts, an ashtray, and a coffee mug with a mandala on it.

"You work in here?" asked Briscoe, pointing to the carton of manuscripts.

"One of our editors dropped those off this afternoon," said McDonald. "Now what is this about?"

"One of the editors who gets a finder's fee?" asked Green.

"No," she said, "it's one of the editors that works for us."

"You don't handle the editing yourselves?"

"The workload can get heavy. We hire freelancers on occasion," she said sharply. "As you know."

"We didn't know," said Briscoe.

"So it's not about taxes," she said. "So why are you here?"

"Taxes?" asked Briscoe. "You expecting a visit from the tax man?"

"One of our editors tried to make us pay comp. It was harassment. He wanted a raise and we wouldn't give him one. Our editors are freelancers. The complaint was thrown out."

"That surprises me," said Briscoe. "They usually

find some excuse to gouge you, don't they? Is business good? How many editors you got?"

"A few," she said. "But they don't work here."

"They're freelancers," said Green.

"Yes."

"Gentlemen!" Avery McDonald appeared at the top of the stairs, combing his hair. He was wearing denim from neck to ankles, and red sneakers. "I suppose you and Monica have met?" He threw an arm around her shoulder and squeezed her.

"Mrs. McDonald was telling us about your editors."

The cheerfulness in his voice disappeared, as if he wondered what she had said. "We screen them carefully even though we can only pay them a dollar a page. They're good, serious workers."

"Takes a lot of pages to buy a house like this," said Briscoe.

"And you have a place in Maine, too?" asked Green. "Nice."

"We have money from our own writings," said Avery.

"Along with your up-front fees," said Green, "you picked up, what was it? Nearly nineteen thousand from Barbara Chesko's manuscript."

"I edited that one personally," said McDonald firmly. "I devoted two entire weekends to it. Didn't I?" Mrs. McDonald nodded. "I'll have to admit it was very frustrating."

"Avery came home in a very bad mood," said Monica, her eyes narrowing. "Very tired."

"Barbara had her own notions about what she should do. Many questionable things." He flicked his hand upward, dismissing the remark. "But that's the prerogative of any artist." His eyebrow rose on the word "artist."

"It's terrible she killed herself," said Monica.

"Publishing can be very frustrating," said Avery. "Now, if you don't mind, we're planning a breakaway until next Tuesday."

"Nice work if you can get it," said Briscoe. "Could we speak with you for just a moment?"

McDonald squeezed his wife again. "We have no secrets."

"What did you talk about with Robert Rosserman on the night Barbara Chesko died?"

McDonald blinked. "On the night she died?"

"Wednesday, the twenty-first of August," said Green.

"I don't remember speaking with Bob at all that day or evening. Let me think." He knit his brows. "No, I don't think so. I didn't go into town that day and I don't recall a telephone conversation."

"The twenty-first?" said Monica. "We were working."

"You didn't meet Rosserman in a bar at Fifty-fourth Street?"

"No," said McDonald.

"He was here all day," said Monica. "We had a deadline."

"It was..." McDonald thought for a moment, "the book with the train, wasn't it?"

"A thriller," said Monica. "The client was in a hurry."

"A witness saw you in Teddy's Tumbler," said Briscoe.

"What witness?" asked McDonald. "It couldn't have been me."

"You know Teddy's?"

"I've been in many places with clients. I couldn't say I know the place."

"Have you ever met with Rosserman in a bar?"

"Does Bob say I was there?"

"He was here," said Monica.

"Either your witness is wrong," said Avery, "or they've confused the day. God knows that's easy to do."

"Maybe you've confused the day. It would have been about seven?" urged Green. "You had an argument with him."

"Is that what Bob said?"

"Look," said Briscoe, "we're interested in what *you* have to say. We're asking *you*. Were you there?"

McDonald was barely controlling himself. "How many times do you want me to say 'no'?"

"And what damned difference does it make?" said Monica. "The bitch killed herself."

"Hey," said Briscoe, "let's calm down."

"I'm having a hard time figuring out what you're so ticked about," said Green, moving closer to Avery McDonald.

He looked up at Green with a wide eye. "If you wish to speak to me further," said McDonald, "you contact my lawyer first!"

"Now, get out," said Monica.

"Thank you for the hospitality," said Briscoe.

Nostrils flaring, Green slammed the car door as Briscoe sat next to him. Briscoe was grinning. "Some pit bull she is," he laughed. "What the hell did we say?"

"She needs a good slap," said Green. "Both of them."

148

"Now, now, Ed. Maybe the barman mixed up the day, right?" He leaned down to take another look at the house as Green pulled away. "Like the Naval Observatory mixes up the day."

"They're lying," snarled Green. "Why is everybody lying if it's a suicide? Are the three of them in it together? Is that it?"

"I nonetheless protest and I want it on the record," said John Ellis. "The bartender was shown a photograph of Mr. Rosserman just a few days ago. That could give him the impression that the detectives want him to identify Bob in this lineup."

"We didn't say who he was, counselor," said Briscoe. "We asked if he recognized either picture. He said Rosserman looked like the man arguing on the night Mrs. Chesko was murdered."

"Well, first of all," said Ellis, "you've got absolutely nothing that proves Barbara Chesko was murdered. And this lineup is going to get tossed if you try to introduce it in court."

"Do you do much criminal law, Mr. Ellis?" Southerlyn said calmly. "There's nothing improper in the bartender identifying the picture and then later, identifying the man. You don't even know that the bartender will identify your client."

"The picture tells him what man to identify! It isn't like he was given a photo array. He was given a picture of Bob."

"You know," said Briscoe, "if he'd just come clean with us, all this might work out for the better."

"The detective's right," said Southerlyn.

"Bob Rosserman has tried to be cooperative and you try to cook up a murder charge on him. It's a shame. He's a good man."

"We don't 'cook up' things, Mr. Ellis," said Southerlyn. "And we haven't charged Mr. Rosserman with anything, yet."

"Even good men make mistakes," said Green. "If he'd just tell us what happened…"

"The only mistake here, detective," said Ellis, "is thinking he's capable of pushing a woman out of a window."

"Ready," said Van Buren, sticking her head in the door.

"Shall we continue?" Southerlyn asked Ellis.

"Just be on notice," he shrugged.

Green went to get the bartender. The man squinted in the dim light. "How am I supposed to recognize anyone in here?" he said.

"There," said Van Buren. The light illuminates the other side of the one-way window.

"Step up to the glass," said Southerlyn. "They can't see you. Do you recognize anyone as having been in Teddy's on the night of August twenty-first?"

"Wow," said the bartender. "It's like in the movies."

Lieutenant Van Buren rolled her eyes. "Take your time, sir."

"Could I have number three step forward?"

Briscoe, who was standing in the back with Green, raised an eyebrow. Green shook his head in dismay.

"Number three, step forward," Van Buren said through the intercom.

The man complied. His name was Trent MacIlhenny, a fuzzy-haired janitor. All of the five in the lineup had been selected for their Larry Fine-like hair.

"That's okay," said the bartender. "He can step back. It *is* just like the movies."

"Mr. Carstairs," snapped Southerlyn, "this isn't for your entertainment. This is a serious business."

"I'm sorry, I'm sorry," he said quickly. "I just—I'm sorry. It's number two over there. That's him."

"You're sure?" asked Southerlyn.

"Oh, yeah, two. He was arguing with the man with the goat."

"Thank you, Mr. Carstairs," said Van Buren.

Briscoe escorted him to the door. "Wait out here for just a minute," he said.

"This identification means nothing," said Ellis. "There will be a brief, count on that. I want to consult my client."

"Now?" asked Southerlyn.

"Yes," said Ellis. "When did you think?"

"There, there," said Southerlyn. "Let's be a gentleman, eh?"

"I'll get you a room," said Van Buren. Ellis thanked the lieutenant and they left.

"All right, then," said Southerlyn, "where is Leo Herlihy and Avery McDonald?"

"In room four," said Briscoe. "McDonald is getting cold feet about the lineup. Herlihy was talking him back into it."

"He doesn't have to do it," said Green. "We know he was the man with Rosserman."

"What I don't understand is why he denies it," said Southerlyn.

"He says over and over it wasn't that Wednesday," said Briscoe. "The only reason I see is that he doesn't

152

want to be anywhere near the Waterloo and the body of Barbara Chesko. It might hurt his racket to have clients dying."

"Is there any possibility that the two of them…?"

"I think McDonald might know something, but Rosserman? We've caught him in lies. He has a motive. He was in the neighborhood. He invented a suicide note and his attorney has the attitude of a man with his back to the wall," said Briscoe.

"What you want to bet they're discussing a deal?" said Green, offering a palm. Briscoe slapped it.

"Case closed," said Briscoe. "On to bigger and better."

"Don't underestimate Ellis," said Southerlyn. "It's true he handles mostly libel, but that's why he does the bulldog in different voices."

"Did I hear you say 'good men make mistakes' to Ellis?" asked Briscoe. "Since when is murder a mistake?"

"I was trying to bait a plea," said Green.

"It would be a gift if they make a deal," said Southerlyn in a near whisper. "A grumpy judge might not even let a jury hear it if we can't prove she was pushed. But maybe they think there's more to our case than there is."

"Ellis is not very experienced in criminal law, you said," Briscoe remarked.

"Let's get the McDonald lineup going," said Southerlyn.

"We've got some guys waiting," said Briscoe.

They had just stepped through the door into the outer office when Green stopped and raised his vibrating cell phone. "Hey ho," he said, looking at the caller ID, "it's the lab."

Green turned his back to the noisy end of the corridor and covered his free ear. "Ed Green."

"Here we go," said Briscoe. "The DNA!"

"That might shake the truth out of him," said Southerlyn.

Green glanced at Briscoe and Southerlyn and rolled his eyes. "And that means?" he said into the phone. "You're kidding me," said Green. He looked like he was going to throw the phone across the room. "Yeah. Okay. Sure."

He made another throwing motion. "It's not his."

"What?" moaned Briscoe.

"The condom wrapper was torn open with the mouth. It did have saliva on it. The saliva is Barbara Chesko's."

"She tore the condom open?" asked Briscoe.

"Never mind the wrapper," said Southerlyn. "What about the semen on the bedspread? It's not—?"

"It's somebody other than Rosserman."

"Are they sure?" asked Southerlyn.

Green looked at her incredulously. "Even if they aren't sure, does it matter?" said Briscoe. "It isn't him."

"Besides the semen stain," said Green, "they found a hair on the bedspread but no follicle. It seems to be a middle-aged white man's, gray, but there's no way to prove it's absolutely Rosserman's."

Briscoe shook his head. "Maybe he pushed her because she was meeting someone else. He's still acted guilty."

"He lied," said Southerlyn. "Even if she is a suicide, I could charge him with impeding the investigation."

"For what that's worth," said Green.

"Then we ought to throw McDonald in as well. I don't like liars," said Briscoe.

"He lied because he didn't want us to know he was in the neighborhood," said Green.

Southerlyn smiled. "You must have a direct wire to my brain, Ed. I was just thinking the same thing."

"You think maybe a little DNA from Mr. McDonald might be illuminating?" said Briscoe.

"Exactly," said Southerlyn.

"So, what do we do with Rosserman?" said Green. "Send him home?"

"Maybe he wasn't in the room," said Southerlyn.

"Let's just hope," said Briscoe, "it wasn't the maid banging the bellboy before Mrs. Chesko got there."

"Or after she went out the window," said Green, thinking.

"How soon do we have to tell him about the DNA tests?" said Briscoe. "He's not under arrest. I'd like to tell him the DNA identifies him, sweat him until he shrivels."

"You can't do that," said Southerlyn. "We can't hold him when he's been exculpated. Does the word 'lawsuit' ring a bell?"

"Hey," said Briscoe, "he's here voluntarily, right?" Southerlyn's expression was firm. "Okay, I know. I was just saying I'd like to sweat him."

"Tell him we're considering obstruction charges," she said. "Then send him home to simmer for the rest of the year." She crossed her arms and was sliding her foot in and out of her right gray pump when a uniformed officer approached.

"You with the D.A.'s office? The lawyer's asking for you."

"Herlihy?" she said.

"No, he said he was Joseph Ellis."

"Should we do McDonald first?" said Briscoe.

"Let's see what they want," said Southerlyn.

"Probably an apology," said Briscoe.

The interrogation room smelled of old sweat and frayed nerves. Ellis waited for them, drumming a Mont Blanc pen on his leather briefcase, and staring at his client, who was holding his head like he was trying to keep it from exploding.

When they stepped in, Ellis rose slightly from his seat and tried to find the right words.

"Well?" asked Southerlyn.

"My client has something to tell you," he finally said. Rosserman mumbled to the tabletop. "I was there."

"Excuse me?" said Briscoe.

"I was there. I was there in the room."

Briscoe looked at Southerlyn. Rosserman must have thought the DNA would match his. Had Barbara Chesko entertained two men that evening? Southerlyn stared poker-faced at Ellis, who twisted his pen sheepishly. Briscoe could almost hear the gears of her mind grinding out a new set of tactics.

"Speak up," said Green, putting his face inches from Rosserman's ear.

"I was there," said Rosserman. "In the room with Barbara."

"You fought?" asked Briscoe.

"You pushed her?" asked Green.

"No!" said Rosserman. "And we didn't fight!" He glared into Green's eyes, then slowly pulled his head back, and lowered his eyes. "Not really. Not a fight. She was upset when I got there. She shouted some. She was shattered. She cried and shook and threw herself on the bed. But she was calm by the time I left."

"Dead people generally are," said Briscoe.

"She *wasn't* dead," said Rosserman. "She was standing by the window, sniffing. I had no idea she was going to kill herself. I thought she'd get over it. She seemed to be getting better. She was talking about finding an agent. I promised to help her find an agent. I'd always made excuses not to do it."

"She was optimistic?" asked Southerlyn.

"No, I guess not really, but she seemed to be talking herself there."

"And you encouraged her," said Green.

"Again," added Southerlyn.

Rosserman cast about for something to say. "She was very upset. What was I supposed to do? Tell her there wasn't a chance in hell she'd get published?"

"Maybe you wouldn't be here if you'd told her that a year ago," said Southerlyn.

"You seem to have no trouble lying to us. What made her special?" said Green.

Rosserman held his head. For a moment Briscoe thought the man might break down and cry. Ellis patted Rosserman's upper arm twice, as if he felt obligated to do so.

"And you went over there because of the note?" asked Green.

"I told you," said Rosserman, "I didn't get that until later."

"With all due respect," said Green, "you told us a lot."

"And lo and behold," said Briscoe, "a lot wasn't true."

"Has Mr. Ellis explained the concept of obstruction of justice?" said Southerlyn. "You've cost the taxpayers a lot of money with your fabrications."

Rosserman looked for help from Ellis. Ellis sat back and twisted his pen as if to say: you made this your party, not mine. "I didn't think you'd want to prove this was murder. She killed herself. It's obvious. You've got no reason to think otherwise."

"Oh, we have reasons," said Green. "How about physical evidence she was pushed? How about your job?"

"How about you fabricated the suicide note?" asked Briscoe.

"I didn't fabricate the note!"

Green moved close to his ear again. "Oh?"

"It was in my mailbox!"

Ellis finally interrupted. "Look," he said, "Can't we start with a clean slate? Bob decided, of his own free will, to completely and honestly reveal all he knows. There is no reason to treat him as a criminal."

"Unless maybe, just possibly, he is," said Briscoe.

"This is nuts!" said Rosserman. "She was a disturbed woman. She killed herself."

Southerlyn took a seat opposite him. "I'll tell you what, Mr. Rosserman. You tell me the whole story, from the beginning. The whole truth and nothing but the truth. We can't do anything for you unless you help us."

"And you haven't been very helpful," said Briscoe.

Ellis said, "Take your time, Bob. If you didn't do it, you have nothing to fear, right?"

"If?" thought Southerlyn. Rosserman's own attorney didn't know whether to believe him.

Just because Rosserman hadn't left a matchable sample didn't mean he hadn't had sex with her, thought Briscoe. He launched a shot from three-point range. "What if we told you the DNA on the bed matches yours?"

Rosserman shook his head. "That's crazy! I was there. I didn't have sex. The situation was bad enough. That's all I needed, to make her think I wanted to continue the relationship!" He tapped the table with four bunched fingers. "I *did not* have sex with her."

The shot had not only missed the rim, but the backboard as well. Then who did have sex with her? thought Briscoe. He glanced at Green and they both seemed to know what the other was thinking.

The bartender will identify Avery McDonald and the DNA will confirm it.

Southerlyn silently watched McCoy work his technique again. She had seen a dozen variations of this one, when McCoy tried to look like he knew more than he did. If you could get the person you were questioning to believe that, they'd often simply tell you what you wanted. He looked at Herlihy, Avery McDonald's attorney, who was smiling a bit smugly, then at Monica McDonald, who divided her infuriated glare between McCoy and Southerlyn. Avery McDonald had crossed his arms. His bored expression said "Do your worst, I'm not impressed," but there was a slight twitch in his left eyebrow. McDonald looked down, copping a glance at Southerlyn's crossed legs. It made her skin crawl.

"You're going to offer a deal?" said Herlihy. "Forget about it. You have no case."

"Monica and I want no deal," said McDonald.

"Monica doesn't even have to be here. I didn't invite Monica, did I, Mr. Herlihy?"

"Not specifically," said Herlihy, momentarily confused. "As she is a codefendant, I assumed..."

"This is only partly about the McDonalds' crooked editing operation. This is about Barbara Chesko." He paused for effect. Herlihy put a hand on his client's shoulder. "Don't play coy, Jack. Avery's already told you he doesn't know anything about that. You're barking up the wrong tree if you think this grand larceny case will create a witness against Bob Rosserman."

"Oh," said McCoy, "the larceny case is another matter altogether. Your client can contemplate its nuttiness in his upstate cell. But it might turn out to be the least of his worries, isn't that right, Mr. McDonald?"

McDonald's eyebrows both rose. He seemed to want to stare down McCoy, but gave it up quickly, turning to Herlihy, then to his wife. "Barbara was our client."

"Mr. McDonald, you told us you were home on the night of Wednesday, August twenty-first, that you weren't in the city in the early morning hours of the twenty-second, when Mrs. Chesko died."

"Yes," said Herlihy, "and Mrs. McDonald confirms it."

"He never left the house all day," said Monica McDonald. "We ate leftover pizza and went to bed early."

"It gave me heartburn," nodded Avery.

"But both the bartender and Bob Rosserman say that Mr. McDonald was in Teddy's Tumbler, until about seven."

"They're wrong," said Avery.

"The bartender admits he isn't sure," said Herlihy.

"But we're sure," said McCoy. "Have you got something to tell us?" he asked McDonald. "I can throw in an obstruction of justice charge, if you like."

"Don't say anything, Avery," said Herlihy. "If you're

going to accuse him of lying, you'd better have a basis."

"Mr. McDonald," said McCoy, "has a cell phone. Mr. McDonald's cell phone placed four calls that Wednesday night."

"You can't identify where a phone was calling from," said Herlihy.

"You're right. But I can identify where it was calling *to*, can't I?" He let that sink in. McDonald looked at Herlihy and shrugged. McCoy shoved a sheet of phone records across the table. "Three of those calls went to your home in Peekskill. Do you call the kitchen from the bathroom?"

"I went to the grocery to get the frozen pizza, and then I was reminded of something I needed to tell Monica."

"Oh, come off it," said McCoy. "One call is at 5:46. The next is at 7:10. The third is at 9:02. That's a long trip to the grocer's. The first and last calls are only a minute long. The one at 7:10 is only two minutes. Barely enough time to discuss whether to have pepperoni or sausage."

"Wait, Avery," said Monica, grabbing his arm. "August. Isn't that when you lost a phone on the subway?"

"Mrs. McDonald," said McCoy sharply, "I can add obstruction to your charges like *that!*" He snapped his fingers. "It's the same cell phone he used this morning. Now you can stop covering for him immediately, or I can name you an accessory."

"Be quiet, Monica," said Herlihy. "Accessory to what?"

"A wife can't testify against her husband," snapped Monica.

"But she can go to jail for participating in the crime as an accessory," said McCoy.

"Perhaps," said Southerlyn, "Mrs. McDonald should have separate representation, Mr. Herlihy. They might have conflicting interests. Don't you think that's the ethical thing?"

"A cheap trick isn't going to tear us apart!" said Monica.

"Please," said Herlihy. "I'll handle this. What are you saying, Jack?"

"Why don't you let Mr. McDonald explain?" said McCoy.

Avery McDonald had watched the exchanges blinking, twisting his cane, his prodigious eyebrows bobbing, as if trying to create some explanation that would get him out of this.

"Or do I have to bring up the fourth telephone call, the one—" he tapped the list "—at 7:13?"

McDonald didn't move.

"The one to the Waterloo Hotel."

"I—I don't know what you mean."

McCoy decided to bluff. "There are security cameras in the Waterloo Hotel. They were operating that Wednesday night."

"All right, then," said McDonald. "I was there."

McCoy had chosen not to mention that no one had been able to make out Avery McDonald between seven and eight. A busload of tourists had been streaming in just before 7:30, as others poured out of the hotel for an evening in the Big Apple. It might have been possible to enhance the tape and spot McDonald, but the quality was so poor there was no guarantee that it would work.

"Yes," he said, "I went to the Waterloo Hotel."

Monica lowered her head and squeezed her flattened hands between her heavy thighs. "So what?" snorted McDonald.

"You don't need to say anything, Avery," said Herlihy.

"No," he said defiantly, "I want to clear this up."

"You and I need to talk," said Herlihy.

"No, I've got nothing to be ashamed of. Bob told me how upset she was, Barbara. I knew that publishing had become her obsession and, frankly, I was worried about her."

"I'll bet you were," said McCoy.

"I was, whether you believe that or not. Barbara and I had worked quite closely on her novel."

"How closely?" said Southerlyn.

"She engaged me to do a complete restructuring of her novel and some time later I did a detailed line edit with her."

"And was it good for you?" asked McCoy.

"What do you mean?" said McDonald. "It took a three-day weekend both times. Dawn to dusk. She rented a place in the Adirondacks so we wouldn't be disturbed. It was exhausting."

"I'll bet it was," said McCoy.

"We're not going to discuss editing," said Herlihy. "Not while you have charges pending trial."

"I want to know what that sneer of yours implies," demanded McDonald. "Monica spent half of one of those weekends in the Adirondacks with us as well."

"How inconvenient," said McCoy. He laced his fingers and leaned across the desk. "Mr. McDonald, I've questioned drug dealers, wife-beaters, Ku Kluxers and just about every kind of human being that breathes, but you are, by far, the most brazen I've ever met. Do you really think that we won't be able to match the DNA on the bedspread from the Waterloo Hotel with you?"

McDonald blinked. "You haven't got any DNA from me."

"Just because Barbara provided the condom doesn't mean you didn't leave any trace of your 'off-the-page' activities."

"Whoa!" said Herlihy. "And exactly what are you comparing the DNA in the hotel with? You haven't given them a sample, have you, Avery?"

"You can get DNA off a water glass, did you know that?" said McCoy. "From a hair that has fallen on a table. Or from a Starbucks cup that was left behind."

McDonald's eyes widened. The bluff had struck its target.

Southerlyn had been carefully watching Monica. The woman had been sitting with crossed arms, but looked up and rested her hands on her thighs when she recognized that they were talking about sex. When she noticed Southerlyn staring, her face twisted in anger. "What are you looking at?" she snapped. "You think this is supposed to be a big surprise to me?" She crossed her arms again. "Avery and I are working it out. We love each other."

Herlihy raised his hands. "Monica! I think I'd better have a conference with my clients."

"No. I want to clear this up," said McDonald. "Yes, I'm fallible, what man is not? Maybe a man with no zest for life!"

"Or maybe a man with a sense of decency," said Southerlyn.

"Art is not about decency," sneered McDonald. "Picasso, Hemingway, Diego Rivera..."

McCoy sneered. "Mr. McDonald, you're the author of *Death Watch*, *The Man's Guide to Studliness*, and a *Happy Hours* novelization. Don't try to wrap yourself in the cloak of genius."

McDonald's eyebrows twitched as he fought back his fury. "And what have you published, sir? *What have you published?*"

"Whoa!" said Herlihy. "We're getting a bit afield, aren't we? Jack, I'm not going to sit still as my client is insulted. I think we'd better go. If you have some specific questions..."

"I'd like to know what Mr. McDonald did in Barbara Chesko's hotel room," said McCoy, "It's a simple question."

"You've got no reason to believe my client was with Barbara Chesko on the day she died."

"Oh, really?" said Southerlyn, who had fixed her cool stare on Monica McDonald. The woman was staring down at her shoes.

McCoy turned toward McDonald. "You can cooperate in the investigation."

Herlihy began to rise, but McDonald, without turning his gaze from McCoy, grabbed his attorney's arm.

"No," said McDonald, "I said I wanted to clear this up. I have nothing to hide." Herlihy begged with his eyes, but McDonald continued. "I admit to being fallible," he said, "I *embrace* my own fallibility."

Southerlyn couldn't help rolling her eyes.

"A writer is finished if he is afraid of being fallible." He touched Monica's shoulder. "And I know that often, in pursuing those feelings, I have hurt those I shouldn't—the woman I love most, a woman I don't deserve. She knows everything."

Monica looked at him and weakly smiled.

"I did indeed go up to Barbara Chesko's room."

"When?" asked McCoy.

"After speaking with Bob in Teddy's Tumbler. Bob had just come from meeting with her. He said she was a little calmer than earlier, but that she was very upset, especially with me."

"Because you had fleeced her for over eighteen thousand dollars?"

Herlihy raised a hand as if to block McDonald's answer. "Jack, I won't let Avery talk about the editing contracts in any way. Not until you drop these crazy larceny charges."

"In fact," said McDonald, "she was not upset about the editing. She was angry that Bob had turned down her book."

"So she was angry," said McCoy. "Not depressed?"

"No. She wanted me to make certain that Bob was serious about giving her another chance."

"Another chance?"

"To reconsider her novel."

"She said he had promised to think about it, but that he couldn't guarantee anything. This is what he told me in the bar.

I told her that she didn't need Kirstner and Strawn. They are hardly the only publishers. I told her she needed to put Kirstner and Strawn behind her and begin knocking on agents' doors."

"Avery, I really object to your discussing anything to do with Redux," said Herlihy.

"I've done nothing wrong," said McDonald. "I advised her to begin writing another book, so that she would be ready to follow up on the success of her first."

"So you could take more of her money?" said Southerlyn.

"We're leaving," said Herlihy.

"I could charge Mr. McDonald with murder," said McCoy.

"On the basis of what?" said Herlihy.

"He was there, he had a motive."

"I had no reason!" protested McDonald. "She was quite, well, I'd say happy, when I left. Or at least content."

Southerlyn watched Monica's reaction, which was to glare defiance.

McCoy picked up a pen. "And when did you leave the hotel?"

"After nine."

"How late after nine?"

McDonald thought for a moment. "About half past."

"Nine-thirty?"

McDonald widened his eyes. "Well, it might have been nine twenty-five or it might have been nine thirty-five, mightn't it?"

"You tell me."

"He has told you," said Herlihy. "At or about nine thirty."

"And you called home after you left?"

McDonald shook his head. "I called before I left the room."

"So you called your wife while you were in a hotel with another woman?"

Monica sneered. "Don't project your hang-ups on us."

Southerlyn and McCoy exchanged a glance. Herlihy shrugged as if to say, "What can I tell you? It takes all kinds."

168

Southerlyn crossed her legs. "What did Avery say to you?"

"When he called? He said he would catch the ten oh-two and be home by eleven-thirty."

Avery interrupted. "Unfortunately I didn't get to Grand Central until five past. I didn't get home until around midnight. Well past midnight, actually. The train ran slow."

McCoy turned to Monica. "And you picked him up at the station?"

"I was asleep," she said.

"I walked home," said McDonald. "It's only a few blocks."

"We have separate bedrooms," said Monica.

They both caught something they didn't like in the way McCoy was studying them.

"Apnea," said Avery.

"My snoring's awful," she explained.

McCoy laid down his pencil. "So no one can verify you were in Peekskill around midnight?"

"Maybe someone saw me at the station," said McDonald.

"Do you use a rail pass?" asked Herlihy.

"Cash," said McDonald.

McCoy rolled his pencil under his palm for a second. "I'd like to hear in detail what happened in the hotel room, Mr. McDonald," he said slowly.

"After I talked to Bob, I left the bar and was going to go home, but I began to get worried about her state of mind. I began to think of her alone in that hotel. Well, I tried to tell myself it was merely my imagination, but, as it turned out, my instincts were correct."

"How did you know which room to go to?" asked McCoy.

"I used the house phone in the men's room."

"Of the bar?"

"In the Waterloo. She seemed glad to hear from me. She started pouring out her soul so I went straight up."

"So she opened the door, I assume, and you went in?"

"Her eyes were red. She told me Bob had betrayed her. I explained he had done everything he could, and so on. At first, as she spoke of it, she got more disturbed, but gradually she calmed to the point that I thought it would be safe to leave."

Southerlyn placed her elbow on her knee, resting her chin on her knuckles. "And at what point did you throw her on the bed?"

McDonald raised an eyebrow. "It was more the opposite, I'm afraid. I was holding her, trying to calm her, and she shoved me back. The tender moment evolved into a passionate one."

Monica crossed her arms and looked out the window.

"Maybe you'd rather not hear this," said McCoy.

"Get off it," she said. "He always comes home to me."

"Aren't you lucky?" said Southerlyn.

"Yes, I am," said Monica fiercely.

"Sex isn't love," said McDonald. "Monica knows how much I love her."

There was a long silence.

"Are we through?" asked Herlihy.

"When you were in the room, did you see Barbara's purse?"

"What now?" snorted McDonald. "Are you going to accuse me of stealing *that*?"

"Did you see it?"

"I might have. I don't remember. No! I do remember. She took the condom from her purse."

"And you opened it?"

"Her purse?"

"The condom, Mr. McDonald."

He looked at Monica and then at Herlihy. "She tore it open with her teeth." He repeated his glances at Monica and his attorney. "She put it on me."

"Did you see her laptop in the room?"

"I don't know. I didn't notice it. She carried it with her everywhere. It must have been there. A very fancy bit of machinery. Not that equipment has anything to do with writing!"

McCoy was trying to decide whether to ask about the details of the intercourse. It could make Herlihy finally shut the questioning down. He proceeded gingerly. "We have some medical evidence or I wouldn't ask this," he said.

"I have nothing to hide," said McDonald.

"How many times did you—?"

"Did he what, Mr. McCoy?" interrupted Herlihy.

"Engage in sexual intercourse. No, correct that. How many times did you penetrate Mrs. Chesko?"

"Twice," he said. Monica McDonald showed no expression.

McDonald cleared his throat. "I was trying to leave, I was calling home in fact, but she came out of the bathroom and wouldn't let me go. It's why I missed the train."

"But you said she was happy when you left," said Southerlyn.

"Yes. She was. I have no idea why she might have killed herself. Perhaps she felt lonely, knew that I wouldn't leave Monica, felt the disappointment about her book. I've asked myself a thousand times. Perhaps now someone will publish her book."

"You're breaking me up," said Southerlyn.

"I don't see why we should be subjected to any more of this," said Monica. Serena thought Monica was repressing the urge to slap her.

McCoy moved his head to indicate he couldn't think of anything else. "See you in court," he said.

"I'll buy you some chicken soup to make you feel better afterward," said Herlihy. He held the door for the McDonalds. When they had gone into the outer office, he stepped back toward McCoy. "And, by the way, if you should take a notion to bring fraud charges against my clients, I don't want to hear a word about Barbara Chesko in the prelim or any other venue, Jack."

"What the hell are you talking about, Leo? She was an eighteen-thousand-dollar victim of their scheme!"

"Not a word about her suicide. Not a word about the affair. At no point did she ever complain about the McDonalds' services, which is the only thing relevant. The rest of it is prejudicial. Just because you can't hang a murder on what is really a suicide, don't try to drag it over into a fraud case. A case which will never reach trial because there was never any fraud."

"Plead guilty and there won't be a trial," said McCoy.

"Dream on," said Herlihy.

"**B**ecause nobody asked me," said the computer tech.

"Didn't it occur to you that this would be the normal thing to do?" shouted McCoy. "Why did you wait? Knowing this could have helped our strategy."

The way McCoy saw it, they had wasted a lot of time trying to stick a pin in Rosserman. He had seemed suspicious and the circumstances pointed to him, particularly when he produced the "suicide note," but any defense attorney could turn such an obvious piece of exculpatory evidence into not just an acquittal, possibly even a lawsuit.

McCoy, Southerlyn, Briscoe and Green all looked toward the tech, David Grunion, as if he should take all the blame. McCoy had called the meeting to see what kind of circumstantial homicide case might be assembled from the evidence, if possible, but not to dismantle it. The tech shrugged. "Nobody said to check for deleted stuff until a few hours ago. When the laptop was delivered, the detectives told me to get by the password and see if that note was there. I did that. It wasn't."

He looked at McCoy and blinked. "We've got a lot

173

of work to do, you know. It's not like the city has extra computer guys. And a lot more cases these days have computers in them somewhere."

McCoy rolled his eyes. "It didn't occur to you while you were checking all those deleted files on Rosserman's computer?"

The tech did a slow burn. His bleary eyes narrowed. "Hey, three hours ago, your guys asked me to take a stroll among the deleted files. That's what I did."

"You're understaffed, maybe you need to get back to work."

Grunion rose slowly and left the room without closing the door. Green glanced at McCoy, drumming his fingers on the case files, then stood and banged the door shut.

"So much for that!" said McCoy.

"Look," said Briscoe, "we thought maybe there would be something on her laptop that pointed to murder, a motive or something."

"It's just we should have known this sooner," said McCoy. "Did you get anything that might help us build a fraud case?"

Briscoe shrugged. "Some old Quicken files. They showed what we already knew. Her payments to Redux."

"Jack," said Green, "the computer was discarded in the lobby. The note could have been written by Rosserman on her machine after he killed her, copied on a diskette, then printed elsewhere."

"And why would he erase it, then?" said McCoy. "Why would he write a note to be discovered in his office, that's allegedly by Barbara Chesko, and then try to remove all traces of the fact that it's on her machine where she's supposed to have written it?

Isn't it more likely that she wrote it? We can't know for sure that Rosserman even took the machine out of the hotel room."

"Does it make any sense that she erased her own note?" said Briscoe. "Why would she care? She intends to kill herself when she's writing it."

"The pawnbroker did it? The Santonios?" Southerlyn ventured.

Green shook his head. "They couldn't get past the password."

Briscoe leaned toward the table. "Listen, from the time we talked to McDonald, we knew he was lying, but everybody lies. The interesting question is always 'why?'"

"What's your point?" asked McCoy. "Why would he kill her?"

"I'm not saying he did," said Briscoe. "But he was cheating her."

"And what could Barbara Chesko do about it?" said McCoy. "Whack him in the head like Herman Rauch whacked Rosserman? For McDonald, it was water off a duck's back."

"I push a woman out a window," McCoy continued. "I don't know who's seen what or how quickly the body will be noticed. But I pause to write a phony suicide note? Maybe the obvious thing is staring us in the face and we refuse to accept it. Barbara Chesko killed Barbara Chesko. What have we got to contradict it?"

"Did we get a psychological profile?" asked Green.

Southerlyn lifted a thin file. "Emil Skoda talked to Glenda Atterby, Hannah Wolfe, and Melva Patterson, all women in the writers' group, and looked over the case file. He says there's nothing that particularly constitutes a suicide predictor. Her parents died of old age. She never attempted it before, et cetera, et cetera. The fact that she was brokenhearted over the book doesn't indicate she'd kill herself. On the other hand, there's nothing inconsistent with suicide, either."

"Nothing like a firm conclusion!" said McCoy. "*Our* psychologist, yet!"

"Well, it doesn't affect making a fraud case, does it?" said Southerlyn. "There are many victims other than Barbara Chesko."

McCoy rocked back in his chair. "But none with a suspicious death that we know of. I can see the worth of trying to get it in the jury's minds that the consequences of the fraud were larger than just money. But, I'm also thinking maybe we don't want to touch Chesko's death. God knows how Ellis or Herlihy could twist it around, sowing a lot of confusion."

"Especially Ellis," said Briscoe. "I've seen him in action. He's a twister, force five."

"That's why he makes the big bucks," said McCoy.

Southerlyn straightened the hem of her skirt.

"In some fraud cases people lose their homes or their entire life savings," McCoy continued. "The jury wants to do something to help the victims. When the victims don't lose as much, it doesn't seem as serious, even if the total take is huge."

"Victimizing a million people at ten dollars a head isn't as serious a crime as stealing one man's life savings," said Briscoe. "Ten million dollars versus a hundred thousand."

"That's the way it often goes," said McCoy. "Look at what some corporations get away with." He shook his head. "Well, you play the cards you're dealt. The tech wizards never pinned down the printer, did they?"

Briscoe shook his head. "It wasn't hers and it wasn't Rosserman's or any of the office ones we found."

"There are a lot of printers in New York City," said Green.

"Well," said McCoy, "I guess you guys have better things to do. We'll drop the homicide and build the fraud case. It's all right, Lennie," said McCoy. "You and Ed did a good job."

Southerlyn reached for the computer tech's report and said, "I'm not even sure it's a suicide note anymore: 'YOU HAVE USED ME. RALPH USED ME. AVERY USED ME. I AM ALL USED UP AND WON'T TAKE ANOTHER DAY OF IT. MY LIFE HAS BEEN OVER FOR YEARS. LET THAT BE ON YOUR HEAD—NOT THAT YOU'LL CARE. YOU'VE SHOWN ME HOW MUCH YOU CARE.' Couldn't 'won't take another day of it' be more of a threat against Rosserman rather than the threat of suicide?"

McCoy took the note and read it slowly. "It might be. It could mean 'I'm not going to play anymore.' What's your point?"

She shot a quick laugh. "I haven't the slightest. No, what I'm saying is that if I wanted to fake a suicide note, wouldn't I be more explicit?"

"Good-bye cruel world," said Briscoe. "So you're saying you think it's the genuine article?"

McCoy read the tech's printout again and tossed it on the desk. "Who knows? Let's let the detectives move on."

"You know," said Briscoe, uncrossing his legs and getting ready to rise, "when I was younger I used to think I could tell if a moke was guilty, could feel it in my bones. Now, my bones just creak. I was sure Mc-Donald had something directly to do with the woman's death, but I don't know."

"Maybe something will surface in the larceny trial," said Southerlyn.

McCoy looked at her curiously. "We'll take what we can get, which usually isn't much," he said. "Either it was suicide or McDonald or Rosserman have pulled off the perfect crime. It may sound strange, but I'd sleep a lot better if I could convince myself it was suicide."

Southerlyn and McCoy were in his office about to discuss how to proceed when Arthur Branch called them in for an update. It was a good idea to pick his brain as well. Probably Chesko had been stirring the pot at City Hall again, McCoy thought. Branch didn't usually get this interested in smaller cases, but they would need his support on something as slippery as this one. He and Southerlyn reconvened in Branch's office and Branch listened placidly to the summary of Rosserman's and McDonald's stories. Rosserman had received the manuscript of *Shafted: Memoirs of a Marriage* about a year ago. It didn't take him long to figure out that William Shaft in the novel was really Ralph Chesko, the financier, who was being investigated by the SEC. That caught his interest, he said, and he contacted Mrs. Chesko to try to convince her to recast the novel as a nonfiction book, with as many details as she could remember about his financial dealings. After the first conversation, however, it became clear she didn't have the slightest idea what her husband actually did to bring home the bacon. What's more, he said, she was determined to be a

179

novelist. She was like many people who think of nonfiction writing as some kind of Grub Street occupation, while fiction writing is all freedom and glamour and the immortality of art.

He explained to Mrs. Chesko that the manuscript wasn't really in shape to be published as fiction (or nonfiction for that matter), and she asked what it needed. He explained it wasn't his job to revise manuscripts, not many editors had time to do real editing, and she asked if there might be someone he knew of.

"When I pressed him," said Southerlyn, "he admitted that many people ask for someone to help them. They take the bait, and Rosserman would 'help' by letting the McDonalds reel them in."

"Especially if he implied the book was worth spending the money on, I suppose," said Branch.

"Exactly. He made it look like a favor, when he was actually picking up a fifteen percent commission."

"How often did he do this?" asked McCoy.

"He says four or five times a week. I'd guess he did it more than that. Not all of them would become clients of Redux."

"For how much?" asked Branch.

"Fifteen percent of at least two thousand. Usually more. So three hundred a victim and up."

"The victim we're concerned with is Barbara Chesko. So how's this lead to her death?"

Rosserman's normal routine was to send names and addresses to Monica McDonald, who would mail a letter describing their services. The letter pretended that Rosserman had incidentally mentioned the book (presumably at some glamorous literary cocktail party) to one of the McDonalds, as if the manuscript had made an impression. Usually, he would either get his finder's fee or not, and that would be the end of it.

Occasionally, someone resubmitted, and Rosserman would send the preprinted note that said the book "doesn't fit our needs at this time." They usually took the hint and didn't try again. Barbara Chesko was more determined. Obsessive, he had said.

Several weeks after he turned down her manuscript the first time, Barbara Chesko sent him a silver pen with a thank-you note for recommending the McDonalds. The note said they were working hard on the manuscript and hoped to have it back to him soon.

"He knew all along there was no chance he would buy her book," said Southerlyn. "He had already classified it as an unsalvageable sow's ear."

Branch looked up. "All right, so she showed up again."

"Not with the manuscript," Southerlyn said. "Barbara Chesko called Rosserman about meeting for a drink. At first, he says he resisted, but she said the novel was coming along so wonderfully under the McDonalds' guidance that she wanted to express her gratitude. He decided it wouldn't hurt, but says he took pains to explain he didn't have the final decision on publication."

"Getting himself off the hook," said Branch.

"He said she apologized for making him think she was trying to bribe him. According to Rosserman an attraction developed. It's more likely he saw she was a pushover for what he was pretending to offer: publication. They ended up having dinner at Minos, the Greek restaurant in the Waterloo Hotel. Then they had Greek coffee and ouzos, too many ouzos."

"What a shame!" said McCoy. "He was seduced, poor fellow!"

Branch gave him a cold eye. Southerlyn cleared her throat and continued. Rosserman and Chesko met several more times. She showed up once at his apartment, even though he'd never given her the address. She took him to her apartment. One time she took him to a friend's apartment. All this while he knew he would have to break it off somehow. She badgered him with questions about how books were selected. He blamed most choices on the marketing and sales departments. He'd "spontaneously" kiss her just to shut her up.

So, when the inevitable happened and she turned up with a revised manuscript, he pretended that the editorial board had turned it down. Actually, he had never proposed it to them. He gave her a short list of flaws, supposedly from notes he had made at the meeting. She seemed disappointed and maybe upset, but he was relieved that she didn't call back for a while. He claimed he didn't know she had gone back to Redux, until he received another commission. Avery McDonald told him that she had come back with the list of flaws and insisted they work on it more.

Rosserman didn't hear from her for several more months. Then she appeared at his office with a completely new revision and a bottle of Calvados to celebrate. He explained to her that once the board turned down a book, they almost never considered it again. One shot of Calvados invited another and soon it was dinner again, and she begged him to ask the board to reconsider.

"And he started to feel amorous," sneered Branch,

"so he told her he would plead her case and they went to the Waterloo."

"Not this time. They went to the Waterloo, I mean, but he says he told her that submitting it to him would never work. His bosses had made up their minds."

"I bet he didn't tell her that before the sex," said Branch.

"Three editing jobs!" said Southerlyn. "She submitted her book to Rosserman four times and the McDonalds took her for three editing jobs and almost nineteen thousand dollars. Rosserman took her to bed a half a dozen times, and she paid for it."

McCoy shook his head.

"You're thinking she was stupid," said Southerlyn.

"If she waddles like a duck…"

"Have you ever tried to write a novel?" asked Southerlyn. "Do you have any idea how much work it takes? How much she got her hopes up? People put their souls into it."

"But three payouts!"

"They threw straws and she kept grasping," said Southerlyn.

"Okay, it's a dirty deal," said Branch, "but she didn't have to do it three times. And that's just the money. She thought the sex was buying publication as well."

Southerlyn's tone was icy. "That's a nice thing to say. You're both forgetting who's the victim."

"To this point, she's cooperating in her own victimization," said Branch.

Rosserman said Chesko submitted it for the fourth time after a detailed line edit, and he bit the bullet and told her there was no way that the board would ever accept the book. The season's list was full and they just wouldn't be persuaded to reconsider. He

183

recommended she try it elsewhere. She said that she had, a dozen times. Each time it was turned down with hardly any explanation. Once a different editor at a different publisher had also recommended Redux, she told Rosserman. What if she had an agent? Could Rosserman recommend an agent? She had tried a couple and they had turned her down. He pretended it was unethical to do that, directed her to the public library, and then begged off, saying he had an appointment.

"The woman wouldn't go away," said McCoy.

"Exactly," said Southerlyn. "He said he was beginning to feel like he was being stalked and just wanted it over."

"So you think he killed her?" asked Branch.

"He says he didn't and we're beyond that now," said McCoy.

"So how did she die?"

Chesko showed up at his office and waited through a long afternoon, scribbling on her manuscript and working on her laptop. Rosserman thought he had waited her out. She was trickier than he realized. When he came down in the elevator, she was waiting in the lobby. To keep her from making a scene, he took her arm and led her out on the street. She told him she had a room at the Waterloo, where they could talk. Rosserman refused, but then she began to cry and he agreed to talk, but no more.

"And he pushed her when she threatened his job," said Branch. "Isn't that the theory? Seems easy enough."

"He says they talked," said Southerlyn. "He says they kissed, but she was too pathetic, he says, and he didn't feel like making love."

"He had a sudden attack of conscience, eh? Gave her all his commissions back?"

"Not hardly. He says she said that she just wanted to die, that everything had been taken away from her." Southerlyn picked up the transcript and flipped to a section she had paper-clipped.

Branch took the transcript and read out loud:

...SO I TOLD HER THAT SHE MUSTN'T GIVE UP, THAT HER TALENT WOULD WIN OUT SOMEDAY.

DET. GREEN: BUT YOU DIDN'T BELIEVE THAT?

ROSSERMAN: GOOD GOD NO. I WAS TRYING TO MAKE HER FEEL BETTER. I JUST WANTED OUT OF THERE. I FELT A LITTLE GUILTY.

"Just a 'little guilty,'" said McCoy.

"Right now he's still saying he left her alive at about six-fifteen," said Southerlyn, "and didn't return after McDonald visited her."

"He went home?" asked Branch.

"He says he called Avery McDonald, then met him at Teddy's Tumbler on Fifty-fourth. He said he asked if McDonald might give her a little of the money back. McDonald told him the best way to handle it was just to cut her off, not return her calls, have nothing to do with her. He begged McDonald to talk to her for him, he says, but McDonald was adamant that he wouldn't."

"And Avery McDonald confirms this?" asked Branch.

"He now admits that he went up to the hotel room to calm her down and the conversation turned romantic."

"Oh dear," said Branch. "I doubt Ralph Chesko wants that spread around. She sounds pretty desperate."

McCoy leaned forward. "McDonald says Rosserman told him that Barbara was very upset. He demanded the McDonalds give him a larger percentage of the editing fees. Rosserman denies this."

"So McDonald was the last one to see her alive?"

"That we think," said Southerlyn. "Rosserman could have gone back after McDonald left."

"Or a thief could have gotten in the room," said McCoy.

Branch checked his watch. "So, cut to the chase. Where do you see us going with this?"

"Most cases are circumstantial," said McCoy. "But I doubt we'd get anywhere if we went for any kind of wrongful death."

"Even if you had something," said Branch, "I could see the stalker scenario. Extreme emotional distress is an affirmative defense. Any juror might be persuaded she had pushed him to the edge. It's one of those *Fatal Attraction* things."

Branch spread his hands on his blotter and thought. "Ralph Chesko isn't going to be very happy to hear that the case is 'still under investigation.' He'll know that's a euphemism. He doesn't want to believe his wife might have been a suicide."

"Ex-wife," said McCoy. "We can't even prove, beyond his own say-so, that Rosserman went up to the room. McDonald's DNA proves he was there, but we can't see what his motive would be. He was never before intimidated by the threat of being exposed. And his wife and he have what they used to call an 'open marriage.'"

"I see," said Branch.

"We even thought about manslaughter two, which includes causing or aiding a suicide," shrugged McCoy. "But that's D.O.A., as well. Rosserman absolutely insists he didn't know Barbara Chesko was dead until he got an anonymous phone call the next Monday morning."

"Is there any evidence for this phone call?" asked Branch. "LUDS?"

"The building has its own system. It's cheaper that way if your company sets it up. You can tell who called in to the central unit, but you can't tell who they called. We could have the detectives run it down call by call, but..."

"All I'm hearing is 'bupkis,'" said Branch. "I think I'd better turn my attention to figuring out how to tell Ralph, and his friends in City Hall, that there's no evidence of murder, or anything else. You know, I think it's even harder for someone to have no answer at all than to have a bad one."

"I'm inclined to agree," said McCoy.

"I don't think there will ever be enough evidence for a homicide charge on this, ever. But there is a crime here," said Southerlyn. "The reason, direct or indirect, for her death. The McDonalds are predators. What about a death caused in the commission of a felony?"

"Felony?" said Branch. "What felony? Fraud? You're not suggesting we charge the McDonalds with murder?"

"Just testing the water." Southerlyn crossed her legs and raised her voice. "Morally they're guilty of murder, I think, even if she killed herself. But legally, probably not. However, I am saying they engaged in a scheme constituting a systematic course of conduct with the intent to defraud ten or more persons. That makes Redux a scheme to defraud in the first degree."

.

"An E felony. That's not good enough to charge murder in the commission of a felony," said Branch. "It's not robbery because it wasn't forcible. It might be grand larceny, but that's still not one of the specified felonies. It doesn't qualify."

"On the other hand, grand larceny in the third degree is a D felony," said McCoy. "The McDonalds got more than three thousand out of Mrs. Chesko three times. God knows what they've gotten out of others. According to Detective Gross, they've pulled six figures a year on this scam. Rosserman knew what they were doing and he participated in it."

"Don't try to complicate this by turning it into a conspiracy case," said Branch.

"Serena and I were discussing the possibility," said McCoy. "If we throw fraud or larceny, and conspiracy, at them, maybe Rosserman will provide evidence against the McDonalds."

"He's just as responsible for her death, Jack," said Southerlyn. "Maybe more so."

"Breaking her heart isn't illegal," said Branch.

Southerlyn raised her pen and pointed at Branch. "What about the possibility of arguing that they evinced a depraved indifference to human life because they knew that Barbara Chesko was not stable? They continued to exploit her and it resulted in her death."

"They drove her to it?" said Branch. "I can see the parade of dueling psychologists now, and in the end, what are you left with? Rosserman and McDonald feel just awful that Barbara threw herself down the air shaft, but they're not psychologists so they couldn't have known, and so on. The judge will toss the case even before you could try to get a jury to buy it."

"Under that theory, at least we would be able to hold the McDonalds responsible for her death," said Southerlyn.

"It's too imaginative for me," said McCoy. It wouldn't fly."

"No, you're right," said Southerlyn. "If we argue Mrs. Chesko killed herself, we'll imply she wasn't stable. At least that's how the jury will see. It if we convince them she was unstable, we won't get anyone convicted under a *Gaslight* theory."

"*Gaslight* theory?" smiled McCoy. "I thought you were too young to know that one."

"She is," said Branch.

"The fraud or larceny charges will be difficult enough without trying some creative argument for homicide," said McCoy. "If that looks like legal nattering, it will make the fraud case seem even weaker."

"So get into case law and take them down on larceny," said Branch. "Don't go out on a limb, but with all their lying, you can rattle the saber of obstruction as well."

"I just want them out of business," said Southerlyn.

"Jail would do that," said McCoy. "Even a short sentence."

"Rah, rah," said Branch, rubbing his eyes. "Go about your work while I call Ralph Chesko. That ought to cap off the week. You do realize today is Friday the thirteenth? I'm not a superstitious man, but it *has* been a bad day, all 'round."

ARRAIGNMENT
PART 44
MONDAY, SEPTEMBER 16, 9:24 A.M.

"**M**r. Wise," said Judge Hernandez dryly. "And to what do we owe this pleasure?" He lifted the folder of charges.

"Your Honor," Wise placed his hand on Robert Rosserman's shoulder and smiled at Serena Southerlyn, "I am replacing the attorney of record. The baton has been passed from Mr. Ellis."

"Baton, eh?" said Hernandez. "A big one: grand larceny in the third degree. Five counts. How do you plead, Mr. Rosserman?" Rosserman seemed disoriented and was distracted by a half-dozen gangbangers being led in at the side door. "Mr. Rosserman?"

"My client pleads 'Not Guilty,' on all counts, Your Honor, and as soon as possible I will be filing to dismiss these absurd charges."

"File away," said Southerlyn.

"I didn't steal anything, Your Honor," said Rosserman weakly.

"Your Honor," said Southerlyn, "the defendant by false pretense and by false promise engaged in a conspiracy to wrongfully take so-called editing fees from over two hundred victims. The take on this scheme, over the time the defendant was involved, exceeded eight hundred thousand dollars."

"That's pretty 'grand,'" said Hernandez.

"Your Honor," said Wise, "my client didn't receive anything close to that amount and what he did receive were finder's fees, not the proceeds from a larceny. There was no larceny."

Southerlyn jumped in. "Just because the driver for a holdup doesn't get a full cut doesn't mean—"

"Save it for the trial judge. Mr. Rosserman, you're also charged with conspiracy in the fourth degree to commit the grand larceny. I assume if you say you're not guilty to the larceny, you're not guilty of conspiring to commit larceny."

"Not guilty," said Rosserman, forcing out the words.

"The district attorney's office is looking into further charges as well, Your Honor," said Southerlyn. "Manslaughter. Possibly murder, and almost certainly obstruction."

Hernandez looked surprised.

"This is just laundry-list prosecution," said Wise, "an attempt to make an innocent man swallow a plea."

Hernandez wasn't interested. "When the charges are made, then it becomes my business, not before. A request for bail?"

"Because of the defendant's illegal activities he lost his job and his income and has nothing to bind him to the community," she said. "He was not born in New York and he is unmarried. We request one hundred thousand dollars."

Wise shook his head, "My client has lived in Manhattan for twenty-seven years. He has no record and is not a wealthy man. He is a book editor with little or no opportunity to continue his profession. He is determined to reveal the absurdity of this prosecution and clear his name."

Rosserman wobbled slightly, as if he might fall. "As God is my witness," he croaked, "I've never stolen anything."

"God'd be a good witness," said Hernandez, "but I've never seen Him testify. And Miss Southerlyn, we're talking a D felony here, aren't we? Let's say five thousand, bail or bond. Next." He handed the file to the clerk, who called out the names Monica McDonald and Avery McDonald. Avery McDonald had his chin up, thrusting his goatee defiantly outward. He reminded Southerlyn of a hammy actor she had seen playing Don Quixote in *Man of La Mancha*. Beside him, Monica, a sheepish Sancho Panza, with her head down, her plump cheeks flushed.

"These are codefendants?" asked Hernandez.

A short, scrappy attorney in a fuzzy brown suit pushed between his clients and stuck up his hand as if were hailing a cab. "Leo Herlihy for the defense, Your Honor. Your Honor, I am going to ask for an immediate dismissal of the charges."

"That seems to be a popular tune today," said Hernandez.

"The defendants offered a service and they provided that service," he held up a legal document, "to the letter of that contract."

"The business was a deliberate fraud," said Southerlyn.

"Every jot and tittle of the contract was adhered to!" said Avery McDonald.

"Be quiet, Mr. McDonald. Jots and tittles are findings of fact. If the state is correct, you made a lot of illegal money on jots and tittles. If not, you'll be acquitted. It's not my role to decide."

"Tittles!" snorted one of the gangbangers behind them, light gleaming off two gold teeth.

"So how do you plead, Mr. McDonald?"

"Not guilty!" said McDonald tossing his head back.

"And you, Mrs. McDonald?"

"We did nothing wrong," she said.

"Guilty or not guilty?" said Hernandez. "One or the other."

"Not guilty on all counts," said Herlihy. "And we ask that the McDonalds be released on their own recognizance."

"Your Honor, they accumulated a lot of money in this enterprise," said Southerlyn, "and have a home out of state."

"The state has frozen their accounts!" said Herlihy. "They have access to nothing. And they have work to attend to. They are looking forward to getting these charges out of the way so they can pursue a defamation and false arrest suit."

Judge Hernandez raised his hands. "Sounds entertaining. I am entering the pleas and setting bail or bond at ten thousand dollars. Make sure you dot your jots. Next!"

"**L**ook, Jack," said Joel Wise, "you know you're not serious about these hints you'll pursue homicide charges."

"Who says?" said McCoy, looking around as if to see who said it.

"I didn't kill her!" said Rosserman.

"Calm down, Bob," said Wise. "If they were serious, they would have charged you." He smirked at McCoy. "Look, the only reason you brought it up was to scare my client. Hint that if he doesn't fink out on the McDonalds, you concoct a murder charge."

"Concoct?" said McCoy. "Your client concocted several tales to mislead the police. Maybe we won't need to charge him with a homicide. Obstruction looks like a slam dunk."

"I'll repeat," said Wise, "if you had anything that amounted to evidence, Bob would already be charged. He's not. What you're really after is the McDonalds, am I right? I mean, you must be thinking the real cause of Barbara Chesko's death is Redux."

"Maybe the real cause is Mr. Rosserman pushing her."

194

"Jack," said Wise, "you repeat that again and we'll have a slander and defamation suit."

"How many times do I have to say it?" said Rosserman. "She was alive when I left. I didn't know until a woman called me on Monday. That's all I know."

"I've convicted people on less," said McCoy.

"Maybe some crack-dealing loser with a metal stud in his tongue. When you weren't up against me," said Wise. "But, then, let's not turn this into a pissing match. Mr. Rosserman can give you all the details about the Redux operation. You can bring them down, Jack. Isn't that what you really want?"

"He was as guilty as the McDonalds on Redux," said Southerlyn. "Maybe worse. Without him they wouldn't have known Barbara Chesko or many of the other victims."

"Oh, no," said Wise, "you can't even compare what Bob got out of it compared to them. He got a few hundred here and there. They got ten times that, a hundred times that."

"I wasn't the only editor doing this," said Rosserman. "And there were phony publishers as well."

"What do you mean?" said McCoy.

"Interested?" asked Wise. "Bob didn't defraud anyone. He merely did referrals. He's no more guilty than if he referred these people to an embezzling stockbroker."

"He is if he knows the broker was an embezzler. He is if he accepted commissions on the embezzlement."

Wise shook his head. "You can argue anything you want, that doesn't mean it makes any sense. He never intended any harm."

"Barbara Chesko's death wasn't harmful?"

"No!" said Rosserman, standing. "I don't care what you're trying to call it: murder, manslaughter. I didn't kill her!"

Wise now put both hands on Rosserman, one on his shoulder and another on his forearm. "Calm down, Bob," he said. "That's not even on the table. Jack, if you try to lay that on Bob again, this discussion is over. The only subjects on the table are these ridiculous larceny and conspiracy charges."

McCoy locked his gaze on Rosserman's sweaty face. "I just want Mr. Rosserman to face up to his responsibilities. Things have consequences."

Rosserman seemed to deflate slightly. His eyes teared up and he shook his head. He covered his face with both hands and choked on a few words.

"What was that?" demanded McCoy.

"Bob..." said Wise.

"I didn't do it," said Rosserman through his hands. "For God's sake, there's a suicide note! *She* did it."

"Look, Mr. Rosserman," said Southerlyn, "it isn't only that it will go easier if you admit to your role in Redux's scheme. You'll also feel a lot better."

"I'm not a criminal," said Rosserman. "I won't say that I am." He pulled away from his attorney and left the room.

"Bob," said Wise. "Bob!"

But Rosserman was already gone.

"Well," said Wise, "now you've done it. We might have come to some resolution here, but you keep making him think you want him for murder."

"I want him to know she's dead because of him," said McCoy.

"Bob is just an innocent pawn in Redux's business.

My guess is, you won't even be able to prove that Redux is a fraud, even if he cooperated with you. But the plain and simple of it is that he believes that co-operating is admitting he did wrong."

"My guess is that a jury will change his mind," said McCoy.

Wise picked up his briefcase. "And my guess is that the dealing's over," he said. "Just between you guys and me and the wall, I've been fooled a few times but this one I really believe is innocent. I'll give you a hell of a scrap on it."

"Didn't you tell me and the wall that you believed Bill Burnington was really innocent?"

Wise shrugged. "And I gave you a hell of a scrap, didn't I? So I was wrong. This time I'm not. See you in court."

When Wise closed the door, McCoy threw his pencil on the blotter. "Well, that didn't work worth a damn."

"Give him time to stew," said Southerlyn. "If Rosserman thinks he might get stuck—"

"It was bad strategy," said McCoy. "It would only work if he feels guilty about her. We should have just pushed for him to give us the McDonalds."

"I'd hate to let him off the hook," Southerlyn said.

"He doesn't believe he did anything wrong," said McCoy.

"Nor does Wise," said Southerlyn, "At least in legal terms."

"Which is all that matters," said McCoy.

"By the way," Southerlyn asked, "who was Bill Burnington?"

"A carjacker," smirked McCoy. "Burnington's serving seven to ten."

"This one may be tougher," said Southerlyn.

"Amen," said McCoy, raising his eyebrows.

McCoy held up a letter on Redux stationery. It was enclosed in a plastic holder. "And this is the letter you received?"

The witness, Colonel Mark Aalborg, USAF Retired, slipped on his reading glasses and scrutinized it. "Yes, sir. I received it about a week after Mr. Rosserman turned down my book."

"Move to enter into evidence, people's 75," said McCoy to Judge Samuels.

"No objection," said Wise.

"No objection," said Herlihy, the McDonalds' attorney.

"And what does this letter say to you?"

"It says that Mr. Rosserman recommended my book to them."

"Objection," said Herlihy. "The jury doesn't need Colonel Aalborg's interpretation when the letter is available."

"We can read it out loud," said McCoy.

Samuels pursed her lips and looked over the top of her reading glasses. "If the defense would agree to stipulate…"

"Certainly, Your Honor," said Herlihy.

Wise took the letter and read it carefully. "Yes, it's the same as the others." He handed it back to McCoy. "But I don't know what's served by going over this again and again."

"What's served is demonstrating how many times the defendants engaged in this activity."

"Go on, Mr. McCoy," said the judge.

"So," said McCoy to Colonel Aalborg, "would it be fair to say that this letter encouraged you about your memoir, *I Reached Out and Touched the Face of God*?"

"Yes," said the colonel, "it said that Mr. Rosserman had mentioned to Avery and Monica McDonald that I had sent him a very interesting manuscript. It offered their editing services at a ten-percent discount because of the manuscript's promise. I called them the next day. I got Monica McDonald. She acted like we were old pals or something. I—"

"Objection," said Herlihy. "He's characterizing."

McCoy glanced back at the defense to let the jury know he didn't like being interrupted. Sometimes juries would interpret objections as an attempt to conceal important details from them.

"Just stick to the facts, Mr. Aalborg," said the judge. "What did you say? What did she say?"

"I'm just saying the way she acted."

"I'm sure you remember the old *Dragnet*, Colonel Aalborg," said Samuels. "'Just the facts,' right?" The colonel sat stone-faced as someone chuckled.

"And what did she tell you, Colonel Aalborg?" asked McCoy.

He coughed. "She told me it was clear that my story needed to reach the public. She asked me if I were the kind of man who would feel comfortable doing talk shows and radio interviews."

"Talk shows and radio interviews?"

"She asked if I was free to travel to book signings."

"And what did you say?"

"I said I'd been to hell and back and thought I could survive a book tour."

"Was money mentioned?"

"Eventually. When I first brought it up, she asked me a few questions about my retirement income. She suggested I must have a pretty good retirement after thirty-five years of active duty. I told her I wasn't rich, but had as much as I needed."

"And then?"

"She suggested they could do a thorough editing job to prepare it for submission for five thousand dollars."

"Did you accept this?"

"I asked if that amount included the ten percent discount. She then said that based on Mr. Rosserman's recommendation, she might reduce the fee by another two hundred and fifty." Aalborg cleared his throat. "I said I'd have to think about it. She said she wanted to talk to her husband and see what he said. She said they really believed my story needed to come out. Avery McDonald called me on Monday. He said they might be able to do more for me because of their confidence in the book. They said that successful books tended to increase their own reputation in the industry and so they were sometimes willing to take a deeper cut to land a reputation-enhancing job. He said that Mr. Rosserman had told them it was a 'hell of a book' with enormous potential. He said he was deeply moved by my manuscript, that America needed to hear about patriots like me. Then he said that he didn't want to price himself out of such a great job, so he was offering his absolute minimum, four thousand dollars."

"And you accepted?"

"I hesitated a bit and then he suggested payments or a credit card, so that they could get started right away. He said some mumbo jumbo about striking when the iron was hot."

"Objection," said Herlihy.

"Disregard 'mumbo jumbo,'" said the judge. She peered over her glasses at the colonel.

"I know," he said. "Just the facts. I mailed him a check. I should have known what the real motivation was when he said they would have to wait until the check cleared before beginning."

The judge said, "Colonel…" like a mother growing impatient with a twelfth grader.

"And what was the result of your payment?" asked McCoy.

"After the check cleared, I waited about three weeks, then called. My manuscript, she said—that's Monica McDonald—was in the mail. It showed up postmarked two days *after* I called."

McCoy held up a manuscript with both hands. It was about three inches thick and held together with two rubber bands. "And is this that manuscript, as edited?"

"Yes," said the colonel. "I had it retyped for submission."

"But this is the manuscript they returned to you?"

"Yes, sir."

McCoy asked that it be entered into evidence. The defense attorneys took a glance at it and agreed.

When the procedure was done, Colonel Aalborg continued. "So I took it to a secretarial service called

Tribeca Professional. I had to go back several times to explain, to try to make sense of the gibberish written all over the pages."

"You're referring to the red ink?"

"There were arrows going every which way. Big X's through things. It looked like they'd given it to a two-year-old to play with."

"Just stick to the facts," the judge reminded him.

"But weren't these markings helpful?" asked McCoy. "At first glance, it looks very thorough."

"They were just marks. It made no sense what was slashed. I noticed typos of mine that they hadn't caught. I had typed 'President Jones' once or twice when I meant 'President Johnson,' and *B*, I, E, T-Nam instead of *V*. They wrote things like 'strengthen' or 'reword' with no explanation what they meant."

"And did you confront the McDonalds about this?"

"I left four or five messages, then one day Avery McDonald picked up the phone instead of leaving it to his answering machine. He got pretty huffy and said 'reword' meant 'reword' and that I ought to know what that meant. Oh, and he offered to do a clean copy for me, typed out with only the corrections for another seven hundred. A full rewrite would cost much more."

"Did you find, in the entire manuscript, anything helpful?"

"I learned a lesson about being suckered," said the colonel.

"No more questions," said McCoy.

It was Herlihy's turn first. "Mister, excuse me, Colonel Aalborg, do you have any experience editing for publication?"

"I did a lot in the Air Force, every kind of report."

"With all due respect, Colonel, I didn't ask you that."

"I supervised and corrected many documents and reports."

"But no books, am I right?"

"No."

"So you wouldn't recognize common editing marks, and you might have difficulty with the meaning of certain words commonly used in the book trade."

"What? Like 'reword'? I know what that means."

"Excuse me, Colonel," said Herlihy with a slight grin, "didn't you just tell Mr. McCoy you didn't know what 'reword' meant when it appeared on your manuscript?"

The colonel's eyebrows were twitching and his eyes tightened like they were about to fire rockets. "It means to change the wording. But why reword? How? To what end? Someone scribbled 'reword' on there probably without reading it!"

"That's speculation, isn't it, Colonel? What if someone went over the manuscript quite closely and then wrote 'reword' on it? Would that look any different?"

The colonel didn't answer, he just steamed.

"Is it possible that a more professional writer might recognize the problem to which the word referred?"

"I asked him to explain it; he asked me for more money."

"And the McDonalds'—isn't *their* time valuable? Don't you believe they should be compensated for their work?"

"Badgering, Your Honor," said McCoy.

"Sorry, Your Honor," said Herlihy. "Do you believe they should be compensated for their work?"

"Yes, but they didn't do anything. Why should I pay them again? I demanded my money back, but it was never returned."

Herlihy held the manuscript in front of him and riffled the red-marked pages. "How can you say they didn't do anything? How many weeks did they have it?"

"One question at a time, Your Honor," said McCoy.

"Withdrawn," said Herlihy. "Isn't this really about your disappointment, Colonel Aalborg?"

"It's about being lied to," said the colonel.

"Exactly what lie are you referring to?"

"They said they would edit my book. They said it would be a success."

"But they did edit your book, didn't they?"

"No."

"And they did not ever actually say that your book would be a best-seller, did they?"

"No, but they said it would make a mark!"

"'Would,' Colonel, or 'could'? Isn't it just possible that you were hearing what you wanted to hear?"

"No."

"You've served your country for more than three decades, at the end of the Vietnam conflict, in Desert Storm. You worked your way up the ranks, and America owes you a great debt of gratitude. You have a lot of things to say that need to be said. Is that a fair assessment of your feeling?"

"I've been there and back," said the colonel.

"Did you ever consider hiring a ghost author? Someone who was capable of actually expressing what you wanted to say?"

McCoy shot to his feet. "Your Honor!"

The colonel caught the implication of the question and lost the fire in his eyes.

"No more questions," said Herlihy.

Wise rose and spoke quietly. "Colonel, I just have a few questions for you and then you'll be on your way. Did you ever talk to Mr. Rosserman directly?"

"Not face-to-face."

"And how many letters did you receive from him?"

"Just the rejection letter after he turned down my book."

"And did his letter mention the services of Redux?"

"No," said Aalborg. "It said that if I felt my project was important enough to pursue, I might consider professional editing services."

"So you received just that letter from Mr. Rosserman, and he did not specifically mention the McDonalds?"

"No. Their letter followed his by the end of the week. It said he, Rosserman, had mentioned my book to him. The old one-two. Set 'em up. Knock 'em down."

"I can see how that might seem to you, with your disappointment, Colonel, but did you actually have any contact with Bob Rosserman after that rejection letter?"

"Not directly. I called, said that I appreciated his recommendation to the McDonalds. He thanked me for calling, but that was before they did, ah, what they did. Later, when I saw what I'd got for my money, I tried to call him back. I thought he might intercede for me to get my money back. I thought he might explain exactly what the McDonalds were up to."

"So," said Wise, "even after your experience with

the McDonalds, you were willing to consult Mr. Rosserman?"

"I thought he might know what to do."

"Colonel Aalborg," said Wise quietly, "you were seeking Bob's advice. Doesn't that mean you trusted him?"

"No, it means I didn't know where to turn. I didn't know they were paying him."

"You weren't aware that a small referral fee was involved?"

"No."

"And would you have called him after you received the edited manuscript, if you had known about the fee?"

"Of course. I was desperate. I'd have thought he ought to feel responsible for getting me into it."

"Doesn't that imply that you trusted him?"

"Asked and answered," said McCoy.

"I won't bother you any further, Colonel," said Wise, "and may I add I hope to be reading your memoirs soon."

"Throw a little salt in his wounds," Southerlyn whispered.

"Notice that Wise is cutting Rosserman away from the McDonalds," he said in her ear. "He's pretending he hardly knew them."

"Mr. McCoy?" asked the judge.

The bushy hair, now silvery, had been a familiar sight on the New York literary scene since the late 1950s. Martin Post had burst onto the best-seller list at the age of twenty-five with what was then a shocking novel about the fighting in Burma during World War II. Later, there were novels about the waterfront, an airline mogul, and a corrupt boxing promoter, among others. He also wrote controversial nonfiction, particularly *The Race Game* and *Manchildren*, which angered liberals and conservatives alike. If there were anyone in the city who was known as *the* writer, love him or hate him, it was Martin Post. His name was known even by people who hadn't read him.

McCoy had considered whether the anger Martin Post sometimes inspired might actually hurt with one or more members of the jury and whether he was as loose a cannon as his reputation, but the Author's Guild had offered to file an *amicus curiae* brief on behalf of the state, and Martin Post had led the fight for it. Arthur Branch had recommended that a couple of expert witnesses might be needed to enlighten jurors about the book trade and to clarify how crooked the McDonalds were. When McCoy telephoned Post, the writer was delighted.

When McCoy called Post to the stand, most heads in the courtroom turned to watch for him. The eminent novelist strode to the witness stand and took the oath with a clear voice. He was the kind of person who is always aware he is on a world stage. Judge Samuels even brought herself to nod appreciatively.

"How are you, Your Honor?" said Post.

"Very well," said the judge. "I've enjoyed your work."

"Thank you, Your Honor," he said, as if surprised.

"Mr. Post," asked McCoy, trying to establish Post as a legitimate expert witness, "could you summarize your career as an author for anyone who may not be familiar with it?"

"That's more people than I care to think about," he said. His eyes twinkled. "I'll try not to testify all night."

McCoy could see that Post had immediately won over the jury, which was more than you got out of the scientists or physicians usually used as experts. Post's summary was like his writing, direct and clear, and though some of his most recent novels were a good three inches thick, he finished in a few seconds.

"Thank you, Mr. Post," said McCoy. "Might you mention some of the awards you have won as a writer?"

Post mumbled them as if he were reciting a rap sheet. "Pulitzer, Cassis Prix de Roman, National Book Award, Casa d'Oro prize, et cetera. There was that Oscar, too, for the screenplay. But that's not real writing. Movie writing's not real writing."

"Some wouldn't agree with you," said McCoy.

"Certainly not the people who awarded you the Academy Award."

Post shrugged. He didn't seem to enjoy flattery, even though he enjoyed center stage.

"And you have had considerable experience as an editor?"

"I worked as an editor before my first novel was published and for two years after that. Since then I've mostly edited my own work, which needs a lot, I might add. I also edited my second wife's books, though she denies that now."

There was scattered chuckling in the courtroom.

"You created a cutting-edge magazine in 1973."

"*Tower*. Those were cutting times. But it didn't last long, the magazine, I mean. I don't suppose the age of Aquarius lasted long, either."

"And you were editor in chief of *Tower*?"

"Yes. It was go, go, go. I was a lot younger, then, but I was aging three to one. In the end I decided as much as I hated writing, I hated telling people what to write even more."

"Mr. Post, several weeks ago my office forwarded to you three manuscripts selected at random from among the seven manuscripts seized by the police at the headquarters of Redux."

"Yes. They were manuscripts in the return packages. That is, they were about to be returned to the writers."

"So these manuscripts had been edited by Redux?"

"Well, I couldn't say by whom exactly. They were covered with red ink and there was a letter from Avery McDonald in each."

"And each letter stated that it had been edited."

"Yes."

"And did you examine the editorial marks?"

"Closely. It was a chore. They were ridiculous."

"And what do you mean by that?"

"They didn't say anything significant. Oh, there were chicken scratches on every page, a plethora of them, but they were largely pointless."

"So, in your opinion, there was absolutely nothing helpful to a writer."

"It was all nonsense."

McCoy handed him one of the three manuscripts. "You've flagged several pages. Would you like to show the jury?"

Southerlyn pushed an electronics cart to the front of the courtroom while McCoy raised a projection screen. Post handed a sheet to McCoy, who focused it in the opaque projector.

"This is page one hundred of a manuscript entitled *Summers with Sonny*," said Post. "I think it was supposed to be like *Tuesdays with Morrie*. You see all that red ink..."

"To the untrained eye, it looks like a lot of work was expended on this. What do you make of this effort?"

"Umm, to begin with, look at the commas in this paragraph. "Here the sentence reads, 'Sonny whacked hot and cold about Vietnam bouncing like a basket ball...' Notice the typo, two words for 'basketball.' 'Among opinions, he sometimes thought we ought to drop a nuclear bomb on the Kong. Other times he said we ought to tell them to give us fourty-eight hours to get out of town.'"

"And the editor for Redux inserted commas?"

"There, between 'hot' and 'and.' A high schooler knows it doesn't belong there. Then there's one between 'thought' and 'we.' Why? And is that a comma in red ink between 'basket' and 'ball'? It's as if whoever this is has a quota for inserting commas and doesn't much care where they go. But does this knucklehead mark the obvious errors? You don't 'whack' hot and cold, you 'wax' hot and cold. 'Fourty' is a misspelling for 'forty,' but my absolute favorite is the misspelling of Cong. Unless the author intended to nuke King Kong."

There were more chuckles among the spectators, provoking a grave look from the judge.

"I don't mean to make light," said Post. "My point is that anyone who was really editing this book would have noticed at least one of these things. And the manuscript is rife with things inserted in it that either don't add anything, or definitely damage it. The editor overlooks obvious errors and then compounds the problems. Asleep at the wheel, I'd say."

"And this is a representative page?"

"It is typical."

"What about these lines and more general comments?"

"Well," he said, "this line is supposed to tell the author to move the paragraph, I think. But if you follow the events on the page, this would split off the talk about Vietnam and place it between two paragraphs about Sonny's oiling his wheelchair."

"And what is this handwritten remark here?"

"It says 'More plot!'" Post nearly cracked up and squeezed his nose to keep from laughing.

"Is that funny, Mr. Post?"

"It means absolutely nothing. Plot doesn't come in amounts, so it's impossible to know what the so-called editor means. More incidents? More surprises? What?"

"Perhaps you could comment on the editing in another manuscript," said McCoy.

Post had similar comments on two pages in a second book, and noted a seventy-five-page gap on which no marks at all appeared. Perhaps this was because the pages did not need editing? "God no!" said Post and proceeded to point out, among other unmarked gaffes, that a thin waiter on page 52 had become a fat waiter on page 55. McCoy allowed Post to expose more sloppy editing and weak advice in a third manuscript, then decided the point had been made well enough that he didn't want to bore the jurors.

"In conclusion, Mr. Post, as an expert in the fields of writing and editing, what is your opinion of Redux's editing work on these and the other manuscripts you reviewed?"

"I don't see that they've been edited at all. They've been marked up, but not edited. In my opinion, these customers didn't get anything for their money."

"Objection," said Herlihy.

"On what basis?" said Judge Samuels. "An expert witness is allowed to express an expert opinion."

Herlihy blinked. "We object to the characterization. He said the clients didn't get anything. Obviously, they got something. Just because the controversial Mr. Post doesn't approve of my clients' work doesn't mean the work wasn't done."

"Well, then, I object to Mr. Herlihy's characterization of Mr. Post," said McCoy.

"But I like being thought of as 'controversial'!" said Post.

Chuckling broke out, even among the jury.

Samuels rapped her gavel. "Mr. Post…" warned the judge.

"I apologize," said Post.

"The jury should disregard Mr. Herlihy's characterizations of Mr. Post," she said. "If you want to discredit Mr. Post's qualifications, you'll have to do that on cross."

"Yes, Your Honor," said Herlihy.

"And you can also challenge the assertion that the McDonalds' clients got nothing on your cross-examination, if you choose to do so. An expert witness is allowed to express an opinion. That's what expert witnesses do, counselor. Overruled."

"Yes, Your Honor," he said, sitting.

"It was worthless," interrupted Post.

"You don't have a question, Mr. Post," said the judge. "Now, people, let's try to maintain the dignity of the legal system and get on with it."

"Mr. Post," said McCoy, "for the benefit of the counsel for the defense, could you clarify your last statement concerning the value of the editing jobs which you reviewed?"

"I'll say it again: they were worthless."

"And do you mean by that merely that you disagree with the recommendations given by the editors?"

"No," said Post, "I see dozens of marks, but they are random and meaningless. No one really edited these manuscripts. They simply made them look as if they had been edited."

Herlihy interrupted again. "He's speculating on the motives of the defendants. He's not here as a psychiatrist."

Samuels exhaled and looked toward the jury.

"Disregard Mr. Post's comments about the intent of the editor or editors."

McCoy pursued the issue in another way. "Mr. Post, judging solely from the manuscripts, is it your opinion that the extensive markings constituted editing in a professional sense?"

"Absolutely not."

"Thank you, Mr. Post." McCoy returned to his table.

Herlihy stood. "Mr. Post, we are honored to have you here."

"Thank you." Post looked embarrassed to be flattered again.

Herlihy strolled near the witness box. "Isn't editing really a matter of taste?"

"It is and it isn't."

"Could you clarify that for me and for those of us who are not writers? What is, and what isn't, a matter of taste?"

"There are things which are simply wrong and things which are a matter of taste. Grammatical things, for example. Punctuation. Those kinds of mechanical things. And say you have a character born and bred in Manhattan and he speaks with a Louisiana accent. That's wrong as well. It's what Aristotle calls an inappropriate characterization."

"What if the character feigns a Louisiana accent?"

"Well, if such a thing is justified by the context of the story, it wouldn't be wrong, necessarily."

"I see," said Herlihy, "'the context.' Is that what you mean by taste?"

"No, I mean whether you choose to give a character blonde hair or red."

"Well, suppose the character is of a racial type—Hispanic, African-American—that does not have blond hair, could you give such a character blond hair in a book?"

"If it were justified by the context. Maybe there's a genetic mutation. Maybe the character was exposed to a strange chemical accident. Maybe it's blond out of a box."

"So anything goes then, in fiction?"

"No. If it's justified in the story. It has to be justified by the integrity of the story."

"I'm sorry, Mr. Post, but these concepts are difficult for me. These would be things that one would learn as a writer?"

"Most good writers have an instinct, but they also learn about the integrity of the story as they develop their skills. At least one hopes they do."

"But could there be a difference of opinion about what constitutes this integrity you refer to?"

"Yes. On a certain level. Not on the basic level."

"And these examples we were discussing, a native New Yorker with a Louisiana accent, it wouldn't necessarily be wrong?"

"In certain contexts, no."

"So there's nothing you would describe as being always and absolutely wrong then?"

"In a given manuscript, some things can be absolutely wrong."

"I'm still a little confused." Herlihy turned and grabbed a book off his desk. "Would you mind reading the marked passage, ah, right there?"

Post looked at the text, flipped the book and quickly looked at the spine. "'I doan k'yer what de widder say, he *warn't* no wise man, nuther. He had some of the dadfetchedes' ways I ever see.'"

Herlihy put a photocopy on the opaque projector.

DEAD LINE

"Now, Mr. Post, are there things that are wrong in this passage?"

"We'll give Mark Twain the benefit of the doubt. This is from *Huckleberry Finn*."

"But what about those spellings in there? 'Widder,' 'warn't,' and so on."

"Mark Twain is trying to simulate the speech of the slave Jim. The context of the story makes it appropriate."

"So even spelling is a matter of taste."

"This isn't a matter of taste, here. It would lose a lot by having Jim speak like the president of Harvard." Post hmmphed. "Or like you."

"I see, but don't some people regard all this *simulation*, as you call it, to be offensive to African-Americans? I mean, it makes Jim into a stereotype, doesn't it?"

"No, Jim is almost the only honest person in the book. Huckleberry Finn doesn't understand how society can oppress such a man, not even credit Jim with being a man."

Herlihy nodded. "And what about down here? Would you read the marked passage?"

Post scanned it, glanced up at Herlihy and the judge and read. "'I never see such a nigger. If he got a notion in his head once, there warn't no getting it out again. He was the most down on Solomon of any nigger I ever see.'"

McCoy's eyes met Southerlyn's. There were two black men and one black woman on the jury. Who'd have thought this case would suggest playing the race card?

"If you had been editing this passage, Mr. Post, would you have changed it?" Herlihy asked.

"I certainly hope not!" said Post. "It's intended to simulate Huck Finn's dialect and the time in which he lived."

"But isn't it wrong? Isn't it offensive? Shouldn't it be changed?"

"Good God," said Post. "It's *Huckleberry Finn*. I suppose you'd burn the book."

"But the spellings are wrong," said Herlihy, "the use of the word, pardon me, 'nigger,' is in bad taste, wouldn't you say?"

"It was written over a hundred years ago."

"Should such racist things have been edited from the book?"

"No. If you get racism out of it," said Post, "you don't understand the book."

"Your Honor," said McCoy, "Mark Twain isn't on trial here! And this is hardly the place for a discussion of the merits of *Huckleberry Finn*."

"I'm merely trying to establish exactly on what basis the witness claims that editing is not a matter of individual taste," Herlihy said. "Simply because Mr. Post doesn't agree with the work of my clients doesn't mean there is an intent to defraud."

"I think your point is made, Mr. Herlihy," said the judge.

"I have other examples," he said.

"Are we going to do all of world literature?" snorted McCoy.

"I merely wanted to show there are no quotation marks in James Joyce's *Ulysses*, and no paragraph breaks in *No One Writes to the Colonel* by Nobel prize winner Gabriel García-Márquez."

"This is muddying the water," said McCoy. "The

state will concede there are numerous instances in literature in which writers do not follow convention."

"And that proves there are no absolute rules, doesn't it?" said Herlihy. "One editor may think one thing, while another thinks something different."

"Nonsense!" said Post.

"Be quiet, Mr. Post," said the judge.

"But it's a misrepresentation," Post insisted. "The context and the intent of the author determines…"

"Be quiet," she repeated. Post crossed his arms.

Herlihy picked up another thick book.

"Forget it, Mr. Herlihy," said Samuels, "Mr. McCoy has conceded that many writers do not follow convention. Move on."

"But I want it clear," said McCoy, "that the witness is *not* saying that anything goes, that editing is a matter of taste."

"Is Mr. McCoy's characterization of your opinion correct?" The judge asked Post.

"Yes," said Post. "Just because great authors bend rules, it doesn't mean that there are none. It all depends on the context. An editor assesses the context and follows the internal logic of the individual work."

"Exactly our point," said Herlihy. "It is the editor who assesses."

"Let's move on," said the judge.

"One other question, Mr. Post," said Herlihy. "You undoubtedly are a very busy man. Your time is quite valuable. Can you tell this court what consideration you received from the state for testifying today?"

Wise, who had watched most of the previous questioning with a bemused expression, turned toward Herlihy.

"Nothing," said Post.

Herlihy blinked, then smiled. "So you did it for the publicity?"

Post's eyes flashed. "No, I did it because I don't like to see people taken advantage of. Who knows—"

"Thank you, Mr. Post," said Herlihy.

"Can I finish?" said Post.

"Mr. Herlihy questioned Mr. Post's integrity, Your Honor," said McCoy.

"So I should finish?" said Post.

"Yes," said the judge.

"I am a member of the executive board of the Author's Guild. We do what we can to protect our fellow writers from being exploited. I looked over the materials and it confirmed what I have heard for years, that Redux is a scam."

The judge anticipated Herlihy's objection and spoke to the jury. "What Mr. Post has heard for years is not evidence, nor is his characterization of Redux as a scam. You are here to determine whether the defendants were engaged in a crime. 'Scam' is not a legal term. Mr. Post is not offering a legal opinion."

"Thank you, Your Honor," said Herlihy. "No further questions."

"Mr. Wise, will this be a lengthy cross? It's lunchtime."

"I'll be brief," said Wise, "so Mr. Post can go about the important business of being one of America's greatest authors."

"Just move it along, then," said Judge Samuels.

"Mr. Post," said Wise, "you have had many manuscripts edited by house editors, am I correct?"

"Every one of two dozen or so."

"House editors are editors employed by the publisher, like Mr. Rosserman, am I correct?"

"They're called 'house editors' because they are salaried or under contract to the publishing house."

"In your expert opinion, in the manuscripts from Redux, does the editing look like house editing?"

"No. It's not house editing. It's freelance editing. Either way, it's all nonsense. It's certainly not the kind of editing a real publisher would tolerate. It's not editing at all."

"You have no reason to believe that Bob Rosserman, an editor with Kirstner and Strawn for seventeen years, who has edited over two hundred published books in that time period, had anything to do with the editing of these manuscripts?"

"I doubt he'd have a job if this was what he normally did."

"Thank you, Mr. Post. It's an honor to meet you."

"Thank you."

The judge recessed until two o'clock. After lunch, McCoy intended to question their second expert, Charlotte Hill, an editor at Fleet Publishing. Like Post, she would testify that what she saw on the manuscripts did not constitute editing. Assuming Herlihy didn't find a way to drag that out all afternoon with passages from the Great Books, he planned to turn the questioning of Deena Dunkel, a former employee of Redux, over to Southerlyn, as well as the questioning of two clients of the McDonalds who had also been taken.

As they ate in an unseasonably warm sun on a bench by a falafel cart, both McCoy and Southerlyn thought Herlihy would again try to muddle the issue of what constituted editing. "Pushing that it's all a matter of taste!" she said.

"Then," said McCoy, "the case seems to be about customers who can't face up to their lack of talent, rather than fraud."

"We'll cut Herlihy off as much as possible," she said.

"Right," said McCoy, "but I don't think Samuels is going to let him do too much of that anyway. She'll let him make his point, but not to any length. How do you read the jury?" He took a bite of his sandwich, then looked at it as if there was something odd in the falafel.

"The woman on the end looked like she was going to leap out of the seat and ask Post for an autograph."

"Good, maybe we bought her. She'll have a story to dine out on when the trial's over."

"A couple of the men were counting cracks in the ceiling, though."

"That doesn't mean they're against us."

"Did you recognize Ralph Chesko? He was in the third row from the back."

"Barbara Chesko's ex-husband?"

"Yes," said Southerlyn. "I recognized him from the news stories about his growth fund."

"I guess he wants to see if he needs to hassle City Hall again."

"He looked very sad," said Southerlyn. "He left sometime during the testimony."

The wind whipped up a bit, reminding her it was November.

"Wise isn't putting up much of a fight," said Southerlyn.

"I'm disappointed. When he wants to, he's one of the best."

"If Herlihy can get the McDonalds off, Rosserman will walk."

"And if we get the McDonalds," said McCoy, "he'll claim Rosserman didn't know what they were up to. He's lying so low, you hardly know he's a defendant." McCoy gave up on his sandwich.

"McDonald looks at my legs. He wants me to see him doing it. It makes me feel like I have lice."

"Maybe the jury will see it. We haven't lost yet," said McCoy. He watched a bicycle messenger weave through traffic, then turned back to study Southerlyn, who was running the tip of her pinky across her upper lip. "This case gets to you, doesn't it?"

"They all get to me," she said.

"What's the expression? 'Ice blonde'? You're usually the Grace Kelly of A.D.A.s." She faced him, but didn't say anything. "It's a compliment, Serena," said McCoy. "Don't let the job get to you. The guilty party walks away a lot."

"If we come to accept it, we might as well quit."

"Who said anything about accepting it?" said McCoy.

"**M**iss Dunkle," Southerlyn asked the emaciated witness, "are you familiar with Redux, the book editing company headed by Avery and Monica McDonald?"

"Yes," she said, using her thumb to shove her thick glasses up her nose.

"How are you familiar with them?"

"For about six months last year, I worked for them."

"And of what did your duties consist?"

"I was an editor. I answered the advertisement for freelance book editors. It was in the Columbia University student paper."

"You're a student there, I take it?"

"A grad student in the School of Arts writing program."

"So you are studying to be an editor?"

"Not really. I'm a poet mostly. I'm writing an avant-garde verse drama about Carmen Miranda. But I needed money and I thought if I got the right kind of books, I could do the job."

"And what happened when you answered the ad?"

"Well, it said to call. I thought I might need to send in a résumé or take an editing test."

"Have you had to take editing tests before?"

"Yes, you know, like you've got fifteen minutes to do corrections on something. I did it at a couple of newspapers and at two magazines." She shoved her glasses back up her nose.

"And you didn't get those jobs?"

"No, they took somebody else each time. It wasn't because I did badly, though. I took the test for the *Handy Shopper*. It's like an advertising supplement. I worked there for three months."

"I see. So you saw the advertisement for freelance book editors and telephoned the number in the ad?"

"I talked to Avery, Mr. McDonald. He asked a couple of questions, then said that was good enough for him. He said I didn't need to take a test. He wanted me to start right away."

"Without references?"

"He said he had the feeling he could trust a Columbia student to do a good job, and, frankly, he said, they were too pressed to waste any more time in getting editors on board."

"So you might have been anyone. You might not have been qualified to edit at all."

"Objection," said Herlihy.

"Withdrawn," said Southerlyn. "So what happened next?"

"I met Mr. McDonald outside the public library. It was a nice day so we sat on the steps outside. He was carrying a big, blue Adidas gym bag. He asked me to tell him more about me. I explained I was a graduate student. He asked me if I'd ever published and I explained I was a poet and was working on verse drama. I began to explain what it was about, but he said he was in a bit of a hurry, so he said, 'Let's cut to the chase, darling.' He asked me how many I wanted."

"How many what?"

"That's what I asked him. He said manuscripts. He'd give me the whole bag if I wanted. He said his rate was a dollar a page. It was up to me how much money I made. I asked him what I was supposed to do with them, and he said 'Edit them!' I asked if I could see a sample of what I was supposed to do. He said I was to edit them any way I liked, as long as the writer felt like there were a lot of suggestions for improvement. I then said it would take a lot of time. He said not if I got in the rhythm of it. I could be making fifty dollars an hour."

"That would require your editing fifty pages in an hour?" said Southerlyn.

"Yes. About a minute a page. He said I was to edit them, not rewrite them. To make lots of marks, the customer expected that but not to rewrite it. This just irritated the customers, he said. He also said most of the books were not salvageable."

Southerlyn interrupted. "Not salvageable?"

"Yes. He said I should give them lots of advice, and to always remain positive, even if the books were horrible. I asked why we would edit books that ought to be rewritten and he just said we didn't want to crush their hopes. It was charity."

"Charity. And did you discover how much this charity cost?"

Dunkle shoved her glasses back up her nose. "I later was told that it ran about ten dollars a page."

"And who told you this?"

"Avery, Mr. McDonald. About three months later. It was when I asked him about my income taxes. He told me he wasn't reporting my income, so I didn't have to worry. He mentioned that he was getting about ten dollars a page and most of it went to expenses, but he was willing to give me a raise to a dollar and a quarter."

"So he told you he collected about ten dollars a page. And about how long were the manuscripts?"

"Anywhere between one hundred pages and a thousand. Mostly around three hundred."

"So if he received three thousand dollars, you received about three hundred, and you did the editing?"

"Speculation, Your Honor!" said Herlihy.

"Sustained," said the judge. "Don't generalize about the figures, Ms. Southerlyn. Introduce them if you have them."

"We will, Your Honor."

Southerlyn paused to recapture her train of thought. "After your initial meeting, how many manuscripts did you take home?"

"The whole gym bag. I could hardly schlepp it. I didn't want to take them all. I wanted to try out a couple to see if I'd be good at this. But Mr. McDonald insisted."

"Insisted?"

"He put his hand on my thigh and said he was sure we'd work well together. He said if I didn't want to do them all, he'd pick them up eventually."

"What were his exact words?"

"Something like, 'I'm confident we'll work very well together, darling. If you don't like the work, I'll just pick up the things eventually.'"

"'The things'?"

"Yes, 'the things.'"

"'Eventually?'"

"Yes."

"And you edited the manuscripts?"

"I did my best. I didn't really know what to say on most of them. I called Avery to ask what to do. He wanted me to meet him for lunch in midtown, but I told him I just wanted some questions answered. He got irritated when I asked, and said I should do whatever I thought needed doing, just do it fast. He said it wasn't brain surgery and it didn't much matter. He said that the thing to do was to get them done. So I took his advice and did it fast. If I didn't understand it, I'd just write, 'Make this clearer,' 'Strengthen this chapter,' something like that. I thought he'd fire me, but he didn't. He asked me where my apartment was so that he could pick up the manuscripts, but I met him in the coffee shop at the Mayflower."

"You didn't feel comfortable about meeting him at your apartment?"

"Objection," said Herlihy. "It's not relevant how the witness personally felt about Mr. McDonald."

"Withdrawn," said Southerlyn. "How long did you work for the McDonalds?"

"About a year."

"And about how many manuscripts did you do for them?"

"At least two a week, sometimes four. I was getting at least four hundred dollars a week, sometimes up to seven hundred."

"So that was at least a book a week?"

"Two, usually three. When I found out about the ten dollars a page they were charging, I worked out that they were bringing in about ten thousand a week."

Judge Samuels looked at Herlihy for an objection.

"The 1040s submitted into evidence yesterday show an income averaging $11,372.88 a week for the year in question," said Southerlyn.

The judge nodded.

"And then you had a falling-out with the McDonalds?"

"Yes," said Dunkle. "I stumbled in Central Park near the zoo and broke my wrist. I couldn't write, so I thought I ought to get unemployment. Mr. McDonald was very curt and said I was a freelancer, which meant I got nothing. Mrs. McDonald yelled at me when I called a day later. She said I should stay away from Mr. McDonald or I'd regret it. I hadn't paid any tax on my income and she'd sic the state and the feds on me."

"So what did you do?"

"I talked to a law student I know, Jerry Stern, who told me I couldn't get workman's comp and then he told me that because I was classified as a contract employee, essentially I was self-employed, and no unemployment insurance had been paid. Besides, the McDonalds could claim I had been fired for misconduct and I'd get nothing. I didn't have the money to fight, so I gave up."

"Did you do anything else?"

"The more I thought about it, the madder I got. It wasn't my fault I broke my wrist. I stopped by the police fraud department, and they took my report and said they'd look into it."

"Why did you report it to the Special Frauds Squad?"

"Well, I thought the whole thing was crooked."

"Objection," said Herlihy.

"Is Mr. Herlihy objecting to the question?" asked Southerlyn.

"The witness is not here to tell us whether a crime has been committed," said Herlihy. "That's up to the jury."

"Ms. Dunkle is explaining the motivation for her actions. She is testifying to her state of mind, not giving a legal opinion."

Judge Samuels looked at the jury. "Ms. Dunkle's opinions about whether the defendants committed fraud is only her opinion. The findings of fact whether or not the defendants committed a crime is strictly in your hands."

"No more questions," said Southerlyn.

Herlihy jabbed the air in Deena Dunkle's direction with a pen. "Since you raised the question about your state of mind, did you consider the fact that if you thought the McDonalds were committing a crime, that you also would be committing a crime?"

Dunkle moved her head from side to side, confused. She looked to the prosecution table and to McCoy for an answer. "I gave the people as much help as I could," she finally said. "I didn't know it was crooked."

"It took you six months to decide Redux was engaged in an illegal activity?"

"I don't know when I thought so."

"And you didn't report it as long as you were paid?"

"Not until later."

"After you broke your wrist?"

"Yes."

"Before that you were content to ride the gravy train, weren't you?"

"The witness is not on trial," said Southerlyn.

"Would you have reported Redux to the Special Frauds unit if you hadn't been incapacitated?"

"I was thinking about quitting. Like I said, I tried to help the people as best I could."

"Well," said Herlihy, "if you helped them, then you could hardly call this a fraud, could you?"

"What do you mean?"

"I mean," said Herlihy, "that if people were paying for help on their manuscripts and you provided that help, then this could hardly be considered a fraud, now could it?"

"It wasn't what *I* did. They didn't care what I did. They didn't care about helping. They were stealing people's money."

"People paid Redux for a service. And you were hired to perform that service. Is that stealing? Either you were an accomplice or there was no crime, was there?"

"What they did was wrong," said Dunkle.

"And what about you?"

"Argumentative," objected Southerlyn.

"No more questions," said Herlihy.

"Mr. Wise?" asked the judge.

Wise didn't bother to stand. "Ms. Dunkle, in your time working for Redux, did you ever meet Mr. Rosserman?"

"No. I usually didn't have much contact with anyone other than Mr. McDonald."

"Did you ever hear of Mr. Rosserman while you were working for Redux?"

"I saw his name on a couple of letters in the manuscripts."

"And those were letters from Mr. Rosserman?"

"No, they were from Monica McDonald. They mentioned Mr. Rosserman."

"But otherwise you never understood that he had any working relationship with Redux?"

"No. Not directly."

"No further questions."

Southerlyn stood. "Redirect." The judge nodded. "Ms. Dunkle, do you remember the nature of these letters?"

"Yes. I noticed them because they were all the same. I saw about six of them over a couple of months. They all said that Bob Rosserman of Kirstner and Strawn had said something nice about the manuscript to the McDonalds."

Southerlyn raised exhibits 14, 15, and 16: letters in clear plastic holders. "These state exhibits, would you read them carefully?"

"Out loud?"

"That isn't necessary," said Southerlyn. "I just want to know if they are the same."

Dunkle lowered her head and squinted at them, nearly losing her glasses off the tip of her nose. "They're all the same."

"There are fifteen examples with the same body text entered in evidence," said Southerlyn. "But are these the same as the letters you saw?"

"Oh, yes," she said.

"No more questions," said Southerlyn.

"The state rests," said McCoy.

Samuels faced Herlihy. "Call your first witness," she said.

"Your Honor," interrupted Wise.

"Yes?"

"At this time I feel obligated to move that the court immediately dismiss all charges against my client."

"On what grounds?" snapped McCoy, shooting to his feet.

"I believe we'll hear this out of the presence of the jury," said Judge Samuels. "Ladies and gentlemen, we're going to adjourn for the day and reconvene in the morning. Have a good evening and relax with your families. I remind you not to discuss the case among yourselves, or with anyone else."

T he judge sat back in her leather chair and sucked greedily on a can of Coca-Cola, one she obviously had in mind when adjourning the jury. Southerlyn, McCoy, Wise, and Herlihy all filed in.

"What's this?" said McCoy to Wise. McCoy was grinning, as if Wise's motion were simply another patented Joel Wise maneuver.

"You haven't got a case," he said.

"Not against my people, either," said Herlihy.

"Are you guys on a Twinkie overdose?" said Southerlyn.

"No," said McCoy, "the McDonalds were editing on Twinkies."

"That would be a defense," said Wise, "but my client doesn't need one because you haven't proven your case against him."

Judge Samuels suppressed a burp from drinking too quickly. "Let's hear it," she said.

"It's as simple as People versus Foster," said Wise. "Mr. Rosserman is charged with grand larceny in the second degree. You're guilty of larceny when you steal property."

"Bingo," said McCoy. "'Stealing property' is defined

as wrongfully taking property from the owner. All
three of the defendants wrongfully obtained money
from the victims through false pretense and false
promise."

"What pretense?" said Herlihy. "They promised to
edit their clients' manuscripts and that's what they
did."

"Doodling on a person's book," said Southerlyn,
"isn't editing."

"We've presented plenty of evidence to that effect,"
said McCoy.

"May I speak?" said Wise. "Even if that is true,
which I'll leave for you and Mr. Herlihy to hash out,
how does that apply to Mr. Rosserman? He had
nothing to do with the editing."

"He snagged the victims!" said McCoy.

"He referred people. He did not require them to go
there."

"He gave Redux the gold seal of approval," said
Southerlyn.

"But he gave no assurance on the quality of the
work. He promised these people nothing."

"Let's not forget he was well rewarded for that!"
said McCoy. "He knew what the McDonalds were
doing and he knew that the money he was receiving
was ill-gotten gains."

"You haven't proven that Bob Rosserman knew."

"Oh, come on!" said Southerlyn.

"Calm down," said the judge.

"If he didn't know," said Wise, "he doesn't have
intent."

"I can't believe this," said McCoy. "He knew exactly
what he was doing."

"Whether he knew or not is irrelevant if you haven't

proved intent," said Wise. "That's the state's burden, eh?"

"He wrote the letters, Joel," McCoy said. "He knew he got paid even when the manuscript was hopeless. He intended to get paid, or why would he have written the letters?"

"But you haven't established that Bob had anything other than an honorable intention when referring writers to Redux. Getting paid isn't proof of intent."

"Your Honor," said Herlihy, "that's true of my clients as well. The state hasn't proved the intent to steal. My clients delivered exactly what they promised no more, it's true. But certainly no less."

"One defendant at a time," said Samuels. She crushed the cola can in her grip like a trucker in a highway bar, then dropped it in her wastebasket. Wise caught Southerlyn's eye and smiled slightly, a kind of "how 'bout that!" look.

"My God!" said McCoy. "How many referrals did Rosserman make? I suppose he thought all of these people had potentially publishable books?"

"If they were edited properly, why not?" said Wise. "He had no real way of knowing what the McDonalds were doing."

"He saw the results," said Southerlyn. "He saw Barbara Chesko's novel three times!"

"And he cashed the check three times," said McCoy. "Twenty-seven hundred dollars' worth and some change."

"Of course he cashed his checks," said Wise, but it wasn't illegal to do that, and that's why, Your Honor, I'm moving for a dismissal."

"Wait a second," said Judge Samuels, "who is Barbara Chesko? Has she been mentioned at all in this trial?"

"Mr. Rosserman referred her to the McDonalds. They took money from her three times while he was having an affair with her. She killed herself over all this," said McCoy.

"None of that's in evidence, and you did rest, didn't you?"

"We felt there was sufficient evidence from living witnesses."

"Be that as it may," said Wise, "not a bit of the evidence proves that my client knew the details of what the McDonalds were doing," said Wise. "As far as he knew he was only receiving finder's fees."

"The point is," said McCoy, "that the defendant embarked on a course of action in which it is logical to assume he was aware of the deception. If you regularly drive people in ski masks to convenience stores, you can't claim you don't know what your colleagues are doing. He made a considerable effort to refer clients to the McDonalds. He can't plead ignorance to that."

Samuels smacked her sternum with her fist, still bothered by the carbonation. "Mr. Wise, I didn't give you your pretrial motion for a summary judgment to dismiss, and I'm not going to do it now. I'm going to make you put on your defense."

Wise tilted his head to the side with a wry smile. It had been worth a try.

"I'm not sure whether the state has fully demonstrated Mr. Rosserman's guilty knowledge, but that's a question of fact I'll let the jury decide. It seems to me that he had more than a toe in the water, but if you want to defend him on that basis, go ahead with it. Or any other defense you can muster, including Twinkies, but I'm not going to close the case for you. Not yet."

"Thank you, Your Honor," said McCoy.

"And that's a ditto for your argument, Mr. Herlihy. Mr. Wise may have had some grounds, but the McDonalds?" She twisted her mouth.

"They did exactly what they promised," said Herlihy.

"That's a fact for the jury," said the judge. "Now let's get out of here and reconvene in the morning."

They all thanked her on leaving, but in the outer office Wise pulled McCoy aside. "Can I speak to you for a moment?" Herlihy paused in front of them, squinting with suspicion.

"Nothing personal," said Wise to Herlihy. "Doing the best for my client."

Herlihy said nothing, but plainly wasn't happy. He spun and went out through the outer doors.

Wise leaned toward the judge's administrative assistant, who was getting ready to leave. "Might we use that conference room there for a moment?"

Wise closed the door behind them. "Jack," he said, "Serena, I'm going to make it easy. What would it take to get you to drop these silly charges and let Bob get on with his shattered life?"

"He could admit he pushed Barbara Chesko out of the window," said Southerlyn.

"That would be jumping from a very cold frying pan into a very hot fire," laughed Wise. "He didn't do that and you know it. I'm not offering a plea bargain."

"Then what are we in here for?" asked McCoy.

"Mr. Rosserman was part of the inner circle, eh?

You could use his testimony against the McDonalds.
Let's suppose he could tell you all of their dirty
secrets."

"A coconspirator?" said Southerlyn. "You just told
the judge he knew nothing."

"I just told the judge that you haven't proven your
case. That's different."

"As an accomplice, Rosserman's testimony is no
good without corroboration."

"I'm sure most of what he has told me can be cor-
roborated in various ways, except for maybe the
things Mr. McDonald said."

"What did McDonald say?"

"Maybe he made a few remarks about his clients.
Bob's not a bad guy. He was just trying to enhance
his very small salary. You're treating him like a crack
dealer, for pity's sake."

"Without him, the McDonalds wouldn't have had
any fish to fry," said Southerlyn.

McCoy shook his head. "You're talking about a guy
we suspect was instrumental in a woman's suicide—and you want us to give him a complete pass."

"Aw, come on, Jack, he wouldn't intentionally hurt
a flea. He's wetting himself that he'll never get to be
an editor again. He's just a schmuck who sold a few
names. He's no worse than most credit card companies."

"That's a pretty bad comparison," said McCoy.

"Maybe so," said Wise, "but you get my point. How
about it? Drop everything: larceny, obstruction, any
screwy stuff on Mrs. Chesko. You're not going to
convict him anyhow. This way you can get more on
the McDonalds."

"And they'll just get on the stand and blame him

for the false promises," said Southerlyn. "We can't take this deal. It's indecent."

"Okay, okay," said Wise. "How about a petit larceny plea? That's pretty generous on my part."

"A misdemeanor?"

"He's going to walk out of here," said Wise. "You'll get something if he testifies against the McDonalds."

"Not enough," said McCoy. "We've got to get back to court, Joel."

Wise spread his hands. "If you change your mind…"

McCoy grabbed Southerlyn's arm as she turned to leave. He waited until he was sure Wise was out of hearing. "What's gotten into you? If I'm in the room, you don't turn down or accept any offers, whether you think they're indecent or not."

"Even if he didn't push her, he used her."

"Using is the national pastime," said McCoy.

"You'd let him take a walk?"

"No," said McCoy, releasing his grip. "What do you think I'm doing here? But this case is hanging by a thread. Rosserman's testimony might have tipped the scales our way."

"I'm sorry," said Southerlyn grimly.

McCoy took a deep breath. "No, I'm sorry. When Wise smirks, it gets to me. He looks like a cat and I feel like a canary. I think the judge almost granted his motion."

SUPREME COURT
100 CENTRE STREET
WEDNESDAY, NOVEMBER 20, 9:32 A.M.

Herlihy's first witness, Gregory Arseneaux, was an elderly man, with shock-white hair, a cultivated tan, and a hawk nose as narrow as a Bronze Age cutting tool. His jacket was green velvet and his red silk ascot was secured by a jade stickpin.

Southerlyn leaned to whisper in McCoy's ear. "Frank Lloyd Wright meets Quentin Crisp."

"The ultimate artiste," McCoy whispered. When the man took the oath, his voice had the gravel you usually associate with television gangsters.

"Mr. Arseneaux, you are a resident of Sag Harbor on Long Island?" asked Herlihy.

"Yes, sir. Fifty years, in fact."

"And how did you come to be acquainted with Avery and Monica McDonald?"

"Certainly. When I retired in 1990, I determined to live out my dream of writing. I had been in various commercial enterprises since graduating from Cornell. I have traded in wine, electronics, and pheromone-based colognes from Scandinavia."

"So you were, loosely, in import/export?"

"Often. I made most of a very hefty income on African art."

241

"You seem to have been a versatile businessman."

"Quick as a cat," he said. "Otherwise, you're the mouse."

Herlihy glanced at the judge, sensing she might be losing patience. "And so, you intended to live out your dream of writing?"

"Yes." Arseneaux raised his chin as if to show off his profile. "I had many extraordinary events in my life and I wished to record them before moving on to the next incarnation."

"And you began to write?"

"Yes, but my wife shortly thereafter developed a debilitating disease and required a great amount of time. We had been married in 1980, third for me, second for her, and I was devoted to her. It was crushing to suffer through her illness. She accepted her fate much better than I, which was, perhaps, selfish, but I could not help myself."

"With all due respect, Your Honor," said McCoy, "what is the question?"

"Get to the point," said Judge Samuels.

"Yes, Your Honor," said Herlihy. "So, Mr. Arseneaux, you came to know the McDonalds after your wife died?"

"Virtually her dying words were that I should write and let no obstacle..." Arseneaux choked up.

"Do you need to compose yourself?" asked the judge.

"I'll soldier on," said Arseneaux.

Southerlyn shoved a note to McCoy. "Oh brother," it said.

"I decided, as an homage to Rosalie, that I would write about her final days, about the wisdom that grew in her as she drifted inexorably toward death.

It was a labor of love and yet, it was to be a monument to her as well."

"And the McDonalds?" Herlihy encouraged.

"I completed a first draft in late 1997. I had no idea how to get a book published, so I went to the Long Island Community College and talked with an instructor there. He was barely polite, but he referred me to several books about how to submit a manuscript to a literary agent or to a publisher."

"And one of them referred you to Redux?"

"No, I was getting quite discouraged, but one of the books said one needed dogged determination, so I continued the quest. In the end I had made about forty attempts. It was then I saw an advertisement for the Conshochoken Press in the back of *The Compleat Writer*, a magazine I subscribe to."

"And you sent your manuscript?"

"Yes. The advertisement said that Conshochoken was a small press that intended to expand and was looking for new authors. But when my manuscript arrived, the editor, Marie Du Tour, suggested the editing services of Redux. A week later, the McDonalds wrote to me themselves, and I called them."

"And what was the result of that telephone call?"

Arseneaux raised his chin again. "I was extremely encouraged. Mrs. McDonald seemed to read my mind. I believe she actually wept when we discussed Rosalie."

Monica smiled at Arseneaux and gave a slight nod.

"And you contracted Redux to edit your manuscript?" continued Herlihy.

"Yes," said Arseneaux. "I felt they were good people."

"And when Redux had completed work on your manuscript you were satisfied with the results?"

"Ultimately, I was extremely satisfied, but not at first."

"And why was that?"

"My manuscript was terrible! I could barely read what I had written because of the going over it received."

"It received a thorough going over?"

"Very. Every page was filled with extensive comments."

"And they were helpful comments?"

"In the end, yes."

"Why do you say, 'in the end'?"

"Initially, I was very confused. I have no real experience with editing. I couldn't understand what was being said to me."

"So how, then, did it become helpful?"

"Well, I called Avery and he refused to coddle me. He said I should go back through and read the comments carefully and think about them. Only then, he said, would I really grasp it. Then he hung up. The conversation was shorter than ten minutes."

Herlihy strolled by the jury box. "This was helpful?"

Arseneaux stretched his long fingers over his chest. "A book comes from in here. You have to find the truth within."

"Could you explain that, Mr. Arseneaux?"

"It forced me to look at my manuscript with new eyes, to really face the challenges of my material. I began to see what they were getting at. It took me another two years to complete my revision. It was the hardest work I've ever done, but the result is this." Arseneaux pulled a paperback out of his pocket.

Herlihy held it up for Judge Samuels, carried it past the jury, and then dropped it on the desk between McCoy and Southerlyn. It was an oversized trade paperback, about six by nine. The cover was a color snapshot of an older woman bent over, snipping chrysanthemums for a bouquet. White script letters arched over her. *"Rosalie's Sweet Sorrow"* they said.

"Mr. Arseneaux," said Herlihy, "to what extent is this publication the result of your contact with Redux Incorporated?"

"It is entirely the result. I owe them everything."

"And by that you mean that their editing services made this book, your dream, come true?"

"Entirely."

"Would you consult them in the future?"

"Of course."

"Would you recommend their services to other writers?"

"Absolutely," said Arseneaux, "but with a strong proviso."

"And that would be?"

"That one has to be willing to respond to the challenge. If one is not willing to exert the effort to fully digest what is offered, one cannot expect good results. Their job is not to write the book, it is to force one to become an author. If one is not willing to make that effort, one shouldn't write at all."

"Thank you, Mr. Arseneaux," said Herlihy. "No further questions."

"Mr. Wise?" said Judge Samuels.

"Yes, Your Honor," said Wise. "Mr. Arseneaux, do you know the defendant, Mr. Robert Rosserman?"

"No, I do not."

"Have you ever heard him mentioned by either Avery or Monica McDonald?"

"No."

"Thank you, Mr. Arseneaux," said Wise. "And, oh, congratulations on your book."

"Thank you," said Arseneaux.

"Mr. McCoy?" asked Judge Samuels.

McCoy stood, riffed through Arseneaux's book, then tossed it on the table. "Perhaps you could clarify for me, Mr. Arseneaux, what you are saying. That is, some of the remarks you made. You're saying that Redux puts difficult and confusing marks all over your manuscript and that forces you to rewrite it properly?"

"No. I am saying that the full power of their editorial marks does not come through until the writer confronts them."

"And you couldn't do this without hiring the McDonalds?"

"They are the experts. They are guides who can point one in the proper direction. They cannot make the journey for you."

"I see," said McCoy. "And how much did their guidance cost?"

"It was worth every penny."

"How many pennies, Mr. Arseneaux?"

"Five thousand dollars."

"That much? How long is your book, Mr. Arseneaux? Three hundred pages?"

"Not quite."

McCoy picked up the book and looked at the last page. "Two fifty-two. That's almost twenty dollars a page!"

"It was worth every penny."

"Do you know whether Avery or Monica McDonald edited the manuscript for you, or someone else?"

"Both of them were involved. Monica told me she was very touched by it."

"So you don't know if, perhaps, a student looking for extra money might have knocked off the book in a couple of hours?"

"Objection," said Herlihy.

"So you don't really know who went through the physical process of editing it?" said McCoy.

"Well, it wasn't knocked off in a couple of hours, whoever did it. And in any case it was Redux I contracted. How they go about it is of no concern, as long as they do a good job."

"So you believe they did a good job by you?"

"I have just said so."

McCoy returned to the prosecutor's table and picked up Arseneaux's book. As he walked toward the witness, he flipped the pages. "So, then, after you had your book edited by Redux, you resubmitted it to Marie Du Tour at Conshochoken Press?"

"Yes."

"And they published it?"

"No."

"Why not?"

"It seems they had gone out of business. There was no listing for them, and the mail was returned. Small presses have a difficult time these days against the giant conglomerates."

McCoy turned his back to the witness and faced the jury, pacing casually. "Would it surprise you to know, Mr. Arseneaux, that the telephone company has told us that Conshochoken Press *never* had a listing in Concord, New Hampshire?"

"Well, they were certainly there. She wrote to me."

"Did you ever go there, personally?"

"Of course not. But the editor wrote to me."

"Marie Du Tour?"

"Yes."

"Would it surprise you to learn that the telephone company in Concord has never had a listing for a Marie Du Tour?"

Arseneaux shrugged. "What of it?"

"Would it surprise you to know that neither the Concord city directory, nor the municipal tax authority, nor the property tax records has ever listed a Marie Du Tour?"

Arseneaux blinked, then smiled. "Pseudonyms are hardly unusual in publishing, Mr. McCoy, and I'm sure you are aware that women are often listed under their husband's names."

Avery McDonald nodded, pleased by Arseneaux's response.

"Would it surprise you to know that the New Hampshire Department of Revenue Administration has no record of a Conshochoken Press ever paying business taxes in the state?"

"Perhaps they had yet to make a profit."

"Did it ever occur to you that the address to which you were writing was a mail drop? Mail was received and held for pickup?"

"That's hardly unusual. Many businesses do that."

"In fact, Redux does that, doesn't it? They use a Princeton, New Jersey, mailing address when the McDonalds actually work out of their home in Peekskill."

"Yes, they do that. I don't see why not."

"But the Concord Chamber of Commerce, the

Concord Better Business Bureau, the tax office—no one seems to have heard of Conshochoken Press, nor its editor Marie Du Tour. How do you explain that?"

"I have no knowledge of that."

"Would it surprise you, Mr. Arseneaux, to learn that none of the booksellers, not Amazon.com nor Borders nor Barnes and Noble nor Ingram, the book wholesaler, can offer you a single book published by any company called the Conshochoken Press?"

"Well, the big publishers sometimes squeeze out small presses. I only know she was very encouraging."

"Oh, yes, very encouraging," said McCoy. "This imaginary person encouraged you to seek editing by Redux, didn't she?"

"Objection," said Herlihy. "'Imaginary' person?"

"Well, where is she then?" asked McCoy.

"Simply because she can't be located doesn't mean she's imaginary," said Herlihy.

"Are you prepared to bring in a witness to verify the existence of Marie Du Tour?" McCoy asked Herlihy.

"She wrote to me," interrupted Arseneaux.

"Only speak when you're asked a question," said Judge Samuels. "The jury should disregard 'imaginary.'"

"Can I say 'fictional' person? 'Alleged' person?" said McCoy. "Marie Du Tour is no more real than Aunt Jemima."

"You haven't proven that," said Herlihy.

"Produce her!" said McCoy.

"Let's move on," said Samuels.

McCoy hoped his point had registered with the jury. McCoy read from a copy. "'In case you are uncertain what professional editors might be reliable, I might mention my good friends Avery and Monica McDonald at Redux Incorporated.' Is that what the letter signed 'Marie Du Tour' said?"

"It didn't say I had to use them. It was just a suggestion."

"Did it ever occur to you that Conshochoken Press might be a front?"

Arseneaux didn't answer.

"No? Didn't it occur to you that maybe it was something created to draw in clients for Redux?"

"No. But what if it was?" said Arseneaux. "Marie Du Tour never promised to publish my book. And in any case, everything worked out perfectly. My book is published, isn't it? I owe that all to Avery and Monica."

McCoy looked down at the book. "Mr. Arseneaux, what does the term 'print on demand' mean?"

"It's the latest thing," said Arseneaux. "With the new computer technology it is possible to print only the number of books which are ordered. Books don't have to be warehoused. There is only a setup cost, not the full expense of a print run."

"And then, when people want copies, they're run off like so many Xeroxes?"

"They're not photocopies. You can see that from my book."

"And this publisher, Book Meisters, who accepted your book, the book edited by the McDonalds, how much did you pay them?"

"For the setup fee? Two hundred dollars."

"Anything more?"

"A three hundred and twenty dollar cover design fee, and then there were some minor charges for getting an ISBN number and registering the copyright and like that. All together I paid Book Meisters under one thousand dollars."

"In other words, you *paid* Book Meisters to publish you?"

"You're trying to make it sound like vanity publishing. It's not like that. I'm investing in my own book."

"They didn't pay you?"

"Why should I let some monster conglomerate skim off all the proceeds? I receive eighty percent royalties. No one gives you royalties like that. Those big companies are a monopoly, stuck on an outdated business model."

"Is your book available in bookstores, Mr. Arseneaux?"

"It's available on the Internet."

"So I can't walk into, say, Barnes and Noble and get one off the shelf?"

"The big companies keep the little ones out. The Internet is the future. Bookstores are the old way."

"So, *if* someone knows about your book, and *if* they know where to look on the Internet, they can buy it?"

"Asked and answered," said Herlihy.

"Withdrawn." McCoy tossed the book on the prosecution table. "I'm very glad," he said, "that the McDonalds did well by you."

Herlihy produced two more satisfied clients, one Andy Marszak and one Astara Kundoo. Marszak had written a novel, *Night Fare*, about cabdrivers. He said he was very happy with the work the McDonalds had done and was looking forward to the book's being published. He had no publisher yet, but he emphasized with great optimism some publishers had shown interest.

Southerlyn took over for the questioning of Astara Kundoo, a slender Nigerian woman who had written a book based on African home remedies. It told how, in her words, "to grow herbs to make the potions that would cure the cold, break the fevers, put the romance back in the marriage where romance has gone, and to enlarge mightily the virility of the middle-aged man." These were all remedies she had learned from granmama, she said, and they worked better than "the pills."

She had paid the McDonalds some $7,000, but this included a layout for self-publishing. Afterward she had gone to what Southerlyn pointed out was a "vanity publisher" who would publish whatever the customers were willing to pay for. Miss Kundoo countered that several vanity press books had been picked up by the larger presses to become best-sellers, like *The Bridges of Madison County* and *The Celestine Prophecy*.

Southerlyn asked her where she had heard about that and she said from Monica McDonald. Miss Kundoo then claimed to have sold nearly two thousand copies by mail and was hoping Rodale or one of the other health presses would pick up her book. She was also writing a follow-up book of African recipes, which she intended to have the McDonalds edit and lay out for her again. They would get $10,000 this time, and an endorsement on the book jacket.

After each of these witnesses, Joel Wise would ask if they knew Robert Rosserman. Rosserman had rejected Marszak's book and, yes, he had gotten a letter from Redux shortly after. Astara Kundoo had submitted her book to so many places, she didn't remember whether she had sent it to Kirstner and Strawn, and she always threw away rejection letters to "get the negativity behind, you know." In any case, she had contacted Redux because of a classified ad in the back of one of the writers' magazines.

After Judge Samuels dismissed Miss Kundoo, Herlihy stood with a loose-leaf notebook. "Your Honor, to save the court's time," he said, "I would like to introduce into evidence a collection of letters by satisfied customers of Avery and Monica McDonald. There are twenty-three."

"Objection," said McCoy. "The court has no way to verify these letters, and they amount to presenting twenty-three witnesses which the state has no ability to cross-examine. They could be as imaginary as Marie Du Tour."

"If Mr. McCoy will stipulate to the contents of these letters, it won't be necessary to question each of the writers."

"That's the defense's choice. The people have no way of knowing whether these people are legitimate or not without cross-examination."

"Sidebar," snapped the judge. Herlihy brought the notebook with him. Wise moved up behind McCoy and placed his hands on McCoy's and Herlihy's shoulders. Judge Samuels hunched down.

"What is this, Mr. Herlihy? Blackmail?" she said.

"It's important for the jury to know that there are many people who have been happy with the work Redux has done."

"Your Honor," said McCoy, "given the McDonalds' penchant for fabricating editors who write letters for phantom publishers, might we not assume they would fabricate happy customers?"

"Can you verify the identity of the writers of these letters?" asked Samuels.

"My clients assure me that all of them are willing and ready to testify here in court."

"I'm calling this bluff," said McCoy. "For every so-called 'satisfied' customer who is delighted to have been cheated, I can produce two who aren't happy at all."

"Look," said Samuels, "you're not dealing with Judge Ito here. I'm not about to drag this trial out for either of you. Or Mr. Wise, either."

"You'll get no argument from me," said Wise.

"If I can't cross-examine these letter writers," said McCoy, "it's clearly not best evidence."

"What are we going to do here, people?" said the judge.

"I would be satisfied," said Herlihy, "if the state would be willing to stipulate that Redux has many satisfied customers."

"I won't stipulate to that!" said McCoy. "It's misleading. The only customers who could be happy about getting robbed are delusional. How can we know these letters are for real? Are the McDonalds going to take the oath and swear that they are real?"

"It's up to the defendant to decide whether to testify, Your Honor. Mr. McCoy can't coerce Avery and Monica to testify if they don't want to."

"I know the Constitution, Mr. Herlihy," said Samuels sourly, "but Mr. McCoy has a point. I'm not entirely convinced your clients wouldn't concoct these letters."

"Well, then I have no choice but to call the witnesses," said Herlihy.

"Your Honor," begged McCoy. "It isn't necessary to make the same point over and over again. We say they did a lousy job; they say they didn't. Hasn't there been enough evidence in this respect to let the jury decide?"

The judge thought.

"How about this?" said McCoy, "I am willing to stipulate that the McDonalds are capable of producing many letters which allege that they did a good job. I am not willing, however, to stipulate that the writers of those letters are genuine without a complete investigation."

"That's good enough," said Samuels. "Step back."

"But the point *is* their genuineness," said Herlihy.

"Yes, but he doesn't have to agree with you. Since their provenance has not been established, I can't admit them at all."

"Then I must establish their provenance."

"It isn't necessary to produce the writers of the letters to do that," said the judge, "since the contents, we can assume, say about the same thing."

"You are coercing my clients to appear on the stand."

"Well, if you want the letters…Now step back."

"Might I have a recess to discuss this with my clients?"

The judge looked at her watch. "It's three. I'm for calling it a day."

"You'll get no objection on that from me," said McCoy.

Late that afternoon, Herlihy's office notified the court and the D.A.'s office that they had removed one of their witnesses from their list. McCoy was disappointed; the witness was a suppurating ball of suet who was going to end up mincemeat. After they had checked his background, neither McCoy nor Southerlyn could imagine what Herlihy had thought in listing him as a witness. The purpose must have been to have him attest as a trade professional to the high quality of the McDonalds' work. Herlihy could only have gotten the name from his clients, and perhaps had finally found out the full story.

The witness was named Marlon Friendly. He posed as a literary agent, and sometime in the past had managed to sell some writers' books to publishers for the usual fifteen percent. But since the early 1990s, he made most of his money charging "reading fees" to aspiring authors. He advertised in the back of most writer's magazines, pointing out of the ad like Uncle Sam on the old recruitment poster. "DO YOU HAVE WHAT IT TAKES TO MAKE BOTH OF US RICH?" his ad trumpeted. In small print it explained his fee schedule: $500 to read and comment on a novel, $200 for a short story or children's book, and so on, all refundable if he decided to represent the work to a publisher. Since 1999, not only had he been getting a fee for reading manuscripts, he was also referring these would-be writers to Redux. He might have been getting richer, but his victims certainly weren't.

He had moved the Friendly Agency to Tyler, Texas, from New York City, and was afterward sued by a couple of writers for absconding with their royalties. After a long court proceeding, which he was about to lose, he relocated to New Orleans, Louisiana, and though the judgment against him was still in place and unpaid he seemed to be operating in New Orleans much as he had elsewhere. He would have been a fine witness to testify to Redux's honesty, but he had disappeared, leaving a forwarding address in Belize.

Herlihy's office further notified the court that the defense would rest without calling Avery or Monica McDonald. Joel Wise had listed only Bob Rosserman as a witness, but told Southerlyn after court adjourned that he would not be calling him.

Southerlyn and McCoy discussed the closing statement until about 6:00 P.M., early for a change, then left feeling the odd discomfort of a free night.

The judge nodded in McCoy's direction. "Ready, Mr. McCoy?" Southerlyn had written a note and shoved it toward him.

"Yes, Your Honor," said McCoy. He glanced down at Southerlyn's elegant handwriting. It said, "Do good."

Without expression, he shoved it back to her and rounded the table.

"Ladies and gentlemen of the jury, you have spent many hours listening to the evidence, so much evidence in fact that the essential facts of the case might easily become obscured. You have heard testimony regarding the role of editors and so-called 'book doctors' in the publishing trade. In many ways, New York City is the publishing capital of the world and freelance editing is an important element of that industry. There are many, many honest freelance editors and 'book doctors.' Many.

"The defense, however, would have you confuse the work of those freelance editors with the fraud perpetrated by the McDonalds and supported by their accomplice, Mr. Rosserman. What the McDonalds do is not about improving manuscripts. It is about money. When Mr. Rosserman passes along his list of potential victims, he is not intending to help beginning authors, he is intending to fatten the McDonalds' banking account and his own.

"They don't care about their victims' feelings. They don't care about their victims' dreams of literary success. They hint around, using Mr. Rosserman's name and phony small presses, that all anyone needs is their professional touch. If they edit your manuscript, you can be a bestseller.

"The defense tells you that they didn't promise anything. Do you really believe that? Do you think they could have drawn in over two million dollars in seven years by saying, 'You pay us a minimum of three thousand or up to ten thousand dollars and we'll edit your book and then you can take your chances'? Who would go for that? Would a reasonable person do that? The New York Lottery offers the chance to win millions of dollars, but a ticket in that only costs a buck. How many people would buy those tickets if they were three to ten thousand dollars apiece. You might find a few. But two million dollars' worth? At three thousand a pop, that's well over a hundred manuscripts a year. *Well* over.

"One book edited every three or four days. I don't know about you, but I'd have trouble just reading a different book every three days."

He smiled and strolled along the front of the jury box. "The defense would have you believe that the meaningless scrawls on the manuscripts were valuable editorial comments. Most of the victims who received them do not. The world-renowned author Martin Post doesn't think so. You heard even a former employee of the McDonalds admit that she was encouraged to work at such a rate that she knew that what she had written on the manuscripts was meaningless. Are there any published books that have come out of the Redux editing process? Self-published books. The authors of those books not only paid the McDonalds, they then paid a printer. Self-publishing companies are in the business of printing anything that you're willing to pay for. It's sad."

McCoy pointed at Rosserman. "Has Mr. Rosserman, when he held his position at Kirstner and Strawn, ever published a single work he recommended to the McDonalds? Has he ever used the McDonalds as freelance editors? Don't you think that would be the first defense he would offer? But, if you listen, what do you hear? Question after question by his attorney pushes the view that Mr. Rosserman hardly knew them. He didn't know what they were doing.

"Yet, Mr. Rosserman lost his job at Kirstner and Strawn exactly because he was involved with the McDonalds. He kept it a secret around the office that he was making referrals to Redux. Does this sound like he didn't know what he was involved in? Do you think it is possible that none of the victims he referred to the McDonalds informed him about being deceived by them?"

Wise and Herlihy became as alert as cats. Every time there was the possibility of an explicit reference to Barbara Chesko's death, they braced to leap on it as grounds for a mistrial. But the only time her name had appeared in the trial was on a long list of client victims and their payments.

"This case isn't about dissatisfied customers. It isn't about a matter of taste. It's not about a retired person who isn't happy with what happened to his memoirs.

It's about a deliberate scheme. It's an elaborate pattern of misleading statements and implied promises which have only one purpose—to separate people from their money. Avery McDonald knew what he was doing. Monica McDonald knew what she was doing. And Robert Rosserman knew what he was doing. If you look at the whole picture, you'll see larceny and in amounts well beyond the minimums for grand larceny. They conspired together, then robbed people as surely as if they had used guns and masks. There is no reasonable doubt. Tell them they can't get away with it. Given all the evidence, you must find these defendants guilty."

McCoy let his words sink in, then returned to the prosecution table.

"Mr. Herlihy?" said Judge Samuels.

"Thank you, Your Honor." Herlihy strolled up to the jury box, spread his hands, and smiled. He stood like that for several seconds until his silence had drawn every juror's attention.

"Why are we here?" he said. "Where's the crime? Somewhere in this city people have committed grand larceny. Maybe even at this very moment someone is robbing a bank, or stealing electronics off the back of a truck. Sticking a gun in an innocent woman's face and saying, 'Empty the cash register.'

"My clients, Avery and Monica McDonald, perform a service. People turn over to them their unpolished, and often quite crude, manuscripts and ask them to make them sophisticated. The McDonalds do as all good editors do. They read the manuscript, make an assessment of what the author is trying to do and make suggestions. They don't rewrite the manuscript. Creativity is an individual thing. It is precious. It is unique in every person. In this way, the McDonalds are akin to spiritual advisors. They are trying to help a writer find his, or her, *own* truth.

"You have heard several witnesses attest to the fact that the McDonalds did very good work as far as they are concerned. We could have produced many more such witnesses. The state gave us a number of witnesses who, on the other hand, were not satisfied with the McDonalds' work. Isn't this to be expected in something as individual and creative as the art of writing? We can only speculate on the reasons why a client of the McDonalds might have been unhappy, but surely if they had followed the McDonalds' guidance and their books had been published as a result, would they be complaining about the editing they received?

"Avery and Monica McDonald would like every manuscript they consult on to become a book. They are *professionals*. They do everything they can to make it possible for this to happen. But the competition is tough. Not every book can be published. You can certainly imagine how disappointing this might be, but that's not the point. The point is simple: How is this their fault?

"Yes, the McDonalds are paid for their work. Aren't professionals usually paid for their work? Does the state imagine that this exacting and difficult work should be done for free? No reasonable person would think so. And I'm certain you don't think so, ladies and gentlemen.

"Now, the state took great pains to introduce tax records of the proceeds of Redux Incorporated. And, yes, Avery and Monica made a lot of money doing this. As Mr. McCoy pointed out, Redux has had gross receipts in excess of two million dollars over a seven-year period. They have averaged about three hundred thousand a year. Yes, it sounds like a lot. But compared to what other professionals make, it isn't all that much. They have very special skills. They heal sick books. They don't get nearly as much as the average surgeon. They can't touch what many stockbrokers make, even though they work just as hard. Harder!"

Herlihy turned toward McCoy and Southerlyn. "But when did it suddenly become a crime to earn a living doing what you do best? If we don't like the route a cabdriver takes, do we charge him with larceny? If we decide the pair of shoes we bought doesn't match our clothes, can we charge Florsheim with larceny?

"Earlier in this trial, I read to you the standard contract which Avery and Monica McDonald require each of their clients to sign. This is not one of those contracts with fine print, written in obscure legalese. My clients insisted that the contract be written in plain, easy-to-understand English."

Herlihy slipped on a narrow lensed pair of reading glasses. "This is what it says, you'll remember:

THE FACT THAT WE HAVE ACCEPTED YOUR MANUSCRIPT FOR EDITORIAL REVISION IN NO WAY IMPLIES THAT WE OR ANY EMPLOYEE OF REDUX INCORPORATED IS GUARANTEEING SUBSEQUENT PUBLICATION OR REPRESENTATION BY ANY LITERARY AGENCY. THIS IS STRICTLY A CONTRACT FOR EDITING SERVICES WITH NO OTHER WARRANTIES EXPRESSED OR IMPLIED.

"Let's take another simple example and compare it. Suppose you had a French poodle. Let's say a pedigreed poodle. It's a happy dog and you've enjoyed having it around, but you think maybe you'd like to enter it in a dog show. Well, maybe it needs a little training in how to walk and to hold its head and its tail up. Maybe it needs its coat trimmed and to have its nails clipped. Wouldn't it be better to hire professionals to do this for you?"

The McDonalds looked at each other and nodded almost simultaneously. Maybe they'd high-five each other at the end of Herlihy's remarks, thought McCoy.

"And those professionals could do a great job. They could do the best job possible. The dog could learn to do everything right. It could look truly beautiful. But neither the trainer nor the groomer could guarantee that your dog would win a kennel show. They couldn't guarantee that the kennel club wouldn't, for some reason, decide they no longer wanted poodles in their competition, thus making your dog ineligible to compete.

"After all that time and effort, you'd be angry. You'd be stuck. But could you then turn around and have the trainer and the groomer arrested for stealing your money? Of course not. They did exactly what you contracted them to do. They did it well, and they fulfilled their end of the deal. They cannot promise what they have no control over. Avery and Monica McDonald cannot control what publishers do. Mr. Rosserman has been an editor at an important publisher for many years. But not even he can guarantee that the books he wants published can be published. He has to go through his editorial board and the marketing department and so on. If Mr. Rosserman, as a respected employee of Kirstner and Strawn, cannot promise publication…"

McCoy shot to his feet. "Mr. Rosserman is not a respected employee of Kirstner and Strawn!"

"Mr. McCoy!" The judge reached for her gavel.

"No," said Herlihy, "I'm sorry. I apologize to the jury. Mr. Rosserman is indeed no longer an employee of Kirstner and Strawn. These absurd charges caused his immediate termination after many years of loyal service. I appreciate Mr. McCoy's correcting my slip of the tongue."

McCoy sat. Southerlyn crossed her arms and narrowed her eyes, as if she thought they might have been suckered.

"*When*," Herlihy continued, "when Mr. Rosserman was a senior editor, he could not absolutely promise publication. How can we expect the McDonalds to do so? And that is exactly what is written in the Redux contract. Nothing is misrepresented.

"Ladies and gentlemen, I am astonished the district attorney's office let this case go forward. Grand larceny! It's absurd, and I know you'll do the right thing and vote not guilty on the charges. Thank you for your attention and your patience."

Herlihy gave the rail of the jury box a tiny tap with the tips of his fingers as he smiled and turned away. An Irish charmer, thought Southerlyn, while McCoy was the Irish firebrand.

"Mr. Wise?" said the judge.

"I'll be brief, Your Honor," Wise said, rising and buttoning his suit coat. He patted his worried client on the shoulder and pinched his upper lip as he approached the jury box.

"Good day, ladies and gentlemen of the jury. Like

Mr. Herlihy, I am even more astonished that charges have been proffered against my client. What has Mr. Rosserman done? Did he promise anyone that he would publish them?" Wise moved along the front of the jury box.

"No. And did he do any editing whatsoever on the manuscripts in question?" He turned back toward the jurors. "No.

"All Mr. Rosserman did was to provide the McDonalds with the names of people who might, and I emphasize *might*, want to use the services of Redux. If this is a crime then we might begin arresting all of those folks who mail you catalogs. If the McDonalds were doing anything illegal, and I think you'll agree that Mr. Herlihy has vigorously argued that they did not, then Mr. Rosserman was certainly not party to it. You look like good people. You'll do the right thing. Mr. Rosserman is innocent."

Southerlyn whispered in McCoy's ear. "That *was* brief."

"The cat who ate the canary," said McCoy.

Judge Samuels adjourned for lunch after the closing statements, reconvened at one-thirty, then began the formal, but legally essential charge to the jury. She read from her notes, sipping water as her mouth dried. The attorneys listened carefully for any slips. This was going to be a particularly long set of instructions and might be the basis for an appeal if anything was stated wrong. There wasn't much chance, since the state of New York standardized its jury instructions, but occasionally a judge left out a crucial word or phrase.

"Under our law," she explained, "a person is guilty of grand larceny in the third degree when such person steals property valued in excess of three thousand dollars. The term 'steals property' used in this definition has its own special meaning in our law. I will now give you the meaning of that term.

"A person (or persons, in this case) 'steals property' when, with the intent to deprive another of property or to appropriate the property to himself or herself, such person wrongfully takes property from the owner of the property.

"Some of the terms used in this definition have their own special meaning."

She cleared her throat.

"'Intent' means a conscious objective or purpose. Thus, a person acts with intent to deprive another of property or to appropriate property to himself or herself when such person's conscious objective or purpose is to withhold the property or cause it to be withheld permanently, or to dispose of the property either for the benefit of himself or herself or a third person.

"A person 'wrongfully takes property' from an owner when that person takes property without an owner's consent, and exercises dominion and control over that property for a period of time, however temporary. The term 'wrongfully take' encompasses as well larceny by trick, by false premise, or by false promise."

Judge Samuels then took a deep breath and explained for each of the five counts that in order to find each defendant guilty, the jury needed to determine beyond a reasonable doubt that on the date of the transaction between the victim and the defendants, in the county of New York, that each defendant wrongfully took money from its owner, and that each defendant did so with the intent to appropriate it to himself or herself.

She then went on to explain the charge of conspiracy in the fifth degree, defining conspiracy in legal terms and the fact that the defendants had to have conspired to do a D level felony, such as grand larceny in the third degree.

All the i's had been dotted and the t's had been crossed, thought McCoy, as the jury stood to file out. There was nothing she had missed that he had heard, but who knew? Defense attorneys like Joel Wise were masters of creativity in composing appeals.

Judge Samuels left the court and Southerlyn and McCoy gathered in their papers. "Well, it's in their hands now," he said to her.

"How do you think they looked?" Southerlyn asked.

"Like all juries," said McCoy. "Astonished at the tedium of the legal system. Bored out of their skulls."

SUPREME COURT
100 CENTRE STREET
WEDNESDAY, NOVEMBER 27

Four days had passed, and McCoy was worried. When Branch called to ask about the deliberations, or when Serena Southerlyn dropped in, he put on a brave face, but when the jury adjourned for the weekend with no decision, then reconvened for three more twelve-hour days into the next week, the D.A.s began to wonder what was going on in there. There was, it was true, a lot on the jury's platter: five counts of grand larceny in the third degree, as well as the conspiracy charges. They would have to decide if Avery McDonald was guilty on each of these, then Monica McDonald, then Rosserman. That was eighteen decisions. Sometimes a jury would just take it as a package and vote everyone guilty or not guilty on everything. Sometimes they'd work it like a swap meet. "I'll give you guilty on this one, if you'll give me not guilty on that one."

Finally, all parties to the case reassembled in the courtroom. Judge Samuels looked like she had a headache somewhere off the Richter scale. She sighed and looked back at the jury foreman, an elderly man with a barrel chest and glasses that made him look like he had whale eyes. "So, you're convinced there will be no meeting of the minds on these last counts? You could continue to meet after Thanksgiving."

"No, ma'am," he said. "There's a couple of stubborn ones. Won't listen to reason."

She raised her hands. "I don't need to know details. They're entitled to their assessment. It's sufficient to say you are deadlocked on these ten items." She held up several sheets of paper.

"Yes, ma'am."

"All right, then," she said. "Let's do the bookkeeping."

Southerlyn crossed her arms and stared angrily at the desktop as the verdict on each count was read. McCoy ticked off the results on a yellow legal pad. The pattern became clear very soon.

Regarding the victim Colonel Mark Aalborg:
    Defendant Avery McDonald, no decision.
    Defendant Monica McDonald, no decision.
    Defendant Robert Rosserman, not guilty.
Regarding the victim Julianna Meyer-Steers:
    Defendant Avery McDonald, no decision.
    Defendant Monica McDonald, no decision.
    Defendant Robert Rosserman, not guilty.
Regarding the victim Anthony Michaels:
    Defendant Avery McDonald, no decision.
    Defendant Monica McDonald, no decision.
    Defendant Robert Rosserman, not guilty.

And so on through the remaining two victims, William Schurman and Charlayne Wysocki.

McCoy's stomach had grown gradually more sour as the reading went on. Southerlyn continued to stare at the tabletop, dropping her head as the conspiracy charges were listed.

The jury had hung on Avery and Monica McDonald. They had acquitted Robert Rosserman.

It was a disaster.

"Very well, then," said the judge without looking up from her notepad. "You were at it for a week, so the court owes you its gratitude. The jury is dismissed."

She looked at the defense table. "Mr. Rosserman, because you have been declared not guilty on all counts, you are dismissed." Rosserman blinked, as if afraid he'd wake up. Joel Wise was showing off his big white dentures and pumping Rosserman's hand.

"Thank you, Your Honor," said Wise.

"In the cases against Avery McDonald and Monica McDonald," continued Samuels, "I am declaring a mistrial. You'll be notified if the state wishes to pursue the issue. Court is adjourned," she said, rapping her gavel.

Monica let out a whoop and flung herself on her husband. They spun in a tight circle, bumping against one of the chairs.

Herlihy drifted toward McCoy, offering his hand.

"Congratulations," said McCoy.

"I assume that's the end of it."

Southerlyn broke out of her numbness with a shudder that was noticeable enough to make McCoy turn. But she did not speak.

"We'll let you know," he said, still looking at Southerlyn.

"You'll be wasting the taxpayers' money," said Herlihy.

"Now don't throw down the gauntlet," said McCoy.

"No challenge," said Herlihy. "Just a suggestion."

Southerlyn looked past him at the McDonalds. Monica had grabbed Avery's head in her hands. She kissed him sloppily.

"Tell your clients their celebration may be premature," Southerlyn said, snatching up her briefcase and marching for the back of the courtroom.

"We'll let you know," said McCoy to Herlihy.

JACK MCCOY'S OFFICE
ONE HOGAN PLACE
MONDAY, DECEMBER 2, 10:20 A.M.

"Jack," said Southerlyn, "they're probably buying ads in writers' magazines to troll for more victims this very moment."

McCoy's feet were up on his desk, He brushed lint off his thigh. "I'm trying to be realistic, Serena. The jury was hung."

"But they were in our favor. Ten to two to convict Avery McDonald. Nine to three to convict Monica."

"It only takes one to hang a jury."

"So let the McDonalds go on victimizing people?"

"That isn't what I'm saying, Serena. If we don't come up with a good argument, Arthur will shut it down for sure."

"Sure," she said, "only take on the easy ones."

"That isn't what we do here, Serena, and you know it. Nobody gains if we can't convict them. They go on doing what they're doing. We look like jackasses."

She opened her notepad. "The two stubborn ones were Mrs. Femina and Irving Banks."

"The old woman and the shoe salesman? Well so much for reading faces," said McCoy. "She looked at me like she wanted to give me cookies and milk."

"According to the foreman, they insisted that the

victims shouldn't have signed the contract if they didn't understand it. Banks kept saying 'A contract is a contract or there's no law at all.' Mrs. Femina said writers were nutcases, that fools and their money were soon parted."

"It sounds like she would have been a loose cannon in any case. And the rest of them?"

"There's some trouble there, too, Jack. I talked to three of them other than the foreman. They weren't at all confident they could tell the difference between good editing and bad editing. One said he'd read so many bad books, he wasn't sure the publishers knew. They didn't see anything wrong with self-publishing, either, or print on demand."

"So why did they vote to convict?"

"One said he thought Avery looked cheesy."

"Well, yeah, but other than that?"

"Mostly they bought our argument that the McDonalds were setting out to fleece customers."

"And they didn't believe Rosserman was? Do you know why the third juror voted to acquit Monica McDonald?"

"It was a woman. She thought women usually commit crimes because they were coerced by their men. So much for liberation."

"Hell, Serena, it's true often enough."

"But they all voted to acquit Rosserman on the three monkeys argument."

McCoy shook his head. "Rosserman knew what the deal was."

"Sure he did, and they really thought so, too, but they didn't think we proved it. Most of them thought he knew what he was doing, but wanted something specific."

"Well, if he'd bragged about it to someone...But he didn't. I think the real issue is exactly what I suspected: the crime doesn't seem important. I mean, here we are trying to convince the D.A. it's important. Why would a jury get incensed?"

"We have to make them understand next time."

"I don't think there will be a next time." He saw her expression. "It's triage, Serena. There are a lot of serious crimes out there. Violent ones. Murder. Rape. Battery."

"They're not just taking money, they're spitting on peoples' dreams," said Southerlyn.

"But they're not killing them."

"They killed Barbara Chesko."

"She had to cooperate in that," said McCoy. "The world is not a fragrant place. What can we do?"

"We go to another jury."

"Arthur won't go for that," said McCoy. "No matter what jury we get, the case will look like a contract dispute rather than a criminal case. I'm not the enemy, Serena!"

"I'm sorry," she said. "It infuriates me."

"I saw McDonald ogling you. I understand. But being a creep isn't quite a crime."

She had lowered her head, but suddenly pointed at him. He was startled by the excitement in her eyes. "So we give up a criminal approach. Let's go after them in a civil action."

"Civil?"

"Why not? The district attorney's office can sue. We'll file based on the fact that they preyed on the unsophisticated. We won't have to meet the burden of reasonable doubt and we can take back the money they've stolen, along with punitive damages. We'll

275

be doing good by the people not just of New York, but elsewhere."

"I thought you said they were criminals," said Mc-Coy.

"They are," she said, "but so was O.J. Simpson, right? They could get off the hook again, and then where would we be?"

"We can't recover people's dreams."

"But we can certainly hurt the people who stomped on them."

McCoy thought for a moment. "It sounds good to me," he said. "Cheesiness will carry a lot more weight in a civil trial. I'll pitch it to Arthur and we'll see if he swings."

"We can make it work," she said.

"No, I suspect *you'll* have to make it work," said McCoy, "and if Arthur allows it to go ahead, he may want it on the back burner. They're slow to get on the docket."

"Just keep it on the agenda," she said.

It had already been dark for an hour, and Detective Lennie Briscoe had spent most of the afternoon doing paperwork on the shooting of a janitor who called himself Julio Manzanna. There was no record to prove that a real Julio Manzanna had ever existed except for his paycheck and phony Social Security card. The shooter, an elderly man, who had wandered away from his family in Battery Park, had gotten the gun from God knows where and seemed to imagine that Julio was David Berkowitz. This was sure to turn out as a novelty story in the papers, especially when they found out that the gun had been stolen from a security guard on Long Island a year before.

But it would die down. Julio Manzanna was probably an illegal, and without a weeping family to photograph, he would drop off the news radar as quickly as he dropped to the sidewalk.

Green had gone home early with the flu, and Briscoe was fretting he might catch it, as well. He was thinking about buying a gyro on the way home, when his desk phone rang.

"Lennie," said the sergeant, "a woman wants to see you."

"Tell her the check's in the mail, Gil."

"Really?"

"No, Gil," he said patiently. "I'll be right down. I was leaving anyway."

When he reached the area where visitors were screened, Gil pointed to a middle-aged woman in a plastic raincoat. She jumped to her feet as she saw him. Her jaw was set. She looked like she was getting ready to slug him.

"Detective Briscoe," she said. It wasn't a question.

"Yes, ma'am. Do I know you?"

"You don't remember me?" She held up his card. "You said to call you if I thought of anything."

He was still drawing a blank on her. He knew he hadn't talked to her today. Yesterday?

"You came to my apartment to ask about Barbara Chesko."

"Barbar—Oh, yeah, sure. The woman who killed herself. You were in the writers' group? That was what, six months ago?"

"More like eight months."

"And you're...?"

"Glenda Atterby. I must speak to you in private."

"I was just on my way out, Mrs. Atterby."

"If I wait," she said, "I may not have the nerve. I swore not to say anything." She bit her lip, glanced around her, and swallowed hard. Her hand was shaking as she brought a tissue to her nose.

"It's okay," said Briscoe, taking her by the arm and leading her into a corridor.

"Are you okay?" he asked. "Do you need to sit down?"

"No. I have to do it, detective," she said. "She swore me to secrecy, but..."

"Take it easy," said Briscoe.

"I was reading the papers and I saw that the charges against Avery McDonald were dismissed."

"He was the book guy, wasn't he?"

"Yes."

"I think there was a mistrial," said Briscoe. "They can try him again if they like."

"Will they?"

"The D.A.s do their best. It's just the way it is."

"But he killed Barbara! I know you can't prove he pushed her, but he cheated her and broke her heart."

"I'm sorry, Mrs. Atterby. It's been out of my hands for quite a while. If you have something new, I can give you the number—"

"I want to report a rape," she said, cutting him off.

"You were raped?"

"Not me," she said. "But it could have been."

So much for the gyro, he thought. So much for the early night.

McCoy tried to make himself inconspicuous in the corner, so that Melva Patterson would be more comfortable while Southerlyn questioned her from across the table. Patterson was slender in her torso, but her hips showed her age. "I'll kill Glenda for this," she said.

"Mrs. Patterson," said Southerlyn, "she told the detective because she is concerned about you. Rape is a serious crime."

"Well, it was the pills and the wine or I wouldn't have told her. Yes, I told her that, but it's really nothing for the police. You're not going to get me to press charges."

"Pills and wine?"

"I'd had a root canal that afternoon, but I went to the meeting anyway. The pain started up and I took a couple of Glenda's pills. I had to stay over. I talked too much."

"She said that Avery McDonald raped you. That's why we asked you to come in."

Patterson flipped her hand as if she were brushing off a fly. "I know, I know. It's your job and all that, but there's rape and then there's *rape*, you know."

280

"No, I don't know," said Southerlyn. "Maybe you'd better explain it."

"It isn't like he put a knife to my throat."

"All right," said Southerlyn, "explain it to me and we can all go home."

"I don't have to," said Patterson.

"I think you want to."

"It's just embarrassing, that's all. What's that old expression, getting hoisted on your petard. That's what happened. He provided the petard."

Southerlyn waited.

"You're a lawyer. You're young. You're gorgeous. You still…" She glanced at McCoy. "You still have the boobs God gave you. I married the wrong guy to get out of Pittsburgh and then I tried again and married okay. He wasn't the greatest man, but he left behind good money." She shrugged wearily. "The only thing I can claim for myself is that I won an essay contest in high school and then when Richmond, my husband, died, there didn't seem much point in cooking and cleaning just for me, so I remembered that essay and how the principal gave me the little trophy and said I'd write a great book someday."

Patterson snorted quietly, like someone who's just been told a weak joke. She shook her head and continued. "You can't believe how much I cry when I read the right kind of book. Maybe you can't understand how much I'd like to be able to do that." She waved the thought off. "Anyway, so I saw a notice in the paper about writing classes at the Learning Annex and I met Glenda there and I ended up going to the meetings on a regular basis."

"And this was when Barbara Chesko was a member?"

"She joined a little later. She was...I don't know."
Southerlyn waited.

"She was all wrapped up in the thing. She was always putting on airs and talking about her inspiration and all of that. I didn't like her writing at all. It wasn't any good to me, but Glenda, she's got a heart of gold and she's got her workshop rules. All the criticism is to focus on the writing and to be nonjudgmental about the person. All remarks should be constructive remarks. All this is a good thing. Who can fault it? Writing is lonely. Support is important."

McCoy raised an eyebrow and Southerlyn took the hint. "So it was through Barbara Chesko that you met Avery McDonald?"

"Not directly."

"How then?"

"She held the workshop in her apartment in the Village one week and let it drop that she had a publisher who was interested in her novel. She wouldn't say who it was, but a month or so later, I had my sister's car while she was in Barbados and I offered to drop Barbara off. We stopped in a Barnes and Noble and I found out that the editor who was interested in her novel worked at Kirstner and Strawn. She didn't tell me his name, but she mentioned that he edited Suzanne Lewiston's latest. I called up and found out it was Robert Rosserman."

"You did a little detective work."

Patterson looked at Southerlyn as if she were a child. "My book was three quarters finished. If Barbara could sell hers to this man..."

"And then?"

"And then she told us that her editor had recommended her to an editing firm. We all thought this meant her deal was in the works, but almost a year passed and each time we asked she said that they were still working on it and she'd have a contract soon. She was down some times and up others. One afternoon I met her for coffee and she told me the editor had finished her manuscript. She was in a hurry to meet him at the Waterloo."

"Did she say why?"

"I thought it meant he was married, you know, and I teased her about being wicked. She smirked and said she was much more wicked than I knew, but for the first time she was free, free like women weren't supposed to be free."

"What did she mean by that?"

"I thought she meant she was having sex with a married man. Later from the way she said some things, I just thought it meant some kind of sex, maybe kinky, maybe she was dominant or acting out like a hooker. All she said was the Waterloo was convenient, that he didn't like to go all the way to the Village."

"How romantic," said Southerlyn.

"This was Robert Rosserman?" interrupted McCoy.

"That's what I thought. She was always coy about him. She liked to call him her editor."

"And do you know how many times she met him at the Waterloo?"

"No. But I had the impression it was more than once. And then the last time..."

"Go on," said Southerlyn.

"Barbara was late to the meeting, but Glenda told us that she might have stopped off to get champagne. She was supposed to have big news for us. We gave her a while and then Glenda told me to go ahead with my reading; it was my turn to read that night. I'd just started when the detectives showed up." She leaned toward Southerlyn and jabbed at the tabletop. "Well, it didn't take *me* long to know what had happened."

"And that was?"

"She'd killed herself. That bastard Rosserman strung her along, used her, then told her to take her book and get lost."

"So you called him?"

Patterson hesitated. "Yes. How did you know? The next Monday. I told him he was responsible for her death. He said he had nothing to do with it and he acted surprised. I said he'd been stringing her along, meeting her at the Waterloo, and I might just tell his wife. He said he wasn't married, and then he said he hadn't seen her for some time."

"Did he say how long?" Southerlyn met McCoy's eyes. Rosserman had admitted he was in the Waterloo with Chesko a few nights before Patterson called.

"No."

Patterson hesitated.

"Does my presence make you uncomfortable, Mrs. Patterson?" asked McCoy.

"No."

"Did Rosserman say anything else in his phone call?"

"I did most of the talking after that."

"What do you mean?"

"I told him I had a book and it was a damn good book."

McCoy's jaw dropped.

"You blackmailed him?" asked Serena.

"It's not blackmail," said Patterson. "I told him I wanted him to read it."

"And you didn't suggest that you might expose his relationship with her? You'd already threatened to tell his wife, when you thought he had a wife."

"You think it's easy to get a publisher to read your book? You send the thing in and it comes back the next day with a preprinted slip telling you they don't look at unsolicited manuscripts, or that it 'doesn't fit their needs.' I didn't threaten him with anything."

"You just let it hang in the air."

"He was responsible for her being dead. It's the same as murder. You ought to charge him with murder."

"We believe it was a suicide."

"I don't. But, he's too much of a wimp to kill anybody with his own hands, anyway."

"So he looked at your book? And it was then he sent you to McDonald."

She shook her head. "No. He stalled for a while and said he was waiting for the right moment to bring it before the editorial board. Then he was fired."

"So how did you meet McDonald?"

"He told me if I kept quiet about his relationship with Barbara, he'd set me up with the same editor who had worked on Barbara's book. I asked him what good that would do. Her book hadn't gone anywhere. He told me he would get them to do the work for half price, maybe even free."

Southerlyn winced. McCoy grabbed his head. "He did this knowing that Redux was a phony. Unbelievable!"

"Didn't he realize it wouldn't take long for you to figure out that Redux was a scam?" said Southerlyn.

"But it wasn't, at least not for me. Avery actually rewrote parts of the book."

"Well, that's a novelty."

"I offered to be a witness at the trial, but he said it would be better to keep our arrangement a secret."

Southerlyn winced again. "Wait a minute, Mrs. Patterson. Mrs. Atterby told us you were raped. Did McDonald rape you?"

"Yes. Sort of."

"Would you mind explaining that?"

"I won't press charges."

"Just explain it," said Southerlyn.

"Bob called Redux and Avery called me. He suggested we meet at a Starbucks in midtown. He said he could see there were real possibilities in my book. He said he had worked very closely with Barbara, had even spent two full weekends in a cabin trying to work out the knots in her manuscript. He said they became very close, but she didn't really have the talent and she wasn't entirely cooperative in the editorial changes he had suggested."

"Did he say they were lovers?"

"No. I knew she had been with Bob, but not with Avery."

"I guess this is what she meant by being freer than a woman is supposed to be," said McCoy.

"Like a man with two girlfriends?" said Southerlyn.

"Later," continued Patterson, "I kind of sensed they had been to bed when Avery said that he and Monica had an open marriage and nothing could separate them."

"And you became intimate with McDonald?"

She shifted uneasily. "He came to my apartment to discuss the manuscript. He forced himself on me."

"What do you mean?"

"He grabbed me by the shoulders and forced a kiss

on me. I turned my face away and he said he knew what I wanted. I tried to pull away and we ended up on the floor. He reached under my skirt and ripped off my panties."

"I'm sorry," said Southerlyn.

Patterson blinked. "Look, you think Richmond cared about when I wanted it or how? Sure, I cried. Avery told me he didn't know what had come over him. There was something about me. And so on."

"You didn't scream?"

"Not really."

"Were you afraid of him?"

"A little. No. Not really."

Southerlyn's spine straightened. "Are you telling us this was consensual?"

"No. I didn't want to. It hurt."

"Did you make it clear to him that you didn't want to?"

"I said no, but I didn't really resist."

"In what sense was this a rape then?"

"Just that I didn't want to."

McCoy and Southerlyn looked at each other then at Patterson. Finally she spoke. "Look," said Patterson, "I hadn't had sex for six years. It wasn't good, but a couple of weeks later he called and said he had done more on the manuscript. He apologized. He brought me a box of Italian cookies. I let him do it again."

"And exactly how many times did you let him 'do it'?" asked Southerlyn.

"Four. Not including the first time."

"Thank you for coming in," said Southerlyn.

"Wait," said McCoy. "You don't want to press charges, Mrs. Patterson, and you can see we'd have a difficult time at best in making a charge stick even if you testified."

"It's sick, okay?" she shouted. "I was lonely. He was going to help me with my novel."

Southerlyn stared, but McCoy approached her and spoke quietly. "He made you believe you were trading sex for publication."

"He didn't say that specifically."

"He took advantage of you," said McCoy. "He's a victimizer. He did that to Barbara Chesko and who knows who else. You can't blame yourself."

"I don't have to like myself for it."

"Your anger should be pointed at him," said McCoy. "Will you do something for us? I know we can't make a rape case out of this without your cooperation. And we probably would lose even with it. So that's your choice, no matter how distasteful that is to me. But, you know what Mrs. Patterson? I certainly intend to use this information to inflict some pain on him."

Southerlyn abruptly looked up. "Jack? What are you thinking?"

The McDonalds sat in their chairs, glaring at McCoy. Avery twisting his sporty cane with a pewter knob. The jewel in the pin securing his tie had fallen out of its setting. Monica wore her usual jeans and a worn leather jacket with "Kerouac" embroidered on the back.

Southerlyn crossed her legs to distract McDonald and to irritate Monica, as Leo Herlihy shook McCoy's hand and nodded with a smile in Southerlyn's direction. "Jack," he said, "if this is about the civil suit I really shouldn't be here. Avery and Monica are going to get a good litigator."

"This isn't about the civil action," said McCoy, "and, in fact, they might consider getting separate attorneys for both the civil action and the criminal action."

"We are a team," sneered Monica. "We don't need separate attorneys."

Herlihy put a hand up to silence her. "Criminal action?"

"New evidence has come to light. The charges directly affect Mr. McDonald, but may have a ripple effect on Mrs. McDonald's case."

"Don't try to put us at each other's throats!" said

289

Avery McDonald. "We've survived everything you've thrown at us and anything you intend to throw at us. Our love is inviolable!"

McCoy raised his eyebrows.

"Relax, Avery," said Herlihy. "What new charges? I can't believe you'd reopen that worthless grand larceny case!"

"Maybe it isn't so worthless."

Herlihy sat back and smiled. "I get it. You're going to keep throwing charges until you break them. Civil lawyers, criminal lawyers. You're using the state to bankrupt them."

"Are you behind the IRS thing?" said McDonald.

"IRS?" said McCoy. "They're sniffing at you?"

"Don't play innocent with me," said McDonald.

"Be quiet, Avery!" said Herlihy. "It's a routine tax inquiry, Jack."

"Well, good luck with it," said McCoy. "Let's hope you don't need a tax attorney, too."

"You revive those criminal charges, Jack, and I'll have a judge throw them out. The city will be looking at a major lawsuit, and maybe for another Executive Assistant D.A."

"The charges weren't thrown out the last time and they won't be this time. Especially when we throw in the rape."

"Rape?" said Herlihy. "Did you say 'rape'?"

"It seems we've got a statement that Mr. McDonald forcibly engaged in sexual intercourse with one of his clients."

Avery McDonald almost laughed. "That's ridiculous! I've never forced anyone."

"That's not what the statement said."

"Sir," said McDonald, "I may not be a saint, but I have never committed rape. It isn't necessary."

"This is a wholly different matter, Jack," said Herlihy. "You're trying to connect it with Redux?"

"Sure. When it comes out that Mr. McDonald, the helpful editor, compelled a woman to have sex with him before he worked on her manuscript, I think the jury will be impressed with his consummate professionalism."

"You can't admit anything like this as evidence in a grand larceny trial."

"I'll get it in, Leo. You know I will. And if I don't, it will certainly be on the public record. How will that help the search for clients?"

"You won't have a prayer," Southerlyn said to McDonald. "In my experience, when one woman comes forward, others come out of the woodwork as well."

Monica McDonald's face had reddened. Sweat had beaded on her forehead.

"Are you all right?" asked Southerlyn.

Avery turned to Monica. "Who's been lying about this?"

"I'll have to talk to my client," said Herlihy.

"I deny it!" said McDonald. "This is nonsense! What is there to talk about! This is persecution, pure and simple. He's running for office or something, Leo."

"To save the state time and money," said McCoy, "I'm willing to entertain a plea."

"Hey," said Herlihy, "don't try to bluff me."

"Five years for him. Three years for her. And restitution."

"They're not violent felons! Come off it!"

"I don't know about her," said McCoy. "But he's a

rapist. If I go after him on rape one, what do you think he'll get?"

"Nothing!" said McDonald. "I raped no one. I don't rape. I don't *have* to rape."

The sweat was now pouring from Monica's face. Her skin had taken on a bloodless pallor.

"Your husband's quite a stud, is he?" said Southerlyn. "He wrote the book on the subject: *The Man's Guide to Studliness*."

"All right," said Herlihy, "that's enough. No one says a word." He stood. "For all we know, you're making all this up, Jack." He reached for Avery's arm. Monica seemed unable to rise.

"You've cheated people long enough," said McCoy. "Call me back when you're ready to plea."

He opened his drawer and lifted out a typed statement.

"Melva Patterson," said McCoy.

"I'm sure you remember her," said Southerlyn. "She was a friend of Barbara Chesko's."

McDonald exhaled in a mocking relief. "Her? She was a conniving bitch. She didn't pay me a thing. Not a penny. I did it as a favor to Bob Rosserman."

"What? Threw her down on the floor and raped her? Maybe I should charge Rosserman as well."

Herlihy grabbed McDonald's arm. "Avery!" he said.

"I edited her trashy manuscript as a favor to Bob, to keep you bastards off his back! The whore throws herself out of a window and you start after us! What kind of justice is that?"

"Avery! Shut up! Now!"

McDonald snatched up the statement and flicked it at McCoy, who had straightened his chair and hunched forward, ready to defend himself. Southerlyn's eyes were headlights as she gripped the handle of her briefcase, the only weapon she could think of.

"Melva Patterson," McDonald sneered, "is a talentless slut who threw herself at me. Rape her? She wanted it, she practically begged for it, and then kept asking for more!"

"Avery!" said Herlihy.

"You'd better tell your client to calm down," said McCoy.

Monica's voice startled them all.

"*Bastard!*" she growled. She snatched the cane from Avery McDonald's hand, raised it over her head and brought it down hard across her husband's forehead. He spun backward, falling over his chair. Herlihy stretched his arms out in front of him to try to stop her, but backed away at the fierce anger. Avery McDonald skittered backward on his rump, blinking blood from his eyes. McCoy was trying to round his desk and block Southerlyn from Monica's wild swings. She cracked the cane across her husband's knees. The next blow struck the chair. McCoy shoved Monica in the side and she flopped on the sofa. Two uniforms shoved Herlihy aside and pinned Monica down.

She panted like an overheated husky as one officer snapped handcuffs on her wrist and twisted her arm behind her. She then broke down. "He promised," she sobbed. "No more. He promised..."

"Are you okay?" McCoy asked Southerlyn.

"Just let me sit down," she said, shaking.

McCoy looked at Herlihy, who was breathing hard, but nodded okay. Avery McDonald moaned, simultaneously trying to hold his knee and wipe the stinging blood from his left eye.

One of the cops knelt over McDonald and pressed

a tissue against the scalp wound. The other cop, carefully watching Monica sob, placed the cane on McCoy's desk behind him and used his radio to ask for paramedics.

"Monica," moaned McDonald, "I love you. You know that."

She sniffed. "I can't kill every woman in the city."

"What did you say?" said McCoy.

"I've lived with it long enough. I told him he had to stop. He doesn't. He won't."

Avery spoke through gritted teeth. "Monica! We're not like ordinary couples, we're…"

"You wanted her money. You would have left me for her!"

"That's ri—" He growled in agony. "It's ridiculous!" He rocked back in pain again. "What did you do? Oh, God, Monica, what did you do?"

Southerlyn looked at Herlihy who was staring in astonishment at what had just happened. Even in this moment of confusion, she knew that Herlihy should be advising his client to shut up. But he wasn't going to do it.

"Lie down," said the cop to Avery. "Lie down."

Tears ran down Avery's cheeks. His eyes were closed and he seemed almost as if he were going to fall asleep. "She wasn't rich, you stupid bitch. You're the one I come home to. You, Monica." He began to blubber as the paramedics pushed their way through the crowd that had gathered outside McCoy's door.

As they moved to slide the carrier under him, Monica turned and murmured, "Oh, baby. Oh, baby." She craned her neck in her husband's direction, her arms held behind her by the handcuffs. The cop pushed her back. The paramedics were about to lift up Avery McDonald, but McCoy stepped toward them.

"Wait," he said. The paramedics looked to the cop, who nodded.

McCoy bent toward Monica. "You killed Barbara Chesko."

Her face was swollen with her blubbering, her eyes as puffy as a bad boxer's.

"You went up to the room after Mr. McDonald left."

"I knew what he was doing there." She sniffed. "He met her there before."

"How do you know?"

"Don't say anything," groaned Avery.

She sniffed again and swallowed. "He had matches. He smelled like perfume. It wasn't hard to know." She began blubbering again.

"You hurt me," said Avery, holding his head. "You never hurt me before. Don't say anything."

Southerlyn touched McCoy as if to say, "That's enough." McCoy looked at the hand as if he would bite it off.

"How did you do it? How?"

"Avery didn't know I was in town. She had called the night before. She was crying about her lousy book. I later heard him call her back."

"His cell phone records say he called home," said McCoy. "But you weren't there?"

"His messages were on the machine."

Southerlyn pulled out a tissue and wiped the wet string hanging from Monica's nose. Monica said thank you, then rolled her eyes up toward Southerlyn with total malice. Suddenly, she gagged like she was going to throw up. The cop held McCoy's wastebasket under her chin.

Monica took a deep breath.

"Are you okay?" asked Southerlyn.

"You went up to the room when you saw Mr. Mc-Donald leaving."

She nodded.

"I told her her book was awful. I told her Avery only laid her for her money and she'd better forget about him or I would kill her."

"And then?"

"She said Avery loved her. I said that no, Avery never said that. He's never said that to anyone. He says it's hypocritical." She turned toward him. "He's never said that to me, until tonight." She began to blubber again.

McCoy waited only a second or two before pressing her again. "Mrs. McDonald! You pushed Barbara Chesko?"

She grew still as if seeing it happen again. "She slapped me. We struggled. Then she got stuck in the open window, holding onto the frame, kind of bent in half, her ass hanging out. I had a moment when I thought she was just another stupid woman, over the hill and no threat to me. She was still holding on and I could have left and she would have pulled herself back in. But when I turned I saw her beret. The label said 'cashmere.' Cashmere! It probably cost more than my entire wardrobe and I knew she could have Avery any time she wanted. So I pushed."

"Oh, Monica..." moaned Avery.

"And you took her purse and her laptop?"

She shook her head.

Arthur Branch appeared in the doorway. "What in blue blazes is going on here?" he demanded.

"We're...We're closing a case," said Southerlyn.